n 9

Chas C. Robinson,
    to Eva M. Robinson
6 - 2 - 14

He could only stare at her.   Page 160.

Frontispiece.   *—The Conquest of Canaan.*

The Conquest of Canaan

By BOOTH TARKINGTON

Author of " The Two Vanrevels,"
" The Gentleman from Indiana," etc.

Illustrated by
LUCIUS W. HITCHCOCK

A. L. BURT COMPANY, Publishers
NEW YORK

Published by arrangement with Harper & Brothers.

TO
L. F. T.

CONTENTS

CONTENTS

THE
CONQUEST OF CANAAN

THE
CONQUEST OF CANAAN

ENTER CHORUS

A DRY snow had fallen steadily throughout the still night, so that when a cold, upper wind cleared the sky gloriously in the morning the incongruous Indiana town shone in a white harmony—roof, ledge, and earth as evenly covered as by moonlight. There was no thaw; only where the line of factories followed the big bend of the frozen river, their distant chimneys like exclamation points on a blank page, was there a first threat against the supreme whiteness. The wind passed quickly and on high; the shouting of the school-children had ceased at nine o'clock with pitiful suddenness; no sleigh-bells laughed out on the air; and the muffling of the thoroughfares wrought an unaccustomed peace like that of Sunday. This was the phenomenon which afforded the opening of the morning debate of the sages in the wide windows of the "National House."

Only such unfortunates as have so far failed to visit Canaan do not know that the "National House" is on the Main Street side of the Courthouse Square, and has the advantage of being within two minutes' walk of the railroad station, which is in plain sight of the windows—an inestimable benefit to the conversation of the aged men who occupied these windows on this white morning, even as they were wont in summer to hold against all comers the cane-seated chairs on the pavement outside. Thence, as trains came and went, they commanded the city gates, and, seeking motives and adding to the stock of history, narrowly observed and examined into all who entered or departed. Their habit was not singular. He who would foolishly tax the sages of Canaan with a bucolic light-mindedness must first walk in Piccadilly in early June, stroll down the Corso in Rome before Ash Wednesday, or regard those windows of Fifth Avenue whose curtains are withdrawn of a winter Sunday; for in each of these great streets, wherever the windows, not of trade, are widest, his eyes must behold wise men, like to those of Canaan, executing always their same purpose.

The difference is in favor of Canaan; the "National House" was the club, but the perusal of traveller or passer by was here only the splume blown before a stately ship of thought; and you might hear the sages comparing the Koran with the speeches of Robert J. Ingersoll.

In the days of board sidewalks, "mail-time" had meant a precise moment for Canaan, and even now, many years after the first postman, it remained somewhat definite to the aged men; for, out of deference to a pleasant, olden custom, and perhaps partly for an excuse to "get down to the hotel" (which was not altogether in favor with the elderly ladies), most of them retained their antique boxes in the post-office, happily in the next building.

In this connection it may be written that a subscription clerk in the office of the Chicago *Daily Standard*, having noted a single subscriber from Canaan, was, a fortnight later, pleased to receive, by one mail, nine subscriptions from that promising town. If one brought nine others in a fortnight, thought he, what would nine bring in a month? Amazingly, they brought nothing, and the rest was silence. Here was a matter of intricate diplomacy never to come within that youth his ken. The morning voyage to the post - office, long mocked as a fable and screen by the families of the sages, had grown so difficult to accomplish for one of them, Colonel Flitcroft (Colonel in the war with Mexico), that he had been put to it, indeed, to foot the firing-line against his wife (a lady of celebrated determination and hale-voiced at seventy), and to defend the rental of a box which had sheltered but three missives in four years. Desperation is often inspiration; the Colonel brilliantly subscribed for the *Standard*, forgetting to give his house address, and it took the others just thirteen days to wring his secret from him. Then the *Standard* served for all.

Mail-time had come to mean that bright hour when they all got their feet on the brass rod which protected the sills of the two big windows, with the steam-radiators sizzling like kettles against the side wall. Mr. Jonas Tabor, who had sold his hardware business magnificently (not magnificently for his nephew, the purchaser) some ten years before, was usually, in spite of the fact that he remained a bachelor at seventy-nine, the last to settle down with the others, though often the first to reach the hotel, which he always entered by a side door, because he did not believe in the treating system. And it was Mr. Eskew Arp, only seventy-five, but already a thoroughly capable cynic, who, almost invariably "opened the argument," and it was he who discovered the sinister intention behind the weather of this particular morning. Mr. Arp had not begun life so sourly: as a youth he had been proud of his given name, which had come to him through his mother's family, who had made it honorable, but many years of explanations that Eskew did not indicate his initials had lowered his opinion of the intelligence and morality of the race.

The malevolence of his voice and manner this morning, therefore, when he shook his finger at the town beyond the windows, and exclaimed, with a bitter laugh, "Look at it!" was no surprise to his companions. "Jest look at it! I tell you the devil is mighty smart. Ha, ha! Mighty smart!"

Through custom it was the duty of Squire Buckalew (Justice of the Peace in '59) to be the first to take up Mr. Arp. The others looked to him for it. Therefore, he asked, sharply:

"What's the devil got to do with snow?"

"Everything to do with it, sir," Mr. Arp retorted. "It's plain as day to anybody with eyes and sense."

"Then I wish you'd p'int it out," said Buckalew, "if you've got either."

"By the Almighty, Squire"—Mr. Arp turned in his chair with sudden heat—"if I'd lived as long as you—"

"You have," interrupted the other, stung. "Twelve years ago!"

"If I'd lived as long as you," Mr. Arp repeated, unwincingly, in a louder voice, "and had follered Satan's trail as long as you have, and yet couldn't recognize it when I see it, I'd git converted and vote Prohibitionist."

"*I* don't see it," interjected Uncle Joe Davey, in his querulous voice. (He was the patriarch of them all.) "*I* can't find no cloven-hoof-prints in the snow."

"All over it, sir!" cried the cynic. "All over it! Old Satan loves tricks like this. Here's a town that's jest one squirmin' mass of lies and envy and vice and wickedness and corruption—"

"Hold on!" exclaimed Colonel Flitcroft. "That's a slander upon our hearths and our government. Why, when I was in the Council—"

"It wasn't a bit worse then," Mr. Arp returned, unreasonably. "Jest you look how the devil fools us. He drops down this here virgin mantle on Canaan and makes it look as good as you pretend you think it is: as good as the Sunday-school room of a country church—though *that*"—he went off on a tangent, venomously—"is generally only another whited sepulchre, and the superintendent's mighty apt to have a bottle of whiskey hid behind the organ, and—"

"Look here, Eskew," said Jonas Tabor, "that's got nothin' to do with—"

6

"Why ain't it? Answer me!" cried Mr. Arp, continuing, without pause: "Why ain't it? Can't you wait till I git through? You listen to me, and when I'm ready I'll listen to—"

"See here," began the Colonel, making himself heard over three others, "I want to ask you—"

"No, sir!" Mr. Arp pounded the floor irascibly with his hickory stick. "Don't you ask me anything! How can you tell that I'm not going to answer your question without your asking it, till I've got through? You listen first. I say, here's a town of nearly thirty thousand inhabitants, every last one of 'em—men, women, and children—selfish and cowardly and sinful, if you could see their innermost natures; a town of the ugliest and worst built houses in the world, and governed by a lot of saloon-keepers—though I hope it 'll never git down to where the ministers can run it. And the devil comes along, and in one night—why, all you got to do is *look* at it! You'd think we needn't ever trouble to make it better. That's what the devil wants us to do—wants us to rest easy about it, and paints it up to look like a heaven of peace and purity and sanctified spirits. Snowfall like this would of made Lot turn the angel out-of-doors and say that the old home was good enough for him. Gomorrah would of looked like a Puritan village—though I'll bet my last dollar that there was a lot, and a *whole* lot, that's never been told about Puritan villages. A lot that—"

"*What* never was?" interrupted Mr. Peter Bradbury, whose granddaughter had lately announced her discovery that the Bradburys were descended from Miles Standish. "What wasn't told about Puritan villages?"

"Can't you wait?" Mr. Arp's accents were those of pain. "Haven't I got *any* right to present my side of the case? Ain't we restrained enough to allow of free speech here? How can we ever git anywhere in an argument like this, unless we let one man talk at a time? How—"

"Go on with your statement," said Uncle Joe Davey, impatiently.

Mr. Arp's grievance was increased. "Now listen to *you!* How many more interruptions are comin'? I'll listen to the other side, but I've got to state mine first, haven't I? If I don't make my point clear, what's the use of the argument? Argumentation is only the comparison of two sides of a question, and you have to see what the first side *is* before you can compare it with the other one, don't you? Are you all agreed to that?"

"Yes, yes," said the Colonel. "Go ahead. We won't interrupt until you're through."

"Very well," resumed Mr. Arp, with a fleeting expression of satisfaction, "as I said before, I

8

wish to—as I said—" He paused, in some confusion. "As I said, argumentation is—that is, I
say—" He stopped again, utterly at sea, having
talked himself so far out of his course that he was
unable to recall either his sailing port or his desti-
nation. Finally he said, feebly, to save the confession, "Well, go on with your side of it."

This generosity was for a moment disconcerting;
however, the quietest of the party took up the
opposition — Roger Tabor, a very thin, old man
with a clean-shaven face, almost as white as his
hair, and melancholy, gentle, gray eyes, very unlike those of his brother Jonas, which were dark
and sharp and button-bright. (It was to Roger's
son that Jonas had so magnificently sold the hardware business.) Roger was known in Canaan as
"the artist"; there had never been another of his
profession in the place, and the town knew not the
word "painter," except in application to the useful artisan who is subject to lead-poisoning. There
was no indication of his profession in the attire of
Mr. Tabor, unless the too apparent age of his
black felt hat and a neat patch at the elbow of his
shiny, old brown overcoat might have been taken
as symbols of the sacrifice to his muse which his
life had been. He was not a constant attendant
of the conclave, and when he came it was usually
to listen; indeed, he spoke so seldom that at the

sound of his voice they all turned to him with some surprise.

"I suppose," he began, "that Eskew means the devil is behind all beautiful things."

"Ugly ones, too," said Mr. Arp, with a start of recollection. "And I wish to state—"

"Not now!" Colonel Flitcroft turned upon him violently. "You've already stated it."

"Then, if he is behind the ugly things, too," said Roger, "we must take him either way, so let us be glad of the beauty for its own sake. Eskew says this is a wicked town. It may be—I don't know. He says it's badly built; perhaps it is; but it doesn't seem to me that it's ugly in itself. I don't know what its real self is, because it wears so many aspects. God keeps painting it all the time, and never shows me twice the same picture; not even two snowfalls are just alike, nor the days that follow them; no more than two misty sunsets are alike — for the color and even the form of the town you call ugly are a matter of the season of the year and of the time of day and of the light and air. The ugly town is like an endless gallery which you can walk through, from year-end to year-end, never seeing the same canvas twice, no matter how much you may want to—and there's the pathos of it. Isn't it the same with people— with the characters of all of us, just as it is with our faces? No face remains the same for two successive days—"

"It don't?" Colonel Flitcroft interrupted, with an explosive and rueful incredulity. "Well, I'd like to—" Second thoughts came to him almost immediately, and, as much out of gallantry as through discretion, fearing that he might be taken as thinking of one at home, he relapsed into silence.

Not so with the others. It was as if a firecracker had been dropped into a sleeping poultry-yard. Least of all could Mr. Arp contain himself. At the top of his voice, necessarily, he agreed with Roger that faces changed, not only from day to day, and not only because of light and air and such things, but from hour to hour, and from minute to minute, through the hideous stimulus of hypocrisy.

The "argument" grew heated; half a dozen tidy quarrels arose; all the sages went at it fiercely, except Roger Tabor, who stole quietly away. The aged men were enjoying themselves thoroughly, especially those who quarrelled. Naturally, the frail bark of the topic which had been launched was whirled about by too many side-currents to remain long in sight, and soon became derelict, while the intellectual dolphins dove and tumbled in the depths. At the end of twenty minutes

Mr. Arp emerged upon the surface, and in his mouth was this:

"Tell me, why ain't the Church—why ain't the Church and the rest of the believers in a future life lookin' for immortality at the other end of life, too? If we're immortal, we always have been; then why don't they ever speculate on what we were before we were born? It's because they're too blame selfish — don't care a flapdoodle about what *was*, all they want is to go on livin' forever."

Mr. Arp's voice had risen to an acrid triumphancy, when it suddenly faltered, relapsed to a murmur, and then to a stricken silence, as a tall, fat man of overpowering aspect threw open the outer door near by and crossed the lobby to the clerk's desk. An awe fell upon the sages with this advent. They were hushed, and after a movement in their chairs, with a strange effect of huddling, sat disconcerted and attentive, like school-boys at the entrance of the master.

The personage had a big, fat, pink face and a heavily undershot jaw, what whitish beard he wore following his double chin somewhat after the manner displayed in the portraits of Henry the Eighth. His eyes, very bright under puffed upper lids, were intolerant and insultingly penetrating despite their small size. Their irritability held a kind of hotness, and yet the personage exuded frost, not of the weather, all about him. You could not imagine man or angel daring to greet this being genially—sooner throw a kiss to Mount Pilatus!

"Mr. Brown," he said, with ponderous hostility, in a bull bass, to the clerk — the kind of voice which would have made an express train leave the track and go round the other way—"do you hear me?"

"Oh yes, Judge," the clerk replied, swiftly, in tones as unlike those which he used for strange transients as a collector's voice in his ladylove's ear is unlike that which he propels at delinquents.

"Do you see that snow?" asked the personage, threateningly.

"Yes, Judge." Mr. Brown essayed a placating smile. "Yes, indeed, Judge Pike."

"Has your employer, the manager of this hotel, seen that snow?" pursued the personage, with a gesture of unspeakable solemn menace.

"Yes, sir. I think so. Yes, sir."

"Do you think he fully understands that I am the proprietor of this building?"

"Certainly, Judge, cer—"

"You will inform him that I do not intend to be discommoded by his negligence as I pass to my offices. Tell him from me that unless he keeps the sidewalks in front of this hotel clear of snow I will cancel his lease. Their present condition is

outrageous. Do you understand me? Outrageous!
Do you hear?"

"Yes, Judge, I do so," answered the clerk,
hoarse with respect. "I'll see to it this minute,
Judge Pike."

"You had better." The personage turned himself about and began a grim progress towards the
door by which he had entered, his eyes fixing
themselves angrily upon the conclave at the windows.

Colonel Flitcroft essayed a smile, a faltering one.

"Fine weather, Judge Pike," he said, hopefully.

There was no response of any kind; the undershot jaw became more intolerant. The personage
made his opinion of the group disconcertingly
plain, and the old boys understood that he knew
them for a worthless lot of senile loafers, as great a
nuisance in his building as was the snow without;
and much too evident was his unspoken threat
to see that the manager cleared them out of there
before long.

He nodded curtly to the only man of substance
among them, Jonas Tabor, and shut the door behind him with majestic insult. He was Canaan's
millionaire.

He was one of those dynamic creatures who
leave the haunting impression of their wills behind them, like the tails of Bo-Peep's sheep, like

the evil dead men have done; he left his intolerant image in the ether for a long time after he had gone, to confront and confound the aged men and hold them in deferential and humiliated silence. Each of them was mysteriously lowered in his own estimation, and knew that he had been made to seem futile and foolish in the eyes of his fellows. They were all conscious, too, that the clerk had been acutely receptive of Judge Pike's reading of them; that he was reviving from his own squelchedness through the later snubbing of the colonel; also that he might further seek to recover his poise by an attack on them for cluttering up the office.

Naturally, Jonas Tabor was the first to speak. "Judge Pike's lookin' mighty well," he said, admiringly.

"Yes, he is," ventured Squire Buckalew, with deference; "mighty well."

"Yes, sir," echoed Peter Bradbury; "mighty well."

"He's a great man," wheezed Uncle Joe Davey; "a great man, Judge Martin Pike; a great man!"

"I expect he has considerable on his mind," said the Colonel, who had grown very red. "I noticed that he hardly seemed to see us."

"Yes, sir," Mr. Bradbury corroborated, with an attempt at an amused laugh. "I noticed it, too.

Of course a man with all his cares and interests must git absent-minded now and then."

"Of course he does," said the colonel. "A man with all his responsibilities."

"Yes, that's so," came a chorus of the brethren, finding comfort and reassurance as their voices and spirits began to recover from the blight.

"There's a party at the Judge's to-night," said Mr. Bradbury—"kind of a ball Mamie Pike's givin' for the young folks. Quite a doin's, I hear."

"That's another thing that's ruining Canaan," Mr. Arp declared, morosely. "These entertainments they have nowadays. Spend all the money out of town — band from Indianapolis, chicken salad and darkey waiters from Chicago! And what I want to know is, What's this town goin' to do about the nigger question?"

"What about it?" asked Mr. Davey, belligerently.

"What about it?" Mr. Arp mocked, fiercely. "You better say, 'What about it?'"

"Well, what?" maintained Mr. Davey, steadfastly.

"I'll bet there ain't any less than four thousand niggers in Canaan to-day!" Mr. Arp hammered the floor with his stick. "Every last one of 'em criminals, and more comin' on every train."

"No such a thing," said Squire Buckalew, living

up to his bounden duty. "You look down the street. There's the ten-forty-five comin' in now. I'll bet you a straight five-cent Peek-a-Boo cigar there ain't ary nigger on the whole train, except the sleepin'- car porters."

"What kind of a way to argue is that?" demanded Mr. Arp, hotly. "Bettin' ain't proof, is it? Besides, that's the through express from the East. I meant trains from the South."

"You didn't say so," retorted Buckalew, triumphantly. "Stick to your bet, Eskew, stick to your bet."

"My bet!" cried the outraged Eskew. "Who offered to bet?"

"You did," replied the Squire, with perfect assurance and sincerity. The others supported him in the heartiest spirit of on-with-the-dance, and war and joy were unconfined.

A decrepit hack or two, a couple of old-fashioned surreys, and a few "cut-unders" drove by, bearing the newly arrived and their valises, the hotel omnibus depositing several commercial travellers at the door. A solitary figure came from the station on foot, and when it appeared within fair range of the window, Uncle Joe Davey, who had but hovered on the flanks of the combat, first removed his spectacles and wiped them, as though distrusting the vision they offered him, then, replacing them, scanned anew the approaching figure and uttered a smothered cry.

"My Lord A'mighty!" he gasped. "What's this? Look there!"

They looked. A truce came involuntarily, and they sat in paralytic silence as the figure made its stately and sensational progress along Main Street.

Not only the aged men were smitten. Men shovelling snow from the pavements stopped suddenly in their labors; two women, talking busily on a doorstep, were stilled and remained in frozen attitudes as it passed; a grocer's clerk, crossing the pavement, carrying a heavily laden basket to his delivery wagon, halted half-way as the figure came near, and then, making a pivot of his heels as it went by, behaved towards it as does the magnetic needle to the pole.

It was that of a tall gentleman, cheerfully, though somewhat with ennui, enduring his nineteenth winter. His long and slender face he wore smiling, beneath an accurately cut plaster of dark hair cornicing his forehead, a fashion followed by many youths of that year. This perfect bang was shown under a round black hat whose rim was so small as almost not to be there at all; and the head was supported by a waxy-white sea-wall of collar, rising three inches above the blue billows of a puffed cravat, upon which floated a large, hollow pearl.

ENTER CHORUS

His ulster, sporting a big cape at the shoulders, and a tasselled hood over the cape, was of a rough Scotch cloth, patterned in faint, gray-and-white squares the size of baggage-checks, and it was so long that the skirts trailed in the snow. His legs were lost in the accurately creased, voluminous garments that were the tailors' canny reaction from the tight trousers with which the 'Eighties had begun: they were, in color, a palish russet, broadly striped with gray, and, in size, surpassed the milder spirit of fashion so far as they permitted a liberal knee action to take place almost without superficial effect. Upon his feet glistened long shoes, shaped, save for the heels, like sharp racing-shells; these were partially protected by tan-colored low gaiters with flat, shiny, brown buttons. In one hand the youth swung a bone-handled walking-stick, perhaps an inch and a half in diameter, the other carried a yellow leather banjo-case, upon the outer side of which glittered the embossed-silver initials, "E. B." He was smoking, but walked with his head up, making use, however, of a gait at that time new to Canaan, a seeming superbly irresponsible lounge, engendering much motion of the shoulders, producing an effect of carelessness combined with independence—an effect which the innocent have been known to hail as an unconscious one.

He looked about him as he came, smilingly, with an expression of princely amusement—as an elderly cabinet minister, say, strolling about a village where he had spent some months in his youth, a hamlet which he had then thought large and imposing, but which, being revisited after years of cosmopolitan glory, appeals to his whimsy and his pity. The youth's glance at the court-house unmistakably said: "Ah, I recall that odd little box. I thought it quite large in the days before I became what I am now, and I dare say the good townsfolk still think it an imposing structure!" With everything in sight he deigned to be amused, especially with the old faces in the "National House" windows. To these he waved his stick with airy graciousness.

"My soul!" said Mr. Davey. "It seems to know some of us!"

"Yes," agreed Mr. Arp, his voice recovered, "and I know *it*."

"You do?" exclaimed the Colonel.

"I do, and so do you. It's Fanny Louden's boy, 'Gene, come home for his Christmas holidays."

"By George! you're right," cried Flitcroft; "I recognize him now."

"But what's the matter with him?" asked Mr. Bradbury, eagerly. "Has he joined some patent-medicine troupe?"

"Not a bit," replied Eskew. "He went East to college last fall."

"Do they *make* the boys wear them clothes?" persisted Bradbury. "Is it some kind of uniform?"

"I don't care what it is," said Jonas Tabor. "If I was Henry Louden I wouldn't let him wear 'em around here."

"Oh, you wouldn't, wouldn't you, Jonas?" Mr. Arp employed the accents of sarcasm. "I'd like to see Henry Louden try to interfere with 'Gene Bantry. Fanny'd lock the old fool up in the cellar."

The lofty vision lurched out of view.

"I reckon," said the Colonel, leaning forward to see the last of it—"I reckon Henry Louden's about the saddest case of abused step-father I ever saw."

"It's his own fault," said Mr. Arp—"*twice* not havin' sense enough not to marry. Him with a son of his own, too!"

"Yes," assented the Colonel, "marryin' a widow with a son of her own, and that widow Fanny!"

"Wasn't it just the same with her first husband —Bantry?" Mr. Davey asked, not for information, as he immediately answered himself. "You bet it was! Didn't she always rule the roost? Yes, she did. She made a god of 'Gene from the day he was born. Bantry's house was run for him, like Louden's is now."

"And look," exclaimed Mr. Arp, with satisfaction, "at the way he's turned out!"

"He ain't turned out at all yet; he's too young," said Buckalew. "Besides, clothes don't make the man."

"Wasn't he smokin' a cigareet!" cried Eskew, triumphantly. This was final.

"It's a pity Henry Louden can't do something for his own son," said Mr. Bradbury. "Why don't he send him away to college?"

"Fanny won't let him," chuckled Mr. Arp, malevolently. "Takes all their spare change to keep 'Gene there in style. I don't blame her. 'Gene certainly acts the fool, but that Joe Louden is the orneriest boy I ever saw in an ornery world-full."

"He always was kind of mis*chee*vous," admitted Buckalew. "I don't think he's mean, though, and it does seem kind of not just right that Joe's father's money — Bantry didn't leave anything to speak of—has to go to keepin' 'Gene on the fat of the land, with Joe gittin' up at half-past four to carry papers, and him goin' on nineteen years old."

"It's all he's fit for!" exclaimed Eskew. "He's low down, I tell ye. Ain't it only last week Judge Pike caught him shootin' craps with Pike's nigger driver and some other nigger hired-men in the alley back of Pike's barn."

Mr. Schindlinger, the retired grocer, one of the silent members, corroborated Eskew's information. "I heert dot, too," he gave forth, in his fat voice. "He blays dominoes pooty often in der room back off Louie Farbach's tsaloon. I see him myself. Pooty often. Blayin' fer a leedle money — mit loafers! Loafers!"

"Pretty outlook for the Loudens!" said Eskew Arp, much pleased. "One boy a plum fool and dressed like it, the other gone to the dogs already!"

"What could you expect Joe to be?" retorted Squire Buckalew. "What chance has he ever had? Long as I can remember Fanny's made him fetch and carry for 'Gene. 'Gene's had everything—all the fancy clothes, all the pocket-money, and now college!"

"You ever hear that boy Joe talk politics?" asked Uncle Joe Davey, crossing a cough with a chuckle. "His head's so full of schemes fer running this town, and state, too, it's a wonder it don't bust. Henry Louden told me he's see Joe set around and study by the hour how to save three million dollars for the state in two years."

"And the best he can do for himself," added Eskew, "is deliverin' the *Daily Tocsin* on a second-hand Star bicycle and gamblin' with niggers and riff-raff! None of the nice young folks invite him to their doin's any more."

"That's because he's got so shabby he's quit goin' with em," said Buckalew.

"No, it ain't," snapped Mr. Arp. "It's because he's so low down. He's no more 'n a town outcast. There ain't ary one of the girls 'll have a thing to do with him, except that rip-rarin' tomboy next door to Louden's; and the others don't have much to do with *her*, neither, I can tell ye. That Arie Tabor—"

Colonel Flitcroft caught him surreptitiously by the arm. "*Sh*, Eskew!" he whispered. "Look out what you're sayin'!"

"You needn't mind me," Jonas Tabor spoke up, crisply. "I washed my hands of all responsibility for Roger's branch of the family long ago. Never was one of 'em had the energy or brains to make a decent livin', beginning with Roger; not one worth his salt! I set Roger's son up in business, and all the return he ever made me was to go into bankruptcy and take to drink, till he died a sot, like his wife did of shame. I done all I could when I handed him over my store, and I never expect to lift a finger for 'em again. Ariel Tabor's my grandniece, but she didn't act like it, and you can say anything you like about her, for what I care. The last time I spoke to her was a year and a half ago, and I don't reckon I'll ever trouble to again."

"How was that, Jonas?" quickly inquired Mr. Davey, who, being the eldest of the party, was the most curious. "What happened?"

"She was out in the street, up on that high bicycle of Joe Louden's. He was teachin' her to ride, and she was sittin' on it like a man does. I stopped and told her she wasn't respectable. Sixteen years old, goin' on seventeen!"

"What did she say?"

"Laughed," said Jonas, his voice becoming louder as the recital of his wrongs renewed their sting in his soul. "Laughed!"

"What did you do?"

"I went up to her and told her she wasn't a decent girl, and shook the wheel." Mr. Tabor illustrated by seizing the lapels of Joe Davey and shaking him. "I told her if her grandfather had any spunk she'd git an old-fashioned hidin' for be-havin' that way. And I shook the wheel again." Here Mr. Tabor, forgetting in the wrath incited by the recollection that he had not to do with an inanimate object, swung the gasping and helpless Mr. Davey rapidly back and forth in his chair. "I shook it good and hard!"

"What did she do then?" asked Peter Brad-bury.

"Fell off on me," replied Jonas, violently. "On purpose!"

"I wisht she'd killed ye," said Mr. Davey, in a choking voice, as, released, he sank back in his chair.

"On purpose!" repeated Jonas. "And smashed a straw hat I hadn't had three months! All to pieces! So it couldn't be fixed!"

"And what then?" pursued Bradbury.

"*She* ran," replied Jonas, bitterly—"ran! And Joe Louden — Joe Louden—" He paused and gulped.

"What did he do?" Peter leaned forward in his chair eagerly.

The narrator of the outrage gulped again, and opened and shut his mouth before responding.

"He said if I didn't pay for a broken spoke on his wheel he'd have to sue me!"

No one inquired if Jonas had paid, and Jonas said no more. The recollection of his wrongs, together with the illustrative violence offered to Mr. Davey, had been too much for him. He sank back, panting, in his chair, his hands fluttering nervously over his heart, and closed his eyes.

"I wonder why," ruminated Mr. Bradbury—"I wonder why 'Gene Bantry walked up from the deepo. Don't seem much like his style. Should think he'd of rode up in a hack.

"Sho!" said Uncle Joe Davey, his breath recovered. "He wanted to walk up past Judge

Pike's, to see if there wasn't a show of Mamie's bein' at the window, and give her a chance to look at that college uniform and banjo-box and new walk of his."

Mr. Arp began to show signs of uneasiness.

"I'd like mighty well to know," he said, shifting round in his chair, "if there's anybody here that's been able to answer the question I *put*, yesterday, just before we went home. You all tried to, but I didn't hear anything I could consider anyways near even a fair argument."

"Who tried to?" asked Buckalew, sharply, sitting up straight. "What question?"

"What proof can you bring me," began Mr. Arp, deliberately, "that we folks, modernly, ain't more degenerate than the ancient Romans?"

II

A RESCUE

MAIN STREET, already muffled by the snow, added to its quietude a frozen hush where the wonder-bearing youth pursued his course along its white, straight way. None was there in whom impertinence overmastered astonishment, or who recovered from the sight in time to jeer with effect; no "Trab's boy" gathered courage to enact in the thoroughfare a scene of mockery and of joy. Leaving business at a temporary stand-still behind him, Mr. Bantry swept his long coat steadily over the snow and soon emerged upon that part of the street where the mart gave way to the home. The comfortable houses stood pleasantly back from the street, with plenty of lawn and shrubbery about them; and often, along the picket-fences, the laden branches of small cedars, bending low with their burden, showered the young man's swinging shoulders glitteringly as he brushed by.

And now that expression he wore—the indulgent amusement of a man of the world—began to disintegrate and show signs of change. It became finely grave, as of a high conventionality, lofty, assured, and mannered, as he approached the Pike mansion. (The remotest stranger must at once perceive that the Canaan papers could not have called it otherwise without pain.)

It was a big, smooth-stone-faced house, product of the 'Seventies, frowning under an outrageously insistent mansard, capped by a cupola, and staring out of long windows overtopped with "ornamental" slabs. Two cast-iron deer, painted death-gray, twins of the same mould, stood on opposite sides of the front walk, their backs towards it and each other, their bodies in profile to the street, their necks bent, however, so that they gazed upon the passer-by — yet gazed without emotion. Two large, calm dogs guarded the top of the steps leading to the front-door; they also were twins and of the same interesting metal, though honored beyond the deer by coats of black paint and shellac. It was to be remarked that these dogs were of no distinguishable species or breed, yet they were unmistakably dogs; the dullest must have recognized them as such at a glance, which was, perhaps, enough. It was a hideous house, important-looking, cold, yet harshly aggressive, a house whose exterior provoked a shuddering guess of the brass lambrequins and plush fringes within; a solid house, obviously— nay, blatantly—the residence of the principal citizen, whom it had grown to resemble, as is the impish habit of houses; and it sat in the middle of its flat acre of snowy lawn like a rich, fat man enraged and sitting straight up in bed to swear.

And yet there was one charming thing about this ugly house. Some workmen were enclosing a large side porch with heavy canvas, evidently for festal purposes. Looking out from between two strips of the canvas was the rosy and delicate face of a pretty girl, smiling upon Eugene Bantry as he passed. It was an obviously pretty face, all the youth and prettiness there for your very first glance; elaborately pretty, like the splendid profusion of hair about and above it—amber-colored hair, upon which so much time had been spent that a circle of large, round curls rose above the mass of it like golden bubbles tipping a coronet.

The girl's fingers were pressed thoughtfully against her chin as Eugene strode into view; immediately her eyes widened and brightened. He swung along the fence with the handsomest appearance of unconsciousness, until he reached a point nearly opposite her. Then he turned his head, as if haphazardly, and met her eyes. At once she threw out her hand towards him, waving him a greeting—a gesture which, as her fingers had been near her lips, was a little like throwing a kiss. He crooked an elbow and with a one-two-three military movement removed his small-brimmed hat, extended it to full arm's-length at the shoulder-level, returned it to his head with Life-Guard precision. This was also new to Canaan. He was letting Mamie Pike have it all at once.

The impression was as large as he could have desired. She remained at the opening in the canvas and watched him until he wagged his shoulders round the next corner and disappeared into a cross street. As for Eugene, he was calm with a great calm, and very red.

He had not covered a great distance, however, before his gravity was replaced by his former smiling look of the landed gentleman amused by the innocent pastimes of the peasants, though there was no one in sight except a woman sweeping some snow from the front steps of a cottage, and she, not perceiving him, retired in-doors without knowing her loss. He had come to a thinly built part of the town, the perfect quiet of which made the sound he heard as he opened the picket gate of his own home all the more startling. It was a scream—loud, frantic, and terror-stricken.

Eugene stopped, with the gate half open.

Out of the winter skeleton of a grape-arbor at one side of the four-square brick house a brown-faced girl of seventeen precipitated herself through the air in the midst of a shower of torn card-board which she threw before her as she leaped. She lit upon her toes and headed for the gate at top speed, pursued by a pale young man whose thin arms strove spasmodically to reach her. Scattering snow behind them, hair flying, the pair sped on like two tattered branches before a high wind; for, as they came nearer Eugene (of whom, in the tensity of their flight, they took no note), it was to be seen that both were so shabbily dressed as to be almost ragged. There was a brown patch upon the girl's faded skirt at the knee; the short-ness of the garment indicating its age to be some-thing over three years, as well as permitting the knowledge to become more general than befitting that her cotton stockings had been clumsily darned in several places. Her pursuer was in as evil case; his trousers displayed a tendency to fringedness at pocket and heel; his coat, blowing open as he ran, threw pennants of torn lining to the breeze, and made it too plain that there were but three buttons on his waistcoat.

The girl ran beautifully, but a fleeter foot was behind her, and though she dodged and evaded like a creature of the woods, the reaching hand fell upon the loose sleeve of her red blouse, nor fell lightly. She gave a wrench of frenzy; the antique fabric refused the strain; parted at the shoulder seam so thoroughly that the whole sleeve came away—but not to its owner's release, for she had been brought round by the jerk, so that, agile as she had shown herself, the pursuer threw an arm about her neck, before she could twist away, and held her.

There was a sharp struggle, as short as it was fierce. Neither of these extraordinary wrestlers spoke. They fought. Victory hung in the balance for perhaps four seconds; then the girl was thrown heavily upon her back, in such a turmoil of snow that she seemed to be the mere nucleus of a white comet. She struggled to get up, plying knee and elbow with a very anguish of determination; but her opponent held her, pinioned both her wrists with one hand, and with the other rubbed great handfuls of snow into her face, sparing neither mouth nor eyes.

"You will!" he cried. "You will tear up my pictures! A dirty trick, and you get washed for it!"

Half suffocated, choking, gasping, she still fought on, squirming and kicking with such spirit that the pair of them appeared to the beholder like figures of mist writhing in a fountain of snow.

More violence was to mar the peace of morning. Unexpectedly attacked from the rear, the conqueror was seized by the nape of the neck and one wrist, and jerked to his feet, simultaneously receiving a succession of kicks from his assailant. Prompted by an entirely natural curiosity, he essayed to turn his head to see who this might be, but a twist of his forearm and the pressure of strong fingers under his ear constrained him to remain as he was; therefore, abandoning resistance, and, oddly enough, accepting without comment the indication that his captor desired to remain for the moment incognito, he resorted calmly to explanations.

"She tore up a picture of mine," he said, receiving the punishment without apparent emotion. "She seemed to think because she'd drawn it herself she had a right to."

There was a slight whimsical droop at the corner of his mouth as he spoke, which might have been thought characteristic of him. He was an odd-looking boy, not ill-made, though very thin and not tall. His pallor was clear and even, as though constitutional; the features were delicate, almost childlike, but they were very slightly distorted, through nervous habit, to an expression at once wistful and humorous; one eyebrow was a shade higher than the other, one side of the mouth slightly drawn down; the eyelids twitched a little, habitually; the fine, blue eyes themselves were almost comically reproachful—the look of a puppy who thinks you would not have beaten him if you had known what was in his heart. All of this was in the quality of his voice, too, as he said to his invisible captor, with an air of detachment from any personal feeling:

"What peculiar shoes you wear! I don't think I ever felt any so pointed before."

The rescuing knight took no thought of offering to help the persecuted damsel to arise; instead, he tightened his grip upon the prisoner's neck until, perforce, water—not tears—started from the latter's eyes.

"You miserable little muff," said the conqueror, "what the devil do you mean, making this scene on our front lawn?"

"Why, it's Eugene!" exclaimed the helpless one. "They didn't expect you till to-night. When did you get in?"

"Just in time to give you a lesson, my buck," replied Bantry, grimly. "In *good* time for that, my playful step-brother."

He began to twist the other's wrist—a treatment of bone and ligament in the application of which school-boys and even freshmen are often adept. Eugene made the torture acute, and was apparently enjoying the work, when suddenly—without any manner of warning — he received an astounding blow upon the left ear, which half stunned him for the moment, and sent his hat flying and himself reeling, so great was the surprise and shock of it. It was not a slap, not an open-handed push, nothing like it, but a fierce, well-delivered blow from a clinched fist with the shoulder behind it, and it was the girl who had given it.

"Don't you dare to touch Joe!" she cried, passionately. "Don't you lay a finger on him."

Furious and red, he staggered round to look at her.

"You wretched little wild-cat, what do you mean by that?" he broke out.

"Don't you touch Joe!" she panted. "Don't you—" Her breath caught and there was a break in her voice as she faced him. She could not finish he repetition of that cry, "Don't you touch Joe!"

But there was no break in the spirit, that passion protection which had dealt the blow. Both boys looked at her, something aghast.

She stood before them, trembling with rage and shivering with cold in the sudden wind which had come up. Her hair had fallen and blew across her streaming face in brown witch-wisps; one of the ill-darned stockings had come down and hung about her shoe in folds full of snow; the arm which had lost its sleeve was bare and wet; thin as the arm of a growing boy, it shook convulsively, and was red from shoulder to clinched fist. She was covered with snow. Mists of white drift blew across her, mercifully half veiling her.

Eugene recovered himself. He swung round upon his heel, restored his hat to his head with precision, picked up his stick and touched his banjo-case with it.

"Carry that into the house," he said, indifferently, to his step-brother.

"Don't you do it!" said the girl, hotly, between her chattering teeth.

Eugene turned towards her, wearing the sharp edge of a smile. Not removing his eyes from her face, he produced with deliberation a flat silver box from a pocket, took therefrom a cigarette, replaced the box, extracted a smaller silver box from another pocket, shook out of it a fusee, slowly lit the cigarette—this in a splendid silence, which he finally broke to say, languidly, but with particular distinctness:

"Ariel Tabor, go home!"

The girl's teeth stopped chattering, her lips remaining parted; she shook the hair out of her eyes and stared at him as if she did not understand, but Joe Louden, who had picked up the banjo-case obediently, burst into cheerful laughter.

"That's it, 'Gene," he cried, gayly. "That's the way to talk to her!"

"Stow it, you young cub," replied Eugene, not turning to him. "Do you think I'm trying to be amusing?"

"I don't know what you mean by 'stow it,'" Joe began, "but if—"

"I mean," interrupted the other, not relaxing his faintly smiling stare at the girl—"I mean that Ariel Tabor is to go home. Really, we can't have this kind of thing occurring upon our front lawn!"

The flush upon her wet cheeks deepened and became dark; even her arm grew redder as she gazed back at him. In his eyes was patent his complete realization of the figure she cut, of this bare arm, of the strewn hair, of the fallen stocking, of the ragged shoulder of her blouse, of her patched short skirt, of the whole dishevelled little figure. He was the master of the house, and he was sending her home as ill-behaved children are sent home by neighbors.

The immobile, amused superiority of this proprietor of silver boxes, this wearer of strange and brilliant garments, became slightly intensified as he pointed to the fallen sleeve, a rag of red and snow, lying near her feet.

"You might take that with you?" he said, interrogatively.

Her gaze had not wavered in meeting his, but at this her eyelashes began to wink uncontrollably, her chin to tremble. She bent over the sleeve and picked it up, before Joe Louden, who had started towards her, could do it for her. Then turning, her head still bent so that her face was hidden from both of them, she ran out of the gate.

"*Do* go!" Joe called after her, vehemently. "*Go!* Just to show what a fool you are to think 'Gene's in earnest."

He would have followed, but his step-brother caught him by the arm. "Don't stop her," said Eugene. "Can't you tell when I *am* in earnest, you bally muff!"

"I know you are," returned the other, in a low voice. "I didn't want her to think so for your sake."

"Thousands of thanks," said Eugene, airily. "You are a wise young judge. She couldn't stay—in *that* state, could she? I sent her for her own good."

"She could have gone in the house and your mother might have loaned her a jacket," returned Joe, swallowing. "You had no business to make her go out in the street like that."

Eugene laughed. "There isn't a soul in sight —and there, she's all right now. She's home."

Ariel had run along the fence until she came to

the next gate, which opened upon a walk leading to a shabby, meandering old house of one story, with a very long, low porch, once painted white, running the full length of the front. Ariel sprang upon the porch and disappeared within the house.

Joe stood looking after her, his eyelashes winking as had hers. "You oughtn't to have treated her that way," he said, huskily.

Eugene laughed again. "How were *you* treating her when I came up? You bully her all you want to yourself, but nobody else must say even a fatherly word to her!"

"That wasn't bullying," explained Joe. "We fight all the time."

"Mais oui!" assented Eugene. "I fancy!"

"What?" said the other, blankly.

"Pick up that banjo-case again and come on," commanded Mr. Bantry, tartly. "Where's the mater?"

Joe stared at him. "Where's what?"

"The mater!" was the frowning reply.

"Oh yes, I know!" said Joe, looking at his step-brother curiously. "I've seen it in stories. She's up-stairs. You'll be a surprise. You're wearing lots of clothes, 'Gene."

"I suppose it will seem so to Canaan," returned the other, weariedly. "Governor feeling fit?"

"I never saw him," Joe replied; then caught

himself. "Oh, I see what you mean! Yes, he's all right."

They had come into the hall, and Eugene was removing the long coat, while his step-brother looked at him thoughtfully.

"'Gene," asked the latter, in a softened voice, "have you seen Mamie Pike yet?"

"You will find, my young friend," responded Mr. Bantry, "if you ever go about much outside of Canaan, that ladies' names are not supposed to be mentioned indiscriminately."

"It's only," said Joe, "that I wanted to say that there's a dance at their house to-night. I suppose you'll be going?"

"Certainly. Are you?"

Both knew that the question was needless; but Joe answered, gently:

"Oh no, of course not." He leaned over and fumbled with one foot as if to fasten a loose shoe-string. "She wouldn't be very likely to ask me."

"Well, what about it?"

"Only that—that Arie Tabor's going."

"Indeed!" Eugene paused on the stairs, which he had begun to ascend. "Very interesting."

"I thought," continued Joe, hopefully, straightening up to look at him, "that maybe you'd dance with her. I don't believe many will ask her—I'm afraid they won't—and if you would, even only once, it would kind of make up for"—he faltered —"for out there," he finished, nodding his head in the direction of the gate.

If Eugene vouchsafed any reply, it was lost in a loud, shrill cry from above, as a small, intensely nervous-looking woman in blue silk ran half-way down the stairs to meet him and caught him tearfully in her arms.

"Dear old mater!" said Eugene.

Joe went out of the front-door quickly.

III

OLD HOPES

THE door which Ariel had entered opened upon a narrow hall, and down this she ran to her own room, passing, with face averted, the entrance to the broad, low-ceilinged chamber that had served Roger Tabor as a studio for almost fifty years. He was sitting there now, in a hopeless and disconsolate attitude, with his back towards the double doors, which were open, and had been open since their hinges had begun to give way, when Ariel was a child. Hearing her step, he called her name, but did not turn; and, receiving no answer, sighed faintly as he heard her own door close upon her.

Then, as his eyes wandered about the many canvases which leaned against the dingy walls, he sighed again. Usually they showed their brown backs, but to-day he had turned them all to face outward. Twilight, sunset, moonlight (the Courthouse in moonlight), dawn, morning, noon (Main

43

Street at noon), high summer, first spring, red autumn, midwinter, all were there—illimitably detailed, worked to a smoothness like a glaze, and all lovingly done with unthinkable labor.

And there were "Italian Flower-Sellers," damsels with careful hair, two figures together, one blonde, the other as brunette as lampblack, the blonde—in pink satin and blue slippers—leaning against a pillar and smiling over the golden coins for which she had exchanged her posies; the brunette seated at her feet, weeping upon an unsold bouquet. There were red-sashed "Fisher Lads" wading with butterfly-nets on their shoulders; there was a "Tying the Ribbon on Pussy's Neck"; there were portraits in oil and petrifactions in crayon, as hard and tight as the purses of those who had refused to accept them, leaving them upon their maker's hands because the likeness had failed.

After a time the old man got up, went to his easel near a window, and, sighing again, began patiently to work upon one of these failures—a portrait, in oil, of a savage old lady, which he was doing from a photograph. The expression of the mouth and the shape of the nose had not pleased her descendants and the beneficiaries under the will, and it was upon the images of these features that Roger labored. He leaned far forward, with

44

his face close to the canvas, holding his brushes after the Spencerian fashion, working steadily through the afternoon, and, when the light grew dimmer, leaning closer to his canvas to see. When it had become almost dark in the room, he lit a student-lamp with a green-glass shade, and, placing it upon a table beside him, continued to paint. Ariel's voice interrupted him at last.

"It's quitting-time, grandfather," she called, gently, from the doorway behind him.

He sank back in his chair, conscious, for the first time, of how tired he had grown. "I suppose so," he said, "though it seemed to me that I was just getting my hand in." His eyes brightened for a moment. "I declare, I believe I've caught it a great deal better. Come and look, Ariel. Doesn't it seem to you that I'm getting it? Those pearly shadows in the flesh—"

"I'm sure of it. Those people ought to be very proud to have it." She came to him quietly, took the palette and brushes from his hands and began to clean them, standing in the shadow behind him. "It's too good for them."

"I wonder if it is," he said, slowly, leaning forward and curving his hands about his eyes so as to shut off everything from his view except the canvas. "I wonder if it is!" he repeated. Then his hands dropped sadly in his lap, and he sank

45

back again with a patient kind of revulsion. "No, no, it isn't! I always think they're good when I've just finished them. I've been fooled that way all my life. They don't look the same afterwards."

"They're always beautiful," she said, softly.

"Ah, ah!" he sighed.

"Now, Roger!" she cried, with cheerful sharpness, continuing her work.

"I know," he said, with a plaintive laugh,—"I know. Sometimes I think that all my reward has been in the few minutes I've had just after finishing them. During those few minutes I seem to see in them all that I wanted to put in them; I see it because what I've been trying to express is still so warm in my own eyes that I seem to have got it on the canvas where I wanted it."

"But you do," she said. "You do get it there."

"No," he murmured, in return. "I never did. I got out some of the old ones when I came in this morning, some that I hadn't looked at for years, and it's the same with them. You can do it much better yourself—your sketches show it."

"No, no!" she protested, quickly.

"Yes, they do; and I wondered if it was only because you were young. But those I did when I was young are almost the same as the ones I paint now. I haven't learned much. There hasn't

46

been any one to show me! And you can't learn from print, never! Yet I've grown in what I *see*—grown so that the world is full of beauty to me that I never dreamed of seeing when I began. But I can't paint it—I can't get it on the canvas. Ah, I think I might have known how to, if I hadn't had to teach myself, if I could only have seen how some of the other fellows did their work. If I'd ever saved money to get away from Canaan—if I could have gone away from it and come back knowing how to paint it—if I could have got to Paris for just one month! *Paris*—for just one month!"

"Perhaps we will; you can't tell what *may* happen." It was always her reply to this cry of his.

"*Paris*—for just one month!" he repeated, with infinite wistfulness, and then realizing what an old, old cry it was with him, he shook his head, impatiently sniffing out a laugh at himself, rose and went pottering about among the canvases, returning their faces to the wall, and railing at them mutteringly.

"Whatever took me into it, I don't know. I might have done something useful. But I couldn't bring myself ever to consider doing anything else—I couldn't bear even to think of it! Lord forgive me, I even tried to encourage your father to paint. Perhaps he might as well, poor boy, as to have put

47

all he'd made into buying Jonas out. Ah me! There you go, 'Flower-Girls'! Turn your silly faces to the wall and smile and cry there till I'm gone and somebody throws you on a bonfire. *I'll* never look at you again." He paused, with the canvas half turned. "And yet," he went on, reflectively, "a man promised me thirty-five dollars for that picture once. I painted it to order, but he went away before I finished it, and never answered the letters I wrote him about it. I wish I had the money now—perhaps we could have more than two meals a day."

"We don't need more," said Ariel, scraping the palette attentively. "It's healthier with only breakfast and supper. I think I'd rather have a new dress than dinner."

"I dare say you would," the old man mused. "You're young—you're young. What were you doing all this afternoon, child?"

"In my room, trying to make over mamma's wedding-dress for to-night."

"To-night?"

"Mamie Pike invited me to a dance at their house."

"Very well; I'm glad you're going to be gay," he said, not seeing the faintly bitter smile that came to her face.

"I don't think I'll be very gay," she answered.

"I don't know why I go—nobody ever asks me to dance."

"Why not?" he asked, with an old man's astonishment.

"I don't know. Perhaps it's because I don't dress very well." Then, as he made a sorrowful gesture, she cut him off before he could speak. "Oh, it isn't altogether because we're poor; it's more I don't know how to wear what I've got, the way some girls do. I never cared much and—well, *I'm* not worrying, Roger! And I think I've done a good deal with mamma's dress. It's a very grand dress. I wonder I never thought of wearing it until to-day. I may be"—she laughed and blushed—"I may be the belle of the ball—who knows!"

"You'll want me to walk over with you and come for you afterwards, I expect."

"Only to take me. It may be late when I come away—if a good many *should* ask me to dance, for once! Of course I could come home alone. But Joe Louden is going to sort of hang around outside, and he'll meet me at the gate and see me safe home."

"Oh!" he exclaimed, blankly.

"Isn't it all right?" she asked.

"I think I'd better come for you," he answered, gently. "The truth is, I—I think you'd better not be with Joe Louden a great deal."

"Why?"

"Well, he doesn't seem a vicious boy to me, but I'm afraid he's getting rather a bad name, my dear."

"He's not getting one," she said, gravely. "He's already got one. He's had a bad name in Canaan for a long while. It grew in the first place out of shabbiness and mischief, but it did grow; and if people keep on giving him a bad name the time will come when he'll live up to it. He's not any worse than I am, and I guess my own name isn't too good—for a girl. And yet, so far, there's nothing against him except his bad name."

"I'm afraid there is," said Roger. "It doesn't look very well for a young man of his age to be doing no better than delivering papers."

"It gives him time to study law," she answered, quickly. "If he clerked all day in a store, he couldn't."

"I didn't know he was studying now. I thought I'd heard that he was in a lawyer's office for a few weeks last year, and was turned out for setting fire to it with a pipe—"

"It was an accident," she interposed.

"But some pretty important papers were burned, and after that none of the other lawyers would have him."

"He's not in an office," she admitted. "I didn't

mean that. But he studies a great deal. He goes to the courts all the time they're in session, and he's bought some books of his own."

"Well—perhaps," he assented; "but they say he gambles and drinks, and that last week Judge Pike threatened to have him arrested for throwing dice with some negroes behind the Judge's stable."

"What of it? I'm about the only nice person in town that will have anything to do with him—and nobody except you thinks *I'm* very nice!"

"Ariel! Ariel!"

"I know all about his gambling with darkies," she continued, excitedly, her voice rising, "and I know that he goes to saloons, and that he's an intimate friend of half the riffraff in town; and I know the reason for it, too, because he's told me. He wants to know them, to understand them; and he says some day they'll make him a power, and then he can help them!"

The old man laughed helplessly. "But I can't let him bring you home, my dear."

She came to him slowly and laid her hands upon his shoulders. Grandfather and granddaughter were nearly of the same height, and she looked squarely into his eyes. "Then you must say it is because you want to come for me, not because I mustn't come with Joe."

"But I think it is a little because you mustn't

come with Joe," he answered, "especially from the Pikes'. Don't you see that it mightn't be well for Joe himself, if the Judge should happen to see him? I understand he warned the boy to keep away from the neighborhood entirely or he would have him locked up for dice-throwing. The Judge is a very influential man, you know, and as determined in matters like this as he is irritable."

"Oh, if you put it on that ground," the girl replied, her eyes softening, "I think you'd better come for me yourself."

"Very well, I put it on that ground," he returned, smiling upon her

"Then I'll send Joe word and get supper," she said, kissing him.

It was the supper-hour not only for them but everywhere in Canaan, and the cold air of the streets bore up and down and around corners the smell of things frying. The dining-room windows of all the houses threw bright patches on the snow of the side-yards; the windows of other rooms, except those of the kitchens, were dark, for the rule of the place was Puritanical in thrift, as in all things; and the good housekeepers disputed every record of the meters with unhappy gas-collectors.

There was no better housekeeper in town than Mrs. Louden, nor a thriftier, but hers was one of the few houses in Canaan, that evening, which showed bright lights in the front rooms while the family were at supper. It was proof of the agitation caused by the arrival of Eugene that she forgot to turn out the gas in her parlor, and in the chamber she called a library, on her way to the evening meal.

That might not have been thought a cheerful feast for Joe Louden. The fatted calf was upon the board, but it had not been provided for the prodigal, who, in this case, was the brother that stayed at home: the fête rewarded the good brother, who had been in strange lands, and the good one had found much honor in his wanderings, as he carelessly let it appear. Mrs. Louden brightened inexpressibly whenever Eugene spoke of himself, and consequently she glowed most of the time. Her husband— a heavy, melancholy, silent man with a grizzled beard and no mustache—lowered at Joe throughout the meal, but appeared to take a strange comfort in his step-son's elegance and polish. Eugene wore new evening clothes and was lustrous to eye and ear.

Joe escaped as soon as he could, though not before the count of his later sins had been set before Eugene in detail, in mass, and in all of their depth, breadth, and thickness. His father spoke but once, after nodding heavily to confirm all points of Mrs. Louden's recital.

"You better use any influence you've got with your brother," he said to Eugene, "to make him come to time. I can't do anything with him. If he gets in trouble, he needn't come to me! I'll never help him again. I'm *tired* of it!"

Eugene glanced twinklingly at the outcast. "I didn't know he was such a roarer as all that!" he said, lightly, not taking Joe as of enough consequence to be treated as a sinner.

This encouraged Mrs. Louden to pathos upon the subject of her shame before other women when Joe happened to be mentioned, and the supper was finished with the topic. Joe slipped away through the kitchen, sneakingly, and climbed the back fence. In the alley he lit a cheap cigarette, and thrusting his hands into his pockets and shivering violently—for he had no overcoat,—walked away singing to himself, "A Spanish cavalier stood in his retreat," his teeth affording an appropriate though involuntary castanet accompaniment.

His movements throughout the earlier part of that evening are of uncertain report. It is known that he made a partial payment of forty-five cents at a second-hand book-store for a number of volumes—*Grindstaff on Torts* and some others—which he had negotiated on the instalment system; it is also believed that he won twenty-eight cents playing seven-up in the little room behind Louie Far-bach's bar; but these things are of little import compared to the established fact that at eleven o'clock he was one of the ball guests at the Pike Mansion. He took no active part in the festivities, nor was he one of the dancers: his was, on the contrary, the rôle of a quiet observer. He lay stretched at full length upon the floor of the enclosed porch (one of the strips of canvas was later found to have been loosened), wedged between the outer railing and a row of palms in green tubs. The position he occupied was somewhat too draughty to have been recommended by a physician, but he commanded, between the leaves of the screening palms, an excellent view of the room nearest the porch. A long window, open, afforded communication between this room, one of those used for dancing, and the dim bower which had been made of the veranda, whither flirtatious couples made their way between the dances.

It was not to play eavesdropper upon any of these that the uninvited Joe had come. He was not there to listen, and it is possible that, had the curtains of other windows afforded him the chance to behold the dance, he might not have risked the dangers of his present position. He had not the slightest interest in the whispered coquetries that he heard; he watched only to catch now and then, over the shoulders of the dancers, a fitful glimpse of a pretty head that flitted across the window—the amber hair of Mamie Pike. He shivered in the draughts; and the floor of the porch was cement, painful to elbow and knee, the space where he lay cramped and narrow; but the golden bubbles of her hair, the shimmer of her dainty pink dress, and the fluffy wave of her lace scarf as she crossed and recrossed in a waltz, left him, apparently, in no discontent. He watched with parted lips, his pale cheeks reddening whenever those fair glimpses were his. At last she came out to the veranda with Eugene and sat upon a little divan, so close to Joe that, daring wildly in the shadow, he reached out a trembling hand and let his fingers rest upon the end of her scarf, which had fallen from her shoulders and touched the floor. She sat with her back to him, as did Eugene.

"You have changed, I think, since last summer," he heard her say, reflectively.

"For the worse, *ma chérie?*" Joe's expression might have been worth seeing when Eugene said "*ma chérie*," for it was known in the Louden household that Mr. Bantry had failed to pass his examination in the French language.

"No," she answered. "But you have seen so much and accomplished so much since then. You have become so polished and so—" She paused,

56

and then continued, "But perhaps I'd better not say it; you might be offended."

"No. I want you to say it," he returned, confidently, and his confidence was fully justified, for she said:

"Well, then, I mean that you have become so thoroughly a man of the world. Now I've said it! You *are* offended—aren't you?"

"Not at all, not at all," replied Mr. Bantry, preventing by a masterful effort his pleasure from showing in his face. "Though I suppose you mean to imply that I'm rather wicked."

"Oh no," said Mamie, with profound admiration, "not exactly wicked."

"University life *is* fast nowadays," Eugene admitted. "It's difficult not to be drawn into it!"

"And I suppose you look down on poor little Canaan now, and everybody in it!"

"Oh no," he laughed, indulgently. "Not at all, not at all! I find it very amusing."

"All of it?"

"Not you," he answered, becoming very grave.

"Honestly—*don't* you?" Her young voice trembled a little.

"Honestly — indeed — truly—" Eugene leaned very close to her and the words were barely audible. "You *know* I don't!"

"Then I'm—glad," she whispered, and Joe saw

his step-brother touch her hand, but she rose quickly. "There's the music," she cried, happily. "It's a waltz, and it's *yours!*"

Joe heard her little high heels tapping gayly towards the window, followed by the heavier tread of Eugene, but he did not watch them go.

He lay on his back, with the hand that had touched Mamie's scarf pressed across his closed eyes.

The music of that waltz was of the old-fashioned swingingly sorrowful sort, and it would be hard to say how long it was after that before the boy could hear the air played without a recurrence of the bitterness of that moment. The rhythmical pathos of the violins was in such accord with a faint sound of weeping which he heard near him, presently, that for a little while he believed this sound to be part of the music and part of himself. Then it became more distinct, and he raised himself on one elbow to look about.

Very close to him, sitting upon the divan in the shadow, was a girl wearing a dress of beautiful silk. She was crying softly, her face in her hands.

IV

THE DISASTER

RIEL had worked all the afternoon over her mother's wedding - gown, and two hours were required by her toilet for the dance. She curled her hair frizzily, burning it here and there, with a slate-pencil heated over a lamp-chimney, and she placed above one ear three or four large artificial roses, taken from an old hat of her mother's, which she had found in a trunk in the store-room. Possessing no slippers, she carefully blacked and polished her shoes, which had been clumsily resoled, and fastened into the strings of each small rosettes of red ribbon; after which she practised swinging the train of her skirt until she was proud of her manipulation of it. She had no powder, but found in her grandfather's room a lump of magnesia, that he was in the habit of taking for heart-burn, and passed it over and over her brown face and hands. Then a lingering gaze into her small mirror gave her joy at last: she yearned so hard to see herself charming that she did see herself so. Admiration came and she told herself that she was more attractive to look at than she had ever been in her life, and that, perhaps, at last she might begin to be sought for like other girls. The little glass showed a sort of prettiness in her thin, unmatured young face; tripping dance-tunes ran through her head, her feet keeping the time,—ah, she did so hope to dance often that night! Perhaps—perhaps she might be asked for every number. And so, wrapping an old waterproof cloak about her, she took her grandfather's arm and sallied forth, high hopes in her beating heart.

It was in the dressing-room that tne change began to come. Alone, at home in her own ugly little room, she had thought herself almost beautiful, but here in the brightly lighted chamber crowded with the other girls it was different. There was a big cheval-glass at one end of the room, and she faced it, when her turn came—for the mirror was popular—with a sinking spirit. There was the contrast, like a picture painted and framed. The other girls all wore their hair after the fashion introduced to Canaan by Mamie Pike the week before, on her return from a visit to Chicago. None of them had "crimped" and none had bedecked their tresses with artificial flowers. Her alterations of the wedding-dress had not been successful; the skirt was too short in front and higher on one side than on the other, showing too plainly the heavy-soled shoes, which had lost most of their polish in the walk through the snow. The ribbon rosettes were fully revealed, and as she glanced at their reflection she heard the words, "*Look at that train and those rosettes!*" whispered behind her, and saw in the mirror two pretty young women turn away with their handkerchiefs over their mouths and retreat hurriedly to an alcove. All the feet in the room except Ariel's were in dainty kid or satin slippers of the color of the dresses from which they glimmered out, and only Ariel wore a train.

She went away from the mirror and pretended to be busy with a hanging thread in her sleeve.

She was singularly an alien in the chattering room, although she had been born and lived all her life in the town. Perhaps her position among the young ladies may be best defined by the remark, generally current among them, that evening, to the effect that it was "very sweet of Mamie to invite her." Ariel was not like the others; she was not of them, and never had been. Indeed, she did not know them very well. Some of them nodded to her and gave her a word of greeting pleasantly; all of them whispered about her with wonder and suppressed amusement; but none talked to her. They were not unkindly, but they were young and eager and excited over their own interests,—which were then in the "gentlemen's dressing-room."

Each of the other girls had been escorted by a youth of the place, and, one by one, joining these escorts in the hall outside the door, they descended the stairs, until only Ariel was left. She came down alone after the first dance had begun, and greeted her young hostess's mother timidly. Mrs. Pike—a small, frightened-looking woman with a prominent ruby necklace—answered her absently, and hurried away to see that the imported waiters did not steal anything.

Ariel sat in one of the chairs against the wall and watched the dancers with a smile of eager and benevolent interest. In Canaan no parents, no guardians nor aunts, were haled forth o' nights to duenna the junketings of youth; Mrs. Pike did not reappear, and Ariel sat conspicuously alone; there was nothing else for her to do. It was not an easy matter.

When the first dance reached an end, Mamie Pike came to her for a moment with a cheery welcome, and was immediately surrounded by a circle of young men and women, flushed with dancing, shouting as was their wont, laughing inexplicably over words and phrases and unintelligible monosyllables, as if they all belonged to a secret society and these cries were symbols of things exquisitely humorous, which only they understood. Ariel laughed with them more heartily than any other, so that she might seem to be of them and as merry as they were, but almost immediately she found herself outside of the circle, and presently they all whirled away into another dance, and she was left alone again.

So she sat, no one coming near her, through several dances, trying to maintain the smile of delighted interest upon her face, though she felt the muscles of her face beginning to ache with their fixedness, her eyes growing hot and glazed. All the other girls were provided with partners for every dance, with several young men left over, these latter lounging hilariously together in the doorways. Ariel was careful not to glance towards them, but she could not help hating them. Once or twice between the dances she saw Miss Pike speak appealingly to one of the superfluous, glancing, at the same time, in her own direction, and Ariel could see, too, that the appeal proved unsuccessful, until at last Mamie approached her, leading Norbert Flitcroft, partly by the hand, partly by will-power. Norbert was an excessively fat boy, and at the present moment looked as patient as the blind. But he asked Ariel if she was " engaged for the next dance," and, Mamie having flitted away, stood disconsolately beside her, waiting for the music to begin. Ariel was grateful for him.

"I think you must be very good-natured, Mr. Flitcroft," she said, with an air of raillery.

"No, I'm not," he replied, plaintively. "Everybody thinks I am because I'm fat, and they expect me to do things they never dream of asking anybody else to do. I'd like to see 'em even *ask* 'Gene Bantry to go and do some of the things they get me to do! A person isn't good-natured just because he's fat," he concluded, morbidly, "but he might as well be!"

"Oh, I meant good-natured," she returned, with a sprightly laugh, "because you're willing to waltz with *me*."

"Oh, well," he returned, sighing, "that's all right."

The orchestra flourished into "La Paloma"; he put his arm mournfully about her, and taking her right hand with his left, carried her arm out to a rigid right angle, beginning to pump and balance for time. They made three false starts and then got away. Ariel danced badly; she hopped and lost the step, but they persevered, bumping against other couples continually. Circling breathlessly into the next room, they passed close to a long mirror, in which Ariel saw herself, although in a

64

flash, more bitterly contrasted to the others than in the cheval-glass of the dressing-room. The clump of roses was flopping about her neck, her crimped hair looked frowzy, and there was something terribly wrong about her dress. Suddenly she felt her train to be ominously grotesque, as a thing following her in a nightmare.

A moment later she caught her partner making a burlesque face of suffering over her shoulder, and, turning her head quickly, saw for whose benefit he had constructed it. Eugene Bantry, flying expertly by with Mamie, was bestowing upon Mr. Flitcroft a condescendingly commiserative wink. The next instant she tripped in her train and fell to the floor at Eugene's feet, carrying her partner with her.

There was a shout of laughter. The young hostess stopped Eugene, who would have gone on, and he had no choice but to stoop to Ariel's assistance.

"It seems to be a habit of mine," she said, laughing loudly.

She did not appear to see the hand he offered, but got to her feet without help and walked quickly away with Norbert, who proceeded to live up to the character he had given himself.

"Perhaps we had better not try it again," she laughed.

"Well, I should think not," he returned, with the frankest gloom. With the air of conducting her home he took her to the chair against the wall whence he had brought her. There his responsibility for her seemed to cease. "Will you excuse me?" he asked, and there was no doubt that he felt that he had been given more than his share that evening, even though he was fat.

"Yes, indeed." Her laughter was continuous. "I should think you *would* be glad to get rid of me after that. Ha, ha, ha! Poor Mr. Flitcroft, you know you are!"

It was the deadly truth, and the fat one, saying, "Well, if you'll just excuse me now," hurried away with a step which grew lighter as the distance from her increased. Arrived at the haven of a far doorway, he mopped his brow and shook his head grimly in response to frequent rallyings.

Ariel sat through more dances, interminable dances and intermissions, in that same chair, in which, it began to seem, she was to live out the rest of her life. Now and then, if she thought people were looking at her as they passed, she broke into a laugh and nodded slightly, as if still amused over her mishap.

After a long time she rose, and laughing cheerfully to Mr. Flitcroft, who was standing in the doorway and replied with a wan smile, stepped out quickly into the hall, where she almost ran into her great-uncle, Jonas Tabor. He was going towards the big front doors with Judge Pike, having just come out of the latter's library, down the hall.

Jonas was breathing heavily and was shockingly pale, though his eyes were very bright. He turned his back upon his grandniece sharply and went out of the door. Ariel turned from him quite as abruptly and re-entered the room whence she had come. She laughed again to her fat friend as she passed him, and, still laughing, went towards the fatal chair, when her eyes caught sight of Eugene Bantry and Mamie coming in through the window from the porch. Still laughing, she went to the window and looked out; the porch seemed deserted and was faintly illuminated by a few Japanese lanterns. She sprang out, dropped upon the divan, and burying her face in her hands, cried heart-brokenly. Presently she felt something alive touch her foot, and, her breath catching with alarm, she started to rise. A thin hand, issuing from a shabby sleeve, had stolen out between two of the green tubs and was pressing upon one of her shoes.

" *'Sh!*" said Joe. "Don't make a noise!"

His warning was not needed; she had recognized the hand and sleeve instantly. She dropped back with a low sound which would have been hysterical if it had been louder, while he raised himself on his arm until she could see his face dimly, as he peered at her between the palms.

"What were you going on about?" he asked, angrily.

"Nothing," she answered. "I wasn't. You must go away, and quick. It's too dangerous. If the Judge found you—"

"He won't!"

"Ah, you'd risk anything to see Mamie Pike—"

"What were you crying about?" he interrupted.

"Nothing, I tell you!" she repeated, the tears not ceasing to gather in her eyes. "I wasn't."

"I want to know what it was," he insisted. "Didn't the fools ask you to dance? Ah! You needn't tell me. That's it. I've been here for the last three dances and you weren't in sight till you came to the window. Well, what do you care about that for?"

"I don't!" she answered. "I don't!" Then suddenly, without being able to prevent it, she sobbed.

"No," he said, gently, "I see you don't. And you let yourself be a fool because there are a lot of fools in there."

She gave way, all at once, to a gust of sorrow and bitterness; she bent far over and caught his hand and laid it against her wet cheek. "Oh.

68

Joe," she whispered, brokenly, "I think we have such hard lives, you and I! It doesn't seem right —while we're so young! Why can't we be like the others? Why can't we have some of the fun?"

He withdrew his hand, with the embarrassment and shame he would have felt had she been a boy. "Get out!" he said, feebly.

She did not seem to notice, but, still stooping, rested her elbows on her knees and her face in her hands. "I try so hard to have fun, to be like the rest,—and it's always a mistake, always, always, always!" She rocked herself, slightly, from side to side. "I am a fool, it's the truth, or I wouldn't have come to-night. I want to be attractive—I want to be in things. I want to laugh like they do—"

"To laugh just to laugh, and not because there's something funny?"

"Yes, I do, I do! And to know how to dress and to wear my hair—there must be some place where you can learn those things. I've never had any one to show me! Ah! Grandfather said something like that this afternoon—poor man! We're in the same case. If we only had some one to show us! It all seems so *blind*, here in Canaan, for him and me! I don't say it's not my own fault as much as being poor. I've been a hoyden; I don't feel as if I'd learned how to be a girl yet,

Joe. It's only lately I've cared, but I'm seventeen, Joe, and—and to-day—to-day—I was sent home—and to-night—" She faltered, came to a stop, and her whole body was shaken with sobs. "I hate myself so for crying—for everything!"

"I'll tell you something," he whispered, chuckling desperately. "'Gene made me unpack his trunk, and I don't believe he's as great a man at college as he is here. I opened one of his books, and some one had written in it, '*Prigamaloo Bantry, the Class Try-To-Be*'! He'd never noticed, and you ought to have heard him go on! You'd have just died, Ariel—I almost bust wide open! It was a mean trick in me, but I couldn't help showing it to him."

Joe's object was obtained. She stopped crying, and, wiping her eyes, smiled faintly. Then she became grave. "You're jealous of Eugene," she said.

He considered this for a moment. "Yes," he answered, thoughtfully, "I am. But I wouldn't think about him differently on that account. And I wouldn't talk about him to any one but you."

"Not even to—" She left the question unfinished.

"No," he said, quietly. "Of course not."

"No? Because it wouldn't be any use?"

"I don't know. I never have a chance to talk to her, anyway."

"Of course you don't!" Her voice had grown steady. "You say I'm a fool. What are you?"

"You needn't worry about me," he began. "I can take care—"

"'*Sh!*'" she whispered, warningly. The music had stopped, a loud clatter of voices and laughter succeeding it.

"What need to be careful," Joe assured her, "with all that noise going on?"

"You must go away," she said, anxiously. "Oh, please, Joe!"

"Not yet; I want—"

She coughed loudly. Eugene and Mamie Pike had come to the window, with the evident intention of occupying the veranda, but perceiving Ariel engaged with threads in her sleeve, they turned away and disappeared. Other couples looked out from time to time, and finding the solitary figure in possession, retreated abruptly to seek stairways and remote corners for the things they were impelled to say.

And so Ariel held the porch for three dances and three intermissions, occupying a great part of the time with entreaties that her obdurate and reckless companion should go. When, for the fourth time, the music sounded, her agitation had so increased that she was visibly trembling. "I can't stand it, Joe," she said, bending over him.

6   71

"I don't know what would happen if they found you. You've *got* to go!"

"No, I haven't," he chuckled. "They haven't even distributed the supper yet!"

"And you take all the chances," she said, slowly, "just to see her pass that window a few times."

"What chances?"

"Of what the Judge will do if any one sees you."

"Nothing; because if any one saw me I'd leave."

"Please go."

"Not till—"

"*'Sh!*"

A colored waiter, smiling graciously, came out upon the porch bearing a tray of salad, hot oysters, and coffee. Ariel shook her head.

"I don't want any," she murmured.

The waiter turned away in pity and was re-entering the window, when a passionate whisper fell upon his ear as well as upon Ariel's.

"*Take it!*"

"Ma'am?" said the waiter.

"I've changed my mind," she replied, quickly. The waiter, his elation restored, gave of his viands with the superfluous bounty loved by his race when distributing the product of the wealthy.

When he had gone, "Give me everything that's hot," said Joe. "You can keep the salad."

"I couldn't eat it or anything else," she answered, thrusting the plate between the palms.

For a time there was silence. From within the
house came the continuous babble of voices and
laughter, the clink of cutlery on china. The young
people spent a long time over their supper. By-
and-by the waiter returned to the veranda, de-
posited a plate of colored ices upon Ariel's knees
with a noble gesture, and departed.

"No ice for me," said Joe.

"Won't you please go now?" she entreated.

"It wouldn't be good manners," he responded.
"They might think I only came for supper."

"Hand me back the things. The waiter might
come for them any minute."

"Not yet. I haven't quite finished. I eat with
contemplation, Ariel, because there's more than
the mere food and the warmth of it to consider.
There's the pleasure of being entertained by the
great Martin Pike. Think what a real kindness
I'm doing him, too. I increase his good deeds and
his hospitality without his knowing it or being
able to help it. Don't you see how I boost his
standing with the Recording Angel? If Lazarus
had behaved the way I do, Dives needn't have
had those worries that came to him in the after-
life."

"Give me the dish and coffee-cup," she whispered, impatiently. "Suppose the waiter came and had to look for them? Quick!"

"Take them, then. You'll see that jealousy hasn't spoiled my appetite—"

A bottle-shaped figure appeared in the window and she had no time to take the plate and cup which were being pushed through the palm-leaves. She whispered a syllable of warning, and the dishes were hurriedly withdrawn as Norbert Flitcroft, wearing a solemn expression of injury, came out upon the veranda.

He halted suddenly. "What's that?" he asked, with suspicion.

"Nothing," answered Ariel, sharply. "Where?"

"Behind those palms."

"Probably your own shadow," she laughed; "or it might have been a draught moving the leaves."

He did not seem satisfied, but stared hard at the spot where the dishes had disappeared, meantime edging back cautiously nearer the window.

"They want you," he said, after a pause. "Some one's come for you."

"Oh, is grandfather waiting?" She rose, at the same time letting her handkerchief fall. She stooped to pick it up, with her face away from Norbert and toward the palms, whispering tremulously, but with passionate urgency, "Please *go!*"

"It isn't your grandfather that has come for

you," said the fat one, slowly. "It is old Eskew Arp. Something's happened."

She looked at him for a moment, beginning to tremble violently, her eyes growing wide with fright.

"Is my grandfather—is he sick?"

"You better go and see. Old Eskew's waiting in the hall. He'll tell you."

She was by him and through the window instantly. Norbert did not follow her; he remained for several moments looking earnestly at the palms; then he stepped through the window and beckoned to a youth who was lounging in the doorway across the room.

"There's somebody hiding behind those plants," he whispered, when his friend reached him. "Go and tell Judge Pike to send some of the niggers to watch outside the porch, so that he doesn't get away. Then tell him to get his revolver and come here."

Meanwhile Ariel had found Mr. Arp waiting in the hall, talking in a low voice to Mrs. Pike.

"Your grandfather's all right," he told the frightened girl, quickly. "He sent me for you, that's all. Just hurry and get your things."

She was with him again in a moment, and seizing the old man's arm, hurried him down the steps and toward the street almost at a run.

"You're not telling me the truth," she said. "You're not telling me the truth!"

"Nothing has happened to Roger," panted Mr. Arp. "Nothing to mind, I mean. Here! We're going this way, not that." They had come to the gate, and as she turned to the right he pulled her round sharply to the left. "We're not going to your house."

"Where are we going?"

"We're going to your uncle Jonas's."

"Why?" she cried, in supreme astonishment. "What do you want to take me there for? Don't you know that he's stopped speaking to me?"

"Yes," said the old man, grimly, with something of the look he wore when delivering a clincher at the "National House,"—"he's stopped speaking to everybody."

V

BEAVER BEACH

T HE Canaan *Daily Tocsin* of the following morning "ventured the assertion" upon its front page that "the scene at the Pike Mansion was one of unalloyed festivity, music, and mirth; a fairy bower of airy figures wafting here and there to the throb of waltz-strains; a veritable Temple of Terpsichore, shining forth with a myriad of lights, which, together with the generous profusion of floral decorations and the mingled delights afforded by Minds's orchestra of Indianapolis and Caterer Jones of Chicago, was in all likelihood never heretofore surpassed in elegance in our city. . . . Only one incident," the *Tocsin* remarked, "marred an otherwise perfect occasion, and out of regard for the culprit's family connections, which are prominent in our social world, we withhold his name. Suffice it to say that through the vigilance of Mr. Norbert Flitcroft, grandson of Colonel A. A. Flitcroft, who proved himself a thor-

ough Lecoq (the celebrated French detective), the
rascal was seized and recognized. Mr. Flitcroft,
having discovered him in hiding, had a cordon of
waiters drawn up around his hiding-place, which
was the charmingly decorated side piazza of the
Pike Mansion, and sent for Judge Pike, who came
upon the intruder by surprise. He evaded the
Judge's indignant grasp, but received a well-
merited blow over the head from a poker which
the Judge had concealed about his person while
pretending to approach the hiding-place casually.
Attracted to the scene by the cries of Mr. Flitcroft,
who, standing behind Judge Pike, accidentally received a blow from the same weapon, all the guests
of the evening sprang to view the scene, only to
behold the culprit leap through a crevice between
the strips of canvas which enclosed the piazza.
He was seized by the colored coachman of the Mansion, Sam Warden, and immediately pounced upon
by the cordon of Caterer Jones's dusky assistants
from Chicago, who were in ambush outside. Un-
fortunately, after a brief struggle he managed to
trip Warden, and, the others stumbling upon the
prostrate body of the latter, to make his escape
in the darkness.

"It is not believed by many that his intention
was burglary, though what his designs were can
only be left to conjecture, as he is far beyond the

age when boys perform such actions out of a sense of mischief. He had evidently occupied his hiding-place some time, and an idea of his coolness may be obtained from his having procured and eaten a full meal through an unknown source. Judge Pike is justly incensed, and swears that he will prosecute him on this and other charges as soon as he can be found. Much sympathy is felt for the culprit's family, who feel his shame most keenly, but who, though sorrowing over the occurrence, declare that they have put up with his derelictions long enough, and will do nothing to step between him and the Judge's righteous indignation."

The Pike Mansion, "scene of festivity, music, and mirth" (not quite so unalloyed, after all, the stricken Flitcroft keeping his room for a week under medical supervision), had not been the only bower of the dance in Canaan that evening: another Temple of Terpsichore had shone forth with lights, though of these there were not quite a myriad. The festivities they illumined obtained no mention in the paper, nor did they who trod the measures in this second temple exhibit any sense of injury because of the *Tocsin's* omission. Nay, they were of that class, shy without being bashful, exclusive yet not proud, which shuns publicity with a single-heartedness almost unique in our republic, courting

79

observation neither in the prosecution of their professions nor in the pursuit of happiness.

Not quite a mile above the northernmost of the factories on the water-front, there projected into the river, near the end of the crescent bend above the town, a long pier, relic of steamboat days, rotting now, and many years fallen from its maritime uses. About midway of its length stood a huge, crazy shed, long ago utilized as a freight storeroom. This had been patched and propped, and a dangerous-looking veranda attached to it, overhanging the water. Above the doorway was placed a sign whereon might be read the words, " Beaver Beach, Mike's Place." The shore end of the pier was so ruinous that passage was offered by a single row of planks, which presented an appearance so temporary, as well as insecure, that one might have guessed their office to be something in the nature of a drawbridge. From these a narrow path ran through a marsh, left by the receding river, to a country road of desolate appearance. Here there was a rough enclosure, or corral, with some tumble-down sheds which afforded shelter, on the night of Joseph Louden's disgrace, for a number of shaggy teams attached to those decrepit and musty vehicles known picturesquely and accurately as Night-Hawks. The presence of such questionable shapes in the corral indicated that the dance was on at Beaver Beach, Mike's Place, as surely as the short line of cabs and family carriages on upper Main Street made it known that gayety was the order of the night at the Pike Mansion. But among other differences was this, that at the hour when the guests of the latter were leaving, those seeking the hospitalities of Beaver Beach had just begun to arrive.

By three o'clock, however, joy at Mike's Place had become beyond question unconfined, and the tokens of it were audible for a long distance in all directions. If, however, there is no sound where no ear hears, silence rested upon the country-side until an hour later. Then a lonely figure came shivering from the direction of the town, not by the road, but slinking through the snow upon the frozen river. It came slowly, as though very tired, and cautiously, too, often turning its head to look behind. Finally it reached the pier, and stopped as if to listen.

Within the house above, a piano of evil life was being beaten to death for its sins and clamoring its last cries horribly. The old shed rattled in every part with the thud of many heavy feet, and trembled with the shock of noise—an incessant roar of men's voices, punctuated with women's screams. Then the riot quieted somewhat; there was a clapping of hands, and a violin began to squeak measures intended to be Oriental. The next moment the listener scrambled up one of the rotting piles and stood upon the veranda. A shaft of red light through a broken shutter struck across the figure above the shoulders, revealing a bloody handkerchief clumsily knotted about the head, and, beneath it, the face of Joe Louden.

He went to the broken shutter and looked in. Around the blackened walls of the room stood a bleared mob, applausively watching, through a fog of smoke, the contortions of an old woman in a red calico wrapper, who was dancing in the centre of the floor. The fiddler — a rubicund person evidently not suffering from any great depression of spirit through the circumstance of being "out on bail," as he was, to Joe's intimate knowledge— sat astride a barrel, resting his instrument upon the foamy tap thereof, and playing somewhat after the manner of a 'cellist; in no wise incommoded by the fact that a tall man (known to a few friends as an expert in the porch-climbing line) was sleeping on his shoulder, while another gentleman (who had prevented many cases of typhoid by removing old plumbing from houses) lay on the floor at the musician's feet and endeavored to assist him by plucking the strings of the fiddle.

Joe opened the door and went in. All of the merry company (who were able) turned sharply toward the door as it opened; then, recognizing the new - comer, turned again to watch the old woman. One or two nearest the door asked the boy, without great curiosity, what had happened to his head. He merely shook it faintly in reply, and crossed the room to an open hallway beyond. At the end of this he came to a frowzy bedroom, the door of which stood ajar. Seated at a deal table, and working by a dim lamp with a broken chimney, a close-cropped, red-bearded, red-haired man in his shirt - sleeves was jabbing gloomily at a column of figures scrawled in a dirty ledger. He looked up as Joe appeared in the doorway, and his eyes showed a slight surprise.

"I never thought ye had the temper to git somebody to split yer head," said he. "Where'd ye collect it?"

"Nowhere," Joe answered, dropping weakly on the bed. "It doesn't amount to anything."

"Well, I'll take just a look fer myself," said the red-bearded man, rising. "And I've no objection to not knowin' how ye come by it. Ye've always been the great one fer keepin' yer mysteries to yerself."

He unwound the handkerchief and removed it from Joe's head gently. "*Whee!*" he cried, as a long gash was exposed over the forehead. "I hope ye left a mark somewhere to pay a little on the score o' this!"

Joe chuckled and dropped dizzily back upon the pillow. "There was another who got something like it," he gasped, feebly; "and, oh, Mike, I wish you could have heard him going on! Perhaps you did—it was only three miles from here."

"Nothing I'd liked better!" said the other, bringing a basin of clear water from a stand in the corner. "It's a beautiful thing to hear a man holler when he gits a grand one like ye're wearing to-night."

He bathed the wound gently, and hurrying from the room, returned immediately with a small jug of vinegar. Wetting a rag with this tender fluid, he applied it to Joe's head, speaking soothingly the while.

"Nothing in the world like a bit o' good cider vinegar to keep off the festerin'. It may seem a trifle scratchy fer the moment, but it assassinates the blood-p'ison. There ye go! It's the fine thing fer ye, Joe—what are ye squirmin' about?"

"I'm only enjoying it," the boy answered, writhing as the vinegar worked into the gash. "Don't you mind my laughing to myself."

"Ye're a good one, Joe!" said the other, continuing his ministrations. "I wisht, after all, ye felt like makin' me known to what's the trouble.

There's some of us would be glad to take it up fer ye, and—"

"No, no; it's all right. I was somewhere I had no business to be, and I got caught."

"Who caught ye?"

"First, some nice white people"—Joe smiled his distorted smile—"and then a low-down black man helped me to get away as soon as he saw who it was. He's a friend of mine, and he fell down and tripped up the pursuit."

"I always knew ye'd git into large trouble some day." The red-bearded man tore a strip from an old towel and began to bandage the boy's head with an accustomed hand. "Yer taste fer excitement has been growin' on ye every minute of the four years I've known ye."

"Excitement!" echoed Joe, painfully blinking at his friend. "Do you think I'm hunting excitement?"

"Be hanged to ye!" said the red-bearded man. "Can't I say a teasing word without gittin' called to order fer it? I know ye, my boy, as well as ye know yerself. Ye're a queer one. Ye're one of the few that must know all sides of the world— and can't content themselves with bein' respectable! Ye haven't sunk to 'low life' because ye're low yourself, but ye'll never git a damned one o' the respectable to believe it. There's a few others like ye in the wide world, and I've seen one or two of 'em. I've been all over, steeple-chasin', sailorman, soldier, pedler, and in the *po*-lice; I've pulled the Grand National in Paris, and I've been handcuffed in Hong-Kong; I've seen all the few kinds of women there is on earth and the many kinds of men. Yer own kind is the one I've seen the fewest of, but I knew ye belonged to it the first time I laid eyes on ye!" He paused, then continued with conviction: "Ye'll come to no good, either, fer yerself, yet no one can say ye haven't the talents. Ye've helped many of the boys out of a bad hole with a word of advice around the courts and the jail. Who knows but ye'd be a great lawyer if ye kept on?"

Young people usually like to discuss themselves under any conditions—hence the rewards of palmistry,—but Joe's comment on this harangue was not so responsive as might have been expected. "I've got seven dollars," he said, "and I'll leave the clothes I've got on. Can you fix me up with something different?"

"Aha!" cried the red-bearded man. "Then ye *are* in trouble! I thought it 'd come to ye some day! Have ye been dinnymitin' Martin Pike?"

"See what you can do," said Joe. "I want to wait here until daybreak."

"Lie down, then," interrupted the other. "And

fergit the hullabaloo in the throne - room beyond."

"I can easily do that"—Joe stretched himself upon the bed,—"I've got so many other things to remember."

"I'll have the things fer ye, and I'll let ye know I have no use fer seven dollars," returned the red-bearded man, crossly. "What are ye sniffin' fer?"

"I'm thinking of the poor fellow that got the mate to this," said Joe, touching the bandage. "I can't help crying when I think they may have used vinegar on his head, too."

"Git to sleep if ye can!" exclaimed the Samaritan, as a hideous burst of noise came from the dance-room, where some one seemed to be breaking a chair upon an acquaintance. "I'll go out and regulate the boys a bit." He turned down the lamp, fumbled in his hip-pocket, and went to the door.

"Don't forget," Joe called after him.

"Go to sleep," said the red-bearded man, his hand on the door-knob. "That is, go to thinkin', fer ye won't sleep; ye're not the kind. But think easy; I'll have the things fer ye. It's a matter of pride with me that I always knew ye'd come to trouble."

VI

"YE'LL TAK' THE HIGH ROAD AND I'LL TAK' THE LOW ROAD"

THE day broke with a scream of wind out of the prairies and such cloud-bursts of snow that Joe could see neither bank of the river as he made his way down the big bend of ice. The wind struck so bitterly that now and then he stopped and, panting and gasping, leaned his weight against it. The snow on the ground was caught up and flew like sea spume in a hurricane; it swirled about him, joining the flakes in the air, so that it seemed to be snowing from the ground upward as much as from the sky downward. Fierce as it was, hard as it was to fight through, snow from the earth, snow from the sky, Joe was grateful for it, feeling that it veiled him, making him safer, though he trusted somewhat the change of costume he had effected at Beaver Beach. A rough, workman's cap was pulled down over his ears and eyebrows; a knitted comforter was wound about the lower part of his face; under a ragged overcoat he wore blue overalls and rubber boots; and in one of his red-mittened hands he swung a tin dinner-bucket.

When he reached the nearest of the factories he heard the exhaust of its engines long before he could see the building, so blinding was the drift. Here he struck inland from the river, and, skirting the edges of the town, made his way by unfrequented streets and alleys, bearing in the general direction of upper Main Street, to find himself at last, almost exhausted, in the alley behind the Pike Mansion. There he paused, leaning heavily against a board fence and gazing at the vaguely outlined gray plane which was all that could be made of the house through the blizzard. He had often, very often, stood in this same place at night, and there was one window (Mrs. Pike's) which he had guessed to be Mamie's.

The storm was so thick that he could not see this window now, but he looked a long time through the thickness at that part of the gray plane where he knew it was. Then his lips parted.

"Good-bye, Mamie," he said, softly. "Good-bye, Mamie."

He bent his body against the wind and went on, still keeping to the back ways, until he came to the alley which passed behind his own home, where, however, he paused only for a moment to make a quick survey of the premises. A glance satisfied him; he ran to the next fence, hoisted himself wearily over it, and dropped into Roger Tabor's back yard.

He took shelter from the wind for a moment or two, leaning against the fence, breathing heavily; then he stumbled on across the obliterated paths of a vegetable-garden until he reached the house, and beginning with the kitchen, began to make the circuit of the windows, peering cautiously into each as he went, ready to tap on the pane should he catch a glimpse of Ariel, and prepared to run if he stumbled upon her grandfather. But the place seemed empty: he had made his reconnaisance apparently in vain, and was on the point of going away, when he heard the click of the front gate and saw Ariel coming towards him, her old water-proof cloak about her head and shoulders, the patched, scant, faded skirt, which he knew so well, blowing about her tumultuously. At the sound of the gate he had crouched close against the side of the house, but she saw him at once.

She stopped abruptly, and throwing the water-proof back from her head, looked at him through the driven fog of snow. One of her hands was stretched towards him involuntarily, and it was in that attitude that he long remembered her:

standing in the drift which had piled up against
the gate almost knee-deep, the shabby skirt and
the black water-proof flapping like torn sails, one
hand out-stretched like that of a figure in a tab-
leau, her brown face with its thin features mottled
with cold and unlovely, her startled eyes fixed
on him with a strange, wild tenderness that held
something of the laughter of whole companionship in it mingling with a loyalty and championship
that was almost ferocious—she looked an Undine
of the snow.

Suddenly she ran to him, still keeping her hand
out-stretched until it touched his own.

"How did you know me?" he said.

"*Know you!*" was all the answer she made to
that question. "Come into the house. I've got
some coffee on the stove for you. I've been up
and down the street waiting for you ever since it
began to get light."

"Your grandfather won't—"

"He's at Uncle Jonas's; he won't be back till
noon. There's no one here."

She led him to the front-door, where he stamped
and shook himself; he was snow from head to foot.

"I'm running away from the good Gomorrah,"
he said, "but I've stopped to look back, and I'm a
pretty white pillar."

"I know where you stopped to look back," she

answered, brushing him heartily with her red hands. "You came in the alley way. It was Mamie's window."

He did not reply, and the only visible token that he had any consciousness of this clairvoyance of hers was a slight lift of his higher eyebrow. She wasted no time in getting him to the kitchen, where, when she had removed his overcoat, she placed him in a chair, unwound the comforter, and, as carefully as a nurse, lifted the cap from his injured head. When the strip of towel was disclosed she stood quite still for a moment with the cap in her hand; then with a broken little cry she stooped and kissed a lock of his hair, which escaped, discolored, beneath the bandage.

"Stop that!" he commanded, horribly embarrassed.

"Oh, Joe," she cried, "I knew! I knew it was there—but to *see* it! And it's my fault for leaving you—I *had* to go or I wouldn't have—I—"

"Where'd you hear about it?" he asked, shortly.

"I haven't been to bed," she answered. "Grandfather and I were up all night at Uncle Jonas's, and Colonel Flitcroft came about two o'clock, and he told us."

"Did he tell you about Norbert?"

"Yes—a great deal." She poured coffee into a cup from a pot on the stove, brought it to him, then placing some thin slices of bread upon a grid-iron, began to toast them over the hot coals. "The Colonel said that Norbert thought he wouldn't get well," she concluded; "and Mr. Arp said Norbert was the kind that never die, and they had quite an argument."

"What were you doing at Jonas Tabor's?" asked Joe, drinking his coffee with a brightening eye.

"We were sent for," she answered.

"What for?"

She toasted the bread attentively without replying, and when she decided that it was brown enough, piled it on a warm plate. This she brought to him, and kneeling in front of him, her elbow on his knee, offered for his consideration, looking steadfastly up at his eyes. He began to eat ravenously

"What for?" he repeated. "I didn't suppose Jonas would let you come in his house. Was he sick?"

"Joe," she said, quietly, disregarding his questions—"Joe, have you *got* to run away?"

"Yes, I've got to," he answered.

"Would you have to go to prison if you stayed?" She asked this with a breathless tensity.

"I'm not going to beg father to help me out," he said, determinedly. "He said he wouldn't, and he'll be spared the chance. He won't mind

93

that; nobody will care! Nobody! What does anybody care what *I* do!"

"Now you're thinking of Mamie!" she cried. "I can always tell. Whenever you don't talk naturally you're thinking of her!"

He poured down the last of the coffee, growing red to the tips of his ears. "Ariel," he said, "if I ever come back—"

"Wait," she interrupted. "Would you have to go to prison right away if they caught you?"

"Oh, it isn't that," he laughed, sadly. "But I'm going to clear out. I'm not going to take any chances. I want to see other parts of the world, other kinds of people. I might have gone, anyhow, soon, even if it hadn't been for last night. Don't you ever feel that way?"

"You know I do," she said. "I've told you— how often! But, Joe, Joe, — you haven't any *money!* You've got to have money to *live!*"

"You needn't worry about that," returned the master of seven dollars, genially. "I've saved enough to take care of me for a *long* time."

"Joe, *please!* I know it isn't so. If you could wait just a little while—only a few weeks, —only a *few*, Joe—"

"What for?"

"I could let you have all you want. It would be such a beautiful thing for me, Joe. Oh, I know how you'd feel; you wouldn't even let me give you that dollar I found in the street last year; but this would be only lending it to you, and you could pay me back sometime—"

"Ariel!" he exclaimed, and, setting his empty cup upon the floor, took her by the shoulders and shook her till the empty plate which had held the toast dropped from her hand and broke into fragments. "You've been reading the *Arabian Nights!*"

"No, no," she cried, vehemently. "Grandfather would give me anything. He'll give me all the money I ask for!"

"Money!" said Joe. "Which of us is wandering? *Money?* Roger Tabor give you *money?*"

"Not for a while. A great many things have to be settled first."

"What things?"

"Joe," she asked, earnestly, "do you think it's bad of me not to feel things I *ought* to feel?"

"No."

"Then I'm glad," she said, and something in the way she spoke made him start with pain, remembering the same words, spoken in the same tone, by another voice, the night before on the veranda. "I'm glad, Joe, because I seemed all wrong to myself. Uncle Jonas died last night, and I haven't been able to get sorry. Perhaps it's because I've been so frightened about you, but I think not, for I wasn't sorry even before Colonel Flitcroft told me about you."

"Jonas Tabor dead!" said Joe. "Why, I saw him on the street yesterday!"

"Yes, and I saw him just before I came out on the porch where you were. He was there in the hall; he and Judge Pike had been having a long talk; they'd been in some speculations together, and it had all turned out well. It's very strange, but they say now that Uncle Jonas's heart was weak — he was an old man, you know, almost eighty, — and he'd been very anxious about his money. The Judge had persuaded him to risk it; and the shock of finding that he'd made a great deal suddenly—"

"I've heard he'd had that same shock before," said Joe, "when he sold out to your father."

"Yes, but this was different, grandfather says. He told me it was in one of those big risky businesses that Judge Pike likes to go into. And last night it was all finished, the strain was over, and Uncle Jonas started home. His house is only a little way from the Pikes', you know; but he dropped down in the snow at his own gate, and some people who were going by saw him fall. He was dead before grandfather got there."

"I can't be sorry," said Joe, slowly.

"Neither can I. That's the dreadful part of it!

"Joe, have you got to run away?" Page 92.

—*The Conquest of Canaan.*

They say he hadn't made a will, that though he was sharper than anybody else in the whole world about any other matter of business, that was the one thing he put off. And we're all the kin he had in the world, grandfather and I. And they say"— her voice sank to a whisper of excitement—"they say he was richer than anybody knew, and that this last business with Judge Pike, the very thing that killed him — something about grain — made him five times richer than before!"

She put her hand on the boy's arm, and he let it remain there. Her eyes still sought his with a tremulous appeal.

"God bless you, Ariel!" he said. "It's going to be a great thing for you."

"Yes. Yes, it is." The tears came suddenly to her eyes. "I was foolish last night, but there had been such a long time of *wanting* things; and now—and now grandfather and I can go—"

"You're going, too!" Joe chuckled.

"It's heartless, I suppose, but I've settled it! We're going—"

"*I* know," he cried. "You've told me a thousand times what *he's* said ten times a thousand. You're going to Paris!"

"Paris! Yes, that's it. To Paris, where he can see at last how the great ones have painted,— where the others can show him! To Paris, where

97

we can study together, where he can learn how to put the pictures he sees upon canvas, and where I—"

"Go on," Joe encouraged her. "I want to hear you say it. You don't mean that you're going to study painting; you mean that you're going to learn how to make such fellows as Eugene ask you to dance. Go ahead and *say* it!"

"Yes—to learn how to *dress!*" she said.

Joe was silent for a moment. Then he rose and took the ragged overcoat from the back of his chair. "Where's that muffler?" he asked.

She brought it from where she had placed it to dry, behind the stove.

"Joe," she said, huskily, "can't you wait till—"

"Till the estate is settled and you can coax your grandfather to—"

"No, no! But you could go with us."

"To Paris?"

"He would take you as his secretary."

"Aha!" Joe's voice rang out gayly as he rose, refreshed by the coffee, toast, and warmth she had given him. "You've been story - reading, Ariel, like Eugene! 'Secretary'!"

"Please, Joe!"

"Where's my tin dinner-pail?" He found it himself upon the table where he had set it down. "I'm going to earn a dishonest living," he went on. "I have an engagement to take a freight at a water-tank that's a friend of mine, half a mile south of the yards. Thank God, I'm going to get away from Canaan!"

"Wait, Joe!" She caught at his sleeve. "I want you to—"

He had swung out of the room and was already at the front-door. She followed him closely. "Good-bye, Ariel!"

"No, no! *Wait*, Joe!"

He took her right hand in his own, and gave it a manly shake. "It's all right," he said.

He threw open the door and stepped out, but she sought to detain him. "Oh, have you *got* to go?" she cried.

"Don't you ever worry about me." He bent his head to the storm as he sprang down the steps, and snow-wreaths swirled between them.

He disappeared in a white whirlwind.

She stood for several minutes shivering in the doorway. Then it came to her that she would not know where to write to him. She ran down to the gate and through it. Already the blizzard had covered his footprints.

VII

"GIVE A DOG A BAD NAME"

THE passing of Joseph from Canaan was complete. It was an evanishment for which there was neither sackcloth nor surprise; and though there came no news of him it cannot be said that Canaan did not hear of him, for surely it could hear itself talk. The death of Jonas Tabor and young Louden's crime and flight incited high doings in the "National House" windows; many days the sages lingered with the broken meats of morals left over from the banquet of gossip. But, after all, it is with the ladies of a community that reputations finally rest, and the matrons of Canaan had long ago made Joe's exceedingly uncertain. Now they made it certain.

They did not fail of assistance. The most powerful influence in the town was ponderously corroborative: Martin Pike, who stood for all that was respectable and financial, who passed the plate o' Sundays, who held the fortunes of the town in his left hand, who was trustee for the widow and orphan,—Martin Pike, patron of all worthy charities, courted by ministers, feared by the wicked and idle, revered by the good,—Judge Martin Pike never referred to the runaway save in the accents of an august doomster. His testimony settled it.

In time the precise nature of the fugitive's sins was distorted in report and grew vague; it was recalled that he had done dread things; he became a tradition, a legend, and a warning to the young; a Richard in the bush to frighten colts. He was preached at boys caught playing marbles "for keeps": "Do you want to grow up like Joe Louden?" The very name became a darkling threat, and children of the town would have run had one called suddenly, "*Here comes Joe Louden!*" Thus does the evil men do live after them, and the ill-fame of the unrighteous increase when they are sped!

Very little of Joseph's adventures and occupations during the time of his wandering is revealed to us; he always had an unwilling memory for pain and was not afterwards wont to speak of those years which cut the hard lines in his face. The first account of him to reach Canaan came as directly to the windows of the "National House" as Mr. Arp, hastening thither from the station, satchel in hand, could bring it.

This was on a September morning, two years after the flight, and Eskew, it appears, had been to the State Fair and had beheld many things strangely affirming his constant testimony that this unhappy world increaseth in sin; strangest of all, his meeting with our vagrant scalawag of Canaan. "Not a *blamebit* of doubt about it," declared Eskew to the incredulous conclave. "There was that Joe, and nobody else, stuck up in a little box outside a tent at the Fair Grounds, and sellin' tickets to see the Spotted Wild Boy!" Yes, it was Joe Louden! Think you, Mr. Arp could forget that face, those crooked eyebrows? Had Eskew tested the recognition? Had he spoken with the outcast? Had he not! Ay, but with such peculiar result that the battle of words among the sages began with a true onset of the regulars; for, according to Eskew's narrative, when he had delivered grimly at the boy this charge, "I know you —*you're Joe Louden!*" the extraordinary reply had been made promptly and without change of countenance: "*Positively no free seats!*"

On this, the house divided, one party maintaining that Joe had thus endeavored to evade recognition, the other (to the embitterment of Mr. Arp) that the reply was a distinct admission of identity and at the same time a refusal to grant any favors on the score of past acquaintanceship.

Goaded by inquiries, Mr. Arp, who had little desire to recall such waste of silver, admitted more than he had intended: that he had purchased a ticket and gone in to see the Spotted Wild Boy, halting in his description of this marvel with the unsatisfactory and acrid statement that the Wild Boy was "simply *spotted*," and the stung query, "I suppose you know what a spot *is*, Squire?" When he came out of the tent he had narrowly examined the ticket-seller,—who seemed unaware of his scrutiny, and, when not engaged with his tickets, applied himself to a dirty law - looking book. It was Joseph Louden, reasserted Eskew, a little taller, a little paler, incredibly shabby and miraculously thin. If there were any doubt left, his forehead was somewhat disfigured by the scar of an old wound—such as might have been caused by a blunt instrument in the nature of a poker.

"What's the matter with *you*?" Mr. Arp whirled upon Uncle Joe Davey, who was enjoying himself by repeating at intervals the unreasonable words, "Couldn't of be'n Joe," without any explanation. "Why couldn't it?" shouted Eskew. "It was! Do you think my eyes are as fur gone as yours? I saw him, I tell you! The same ornery Joe Louden, run away and sellin' tickets for a side-show. He wasn't even the boss of it; the manager was about the meanest-lookin' human I ever saw

—and most humans look mighty mean, accordin' to my way of thinkin'! Riffraff of the riffraff are his friends now, same as they were here. Weeds! and *he's* a weed, always was and always will be! Him and his kind ain't any more than jimpsons; overrun everything if you give 'em a chance. Devil-flowers! They have to be hoed out and scattered—even then, like as not, they'll come back next year and ruin your plantin' once more. That boy Joe 'll turn up here again some day; you'll see if he don't. He's a seed of trouble and iniquity, and anything of that kind is sure to come back to Canaan!"

Mr. Arp stuck to his prediction for several months; then he began to waver and evade. By the end of the second year following its first utterance, he had formed the habit of denying that he had ever made it at all, and, finally having come to believe with all his heart that the prophecy had been deliberately foisted upon him and put in his mouth by Squire Buckalew, became so sore upon the subject that even the hardiest dared not refer to it in his presence.

Eskew's story of the ticket-seller was the only news of Joe Louden that came to Canaan during seven years. Another citizen of the town encountered the wanderer, however, but under circumstances so susceptible to misconception that, in a moment of illumination, he decided to let the matter rest in a golden silence. This was Mr. Bantry.

Having elected an elaborate course in the Arts, at the University which was of his possessions, what more natural than that Eugene should seek the Metropolis for the short Easter vacation of his Senior year, in order that his perusal of the Masters should be uninterrupted? But it was his misfortune to find the Metropolitan Museum less interesting than some intricate phases of the gayety of New York—phases very difficult to understand without elaborate study and a series of experiments which the discreetly selfish permit others to make for them. Briefly, Eugene found himself dancing, one night, with a young person in a big hat, at the "Straw-Cellar," a crowded hall, down very deep in the town and not at all the place for Eugene.

Acute crises are to be expected at the "Straw-Cellar," and Eugene was the only one present who was thoroughly surprised when that of this night arrived, though all of the merrymakers were frightened when they perceived its extent. There is no need to detail the catastrophe. It came suddenly, and the knife did not flash. Sick and thinking of himself, Eugene stood staring at the figure lying before him upon the reddening floor. A rabble fought with the quick policemen at the doors, and then the lights went out, extinguished by the proprietor, living up to his reputation for always being thoughtful of his patrons. The place had been a nightmare; it became a black impossibility. Eugene staggered to one of the open windows, from the sill of which a man had just leaped.

"Don't jump," said a voice close to his ear. "That fellow broke his leg, I think, and they caught him, anyway, as soon as he struck the pavement. It's a big raid. Come this way."

A light hand fell upon his arm and he followed its leading, blindly, to find himself pushed through a narrow doorway and down a flight of tricky, wooden steps, at the foot of which, silhouetted against a street light, a tall policeman was on guard. He laid masterful hands on Eugene.

" 'Sh, Mack!" whispered a cautious voice from the stairway. "That's a friend of mine and not one of those you need. He's only a student and scared to death."

"Hurry," said the policeman, under his breath, twisting Eugene sharply by him into the street; after which he stormed vehemently: "On yer way, both of ye! Move on up the street! Don't be tryin' to poke yer heads in here! Ye'd be more anxious to git out, once ye got in, I tell ye!"

A sob of relief came from Bantry as he gained the next corner, the slight figure of his conductor at his side. "You'd better not go to places like the 'Straw-Cellar,'" said the latter, gravely. "I'd been watching you for an hour. You were dancing with the girl who did the cutting."

Eugene leaned against a wall, faint, one arm across his face. He was too ill to see, or care, who it was that had saved him. "I never saw her before," he babbled, incoherently, "never, never, never! I thought she looked handsome, and asked her if she'd dance with me. Then I saw she seemed queer—and wild, and she kept guiding and pushing as we danced until we were near that man—and then she—then it was all done—before—"

"Yes," said the other; "she's been threatening to do it for a long time. Jealous. Mighty good sort of a girl, though, in lots of ways. Only yesterday I talked with her and almost thought I'd calmed her out of it. But you can't tell with some women. They'll brighten up and talk straight and seem sensible, one minute, and promise to behave, and mean it too, and the next, there they go, making a scene, cutting somebody or killing themselves! You can't count on them. But that's not to the point, exactly, I expect. You'd better keep away from the 'Straw-Cellar.' If you'd been caught with the rest you'd have had a hard time, and they'd have found out your real name, too, because it's pretty serious on account of your dancing with her when she did it, and the Canaan papers would have got hold of it and you wouldn't be invited to Judge Pike's any more, Eugene."

Eugene dropped his arm from his eyes and stared into the face of his step-brother.

"Joe Louden!" he gasped.

"I'll never tell," said Joe. "You'd better keep out of all this sort. You don't understand it, and you don't—you don't do it because you care." He smiled wanly, his odd distorted smile of friendliness. "When you go back you might tell father I'm all right. I'm working through a law-school here—and remember me to Norbert Flitcroft," he finished, with a chuckle.

Eugene covered his eyes again and groaned.

"It's all right," Joe assured him. "You're as safe as if it had never happened. And I expect" —he went on, thoughtfully — "I expect, maybe, you'd prefer *not* to say you'd seen me, when you go back to Canaan. Well, that's all right. I don't suppose father will be asking after me—exactly."

"No, he doesn't," said Eugene, still white and shaking. "Don't stand talking. I'm sick."

"Of course," returned Joe. "But there's one thing I would like to ask you—"

"Your father's health is perfect, I believe."

"It—it—it was something else," Joe stammered.

pitifully. "Are they all—are they all—all right at —at Judge Pike's?"

"Quite!" Eugene replied, sharply. " Are you going to get me away from here? I'm sick, I tell you!"

"This street," said Joe, and cheerfully led the way.

Five minutes later the two had parted, and Joe leaned against a cheap restaurant sign-board, drearily staring after the lamps of the gypsy night-cab he had found for his step-brother. Eugene had not offered to share the vehicle with him, had not even replied to his good-night.

And Joe himself had neglected to do something he might well have done: he had not asked Eugene for news of Ariel Tabor. It will not justify him entirely to suppose that he assumed that her grandfather and she had left Canaan never to return, and therefore Eugene knew nothing of her; no such explanation serves Joe for his neglect, for the fair truth is that he had not thought of her. She had been a sort of playmate, before his flight, a friend taken for granted, about whom he had consciously thought little more than he thought about himself — and easily forgotten. Not for-gotten in the sense that she had passed out of his memory, but forgotten none the less; she had never had a place in his imaginings, and so it be-fell that when he no longer saw her from day to day, she had gone from his thoughts altogether

VIII

A BAD PENNY TURNS UP

UGENE did not inform Canaan, nor any inhabitant, of his adventure of the "Straw-Cellar," nor did any hear of his meeting with his step-brother; and after Mr. Arp's adventure, five years passed into the imperishable before the town heard of the wanderer again, and then it heard at first hand; Mr. Arp's prophecy fell true, and he took it back to his bosom again, claimed it as his own the morning of its fulfilment. Joe Louden had come back to Canaan.

The elder Louden was the first to know of his prodigal's return. He was alone in the office of the wooden-butter-dish factory, of which he was the superintendent, when the young man came in unannounced. He was still pale and thin; his eyebrows had the same crook, one corner of his mouth the same droop; he was only an inch or so taller, not enough to be thought a tall man; and yet, for a few moments the father did not recognize his son, but stared at him, inquiring his business. During those few seconds of unrecognition, Mr. Louden was somewhat favorably impressed with the stranger's appearance.

"You don't know me," said Joe, smiling cheerfully. "Perhaps I've changed in seven years." And he held out his hand.

Then Mr. Louden knew; he tilted back in his desk-chair, his mouth falling open. "Good God!" he said, not noticing the out-stretched hand. "Have *you* come back?"

Joe's hand fell.

"Yes, I've come back to Canaan."

Mr. Louden looked at him a long time without replying; finally he remarked:

"I see you've still got a scar on your forehead."

"Oh, I've forgotten all about that," said the other, twisting his hat in his hands. "Seven years wipes out a good many grievances and wrongs."

"You think so?" Mr. Louden grunted. "I suppose it might wipe out a good deal with some people. How'd you happen to stop off at Canaan? On your way somewhere, I suppose."

"No, I've come back to stay."

Mr. Louden plainly received this as no pleasant surprise. "What for?" he asked, slowly.

"To practise law, father."

"What!"

"Yes," said the young man. "There ought to be an opening here for me. I'm a graduate of as good a law-school as there is in the country—"

"You are!"

"Certainly," said Joe, quietly. "I've put myself through, working in the summer—"

"Working!" Mr. Louden snorted. "Sideshows?"

"Oh, worse than that, sometimes," returned his son, laughing. "Anything I could get. But I've always wanted to come back home and work here."

Mr. Louden leaned forward, a hand on each knee, his brow deeply corrugated. "Do you think you'll get much practice in Canaan?"

"Why not? I've had a year in a good office in New York since I left the school, and I think I ought to get along all right."

"Oh," said Mr. Louden, briefly. "You do?"

"Yes. Don't you?"

"Who do you think in Canaan would put a case in your hands?"

"Oh, I don't expect to get anything important at the start. But after a while—"

"With your reputation?"

The smile which had faded from Joe's lips returned to them. "Oh, I know they thought I was a harum-scarum sort of boy," he answered, lightly, "and that it was a foolish thing to run away for nothing; but you had said I mustn't come to you for help—"

"I meant it," said Mr. Louden.

"But that's seven years ago, and I suppose the town's forgotten all about it, and forgotten me, too. So, you see, I can make a fresh start. That's what I came back for."

"You've made up your mind to stay here, then?"

"Yes."

"I don't believe," said Mr. Louden, with marked uneasiness, "that Mrs. Louden would be willing to let you live with us."

"No," said Joe, gently. "I didn't expect it." He turned to the window and looked out, averting his face, yet scoring himself with the contempt he had learned to feel for those who pity themselves. His father had not even asked him to sit down. There was a long silence, disturbed only by Mr. Louden's breathing, which could be heard, heavy and troubled.

At last Joe turned again, smiling as before. "Well, I won't keep you from your work," he said. "I suppose you're pretty busy—"

"Yes. I am," responded his father, promptly. "But I'll see you again before you go. I want to give you some advice."

"I'm not going," said Joe. "Not going to leave Canaan, I mean. Where will I find Eugene?"

"At the *Tocsin* office; he's the assistant editor. Judge Pike bought the *Tocsin* last year, and he thinks a good deal of Eugene. Don't forget I said to come to see me again before you go."

Joe came over to the older man and held out his hand. "Shake hands, father," he said. Mr. Louden looked at him out of small implacable eyes, the steady hostility of which only his wife or the imperious Martin Pike, his employer, could quell. He shook his head.

"I don't see any use in it," he answered. "It wouldn't mean anything. All my life I've been a hard-working man and an abiding man. Before you got in trouble you never did anything you ought to; you ran with the lowest people in town, and I and all your folks were ashamed of you. I don't see that we've got a call to be any different now." He swung round to his desk emphatically, on the last word, and Joe turned away and went out quietly.

But it was a bright morning to which he emerged from the outer doors of the factory, and he made his way towards Main Street at a lively gait. As he turned the corner opposite the "National House," he walked into Mr. Eskew Arp. The old man drew back angrily

"Lord 'a' mercy!" cried Joe, heartily. "It's Mr. Arp! I almost ran you down!" Then, as

Mr. Arp made no response, but stood stock-still in the way, staring at him fiercely, "Don't you know me, Mr. Arp?" the young man asked. "I'm Joe Louden."

Eskew abruptly thrust his face close to the other's. "*No free seats!*" he hissed, savagely; and swept across to the hotel to set his world afire.

Joe looked after the irate, receding figure, and watched it disappear into the Main Street door of the "National House." As the door closed, he became aware of a mighty shadow upon the pavement, and turning, beheld a fat young man, wearing upon his forehead a scar similar to his own, waddling by with eyes fixed upon him.

"How are you, Norbert?" Joe began. "Don't you remember me? I—" He came to a full stop, as the fat one, thrusting out an under lip as his only token of recognition, passed balefully on.

Joe proceeded slowly until he came to the *Tocsin* building. At the foot of the stairway leading up to the offices he hesitated for a few moments; then he turned away and walked towards the quieter part of Main Street. Most of the people he met took no notice of him, only two or three giving him second glances of half-cognizance, as though he reminded them of some one they could not place, and it was not until he had come near the Pike Mansion that he saw a full recognition in the eyes of one of the many whom he knew, and who had known him in his boyhood in the town. A lady, turning a corner, looked up carelessly, and then half-stopped within a few feet of him, as if startled. Joe's cheeks went a sudden crimson; for it was the lady of his old dreams.

Seven years had made Mamie Pike only prettier. She had grown into her young womanhood with an ampleness that had nothing of oversufficiency in it, nor anywhere a threat that some day there might be too much of her. Not quite seventeen when he had last seen her, now, at twenty-four, her amber hair elaborately becoming a plump and regular face, all of her old charm came over him once more, and it immediately seemed to him that he saw clearly his real reason for coming back to Canaan. She had been the Rich-Little-Girl of his child days, the golden princess playing in the Palace-Grounds, and in his early boyhood (until he had grown wicked and shabby) he had been sometimes invited to the Pike Mansion for the games and ice-cream of the daughter of the house, before her dancing days began. He had gone timidly, not daring ever to "call" her in "Quaker Meeting" or "Post-office," but watching her reverently and surreptitiously and continually. She had always seemed to him the one thing of all the world most rare, most mysterious, most unapproachable. She had not offered an apparition less so in those days when he began to come under the suspicion of Canaan, when the old people began to look upon him hotly, the young people coldly. His very exclusion wove for him a glamour about her, and she was more than ever his moon, far, lovely, unattainable, and brilliant, never to be reached by his lifted arms, but only by his lifted eyes. Nor had his long absence obliterated that light; somewhere in his dreams it always had place, shining, perhaps, with a fainter lustre as the years grew to seven, but never gone altogether. Now, at last, that he stood in her very presence again, it sprang to the full flood of its old brilliance —and more!

As she came to her half-stop of surprise, startled, he took his courage in two hands, and, lifting his hat, stepped to her side.

"You—you remember me?" he stammered.

"Yes," she answered, a little breathlessly.

"Ah, that's kind of you!" he cried, and began to walk on with her, unconsciously. "I feel like a returned ghost wandering about—invisible and unrecognized. So few people seem to remember me!"

"I think you are wrong. I think you'll find everybody remembers you," she responded, uneasily.

"No, I'm afraid not," he began. "I—"

" I'm afraid they do!"

Joe laughed a little. "My father was saying something like that to me a while ago. He meant that they used to think me a great scapegrace here. Do you mean that?"

" I'd scarcely like to say," she answered, her face growing more troubled; for they were close on the imperial domain.

" But it's long ago—and I really didn't do anything so outrageous, it seems to me." He laughed again. " I know your father was angry with me once or twice, especially the night I hid on your porch to watch you—to watch you dance, I mean. But, you see, I've come back to rehabilitate myself, to—"

She interrupted him. They were not far from her gate, and she saw her father standing in the yard, directing a painter who was at work on one of the cast-iron deer. The Judge was apparently in good spirits, laughing with the workman over some jest between them, but that did not lessen Mamie's nervousness.

" Mr. Louden," she said, in as kindly a tone as she could, " I shall have to ask you not to walk with me. My father would not like it."

Joe stopped with a jerk.

" Why, I—I thought I'd go in and shake hands with him,—and tell him I—"

Astonishment that partook of terror and of awe spread itself instantly upon her face.

"Good gracious!" she cried. "*No!*"

"Very well," said Joe, humbly. "Good-bye."

He was too late to get away with any good grace. Judge Pike had seen them, and, even as Joe turned to go, rushed down to the gate, flung it open, and motioned his daughter to enter. This he did with one wide sweep of his arm, and, with another sweep, forbade Joe to look upon either moon *or* sun. It was a magnificent gesture: it excluded the young man from the street, Judge Pike's street, and from the town, Judge Pike's town. It swept him from the earth, abolished him, denied him the right to breathe the common air, to be seen of men; and, at once a headsman's stroke and an excommunication, destroyed him, soul and body, thus rebuking the silly Providence that had created him, and repairing Its mistake by annihilating him. This hurling Olympian gesture smote the street; the rails of the car-track sprang and quivered with the shock; it thundered, and, amid the dumfounding uproar of the wrath of a god, the Will of the Canaanite Jove wrote the words in fiery letters upon the ether:

"Cease to be!"

Joe did not go in to shake hands with Judge Pike.

He turned the next corner a moment later, and went down the quiet street which led to the house which had been his home. He did not glance at that somewhat grim edifice, but passed it, his eyes averted, and stopped in front of the long, ramshackle cottage next door. The windows were boarded; the picket-fence dropped even to the ground in some sections; the chimneys sagged and curved; the roof of the long porch sprinkled shingles over the unkempt yard with every wind, and seemed about to fall. The place was desolate with long emptiness and decay: it looked like a Haunted House; and nailed to the padlocked gate was a sign, half obliterated with the winters it had fronted, "For Sale or Rent."

Joe gat him meditatively back to Main Street and to the *Tocsin* building. This time he did not hesitate, but mounted the stairs and knocked upon the door of the assistant editor.

"Oh," said Eugene. "*You've* turned up, have you?"

Mr. Bantry of the *Tocsin* was not at all the Eugene rescued from the "Straw-Cellar." The present gentleman was more the electric Freshman than the frightened adventurer whom Joe had encountered in New York. It was to be seen immediately that the assistant editor had nothing undaintily business-like about him, nor was there the litter on his desk which one might have expected. He had the air of a gentleman dilettante who amused himself slightly by spending an hour or two in the room now and then. It was the evolution to the perfect of his Freshman manner, and his lively apparel, though somewhat chastened by an older taste, might have been foretold from that which had smitten Canaan seven years before. He sat not at the orderly and handsome desk, but lay stretched upon a divan of green leather, smoking a cigar of purest ray and reading sleepily a small verse-looking book in morocco. His occupation, his general air, the furniture of the room, and his title (doubtless equipped with a corresponding salary) might have inspired in an observant cynic the idea that here lay a pet of Fortune, whose position had been the fruit of nepotism, or, mayhap, a successful wooing of some daughter, wife, or widow. Eugene looked competent for that.

"I've come back to stay, 'Gene," said Joe.

Bantry had dropped his book and raised himself on an elbow. "Exceedingly interesting," he said. " I suppose you'll try to find something to do. I don't think you could get a place here; Judge Pike owns the *Tocsin*, and I greatly fear he has a prejudice against you."

"I expect he has," Joe chuckled, somewhat

sadly. "But I don't want newspaper work. I'm going to practice law."

"By Jove! you have courage, my festive prodigal. *Vraiment!*"

Joe cocked his head to one side with his old look of the friendly puppy. "You always did like to talk that noveletty way, 'Gene, didn't you?" he said, impersonally.

Eugene's color rose. "Have you saved up any-thing to starve on?" he asked, crisply.

"Oh, I'm not so badly off. I've had a salary in an office for a year, and I had one pretty good day at the races—"

"You'd better go back and have another," said his step-brother. "You don't seem to comprehend your standing in Canaan."

"I'm beginning to." Joe turned to the door. "It's funny, too—in a way. Well—I won't keep you any longer. I just stopped in to say good-day—" He paused, faltering.

"All right, all right," Eugene said, briskly. "And, by-the-way, I haven't mentioned that I saw you in New York."

"Oh, I didn't suppose that you would."

"And you needn't say anything about it, I fancy."

"I don't think," said Joe,—"I don't think that **you** need be afraid I'll do that. Good-bye."

" Be sure to shut the door, please; it's rather noisy with it open. Good-bye." Eugene waved his hand and sank back upon the divan.

Joe went across the street to the "National House." The sages fell as silent as if he had been Martin Pike. They had just had the pleasure of hearing a telephone monologue by Mr. Brown, the clerk, to which they listened intently: "Yes. This is Brown. Oh—oh, it's Judge Pike? Yes indeed, Judge, yes indeed, I hear you—ha, ha! Of course, I understand. Yes, Judge, I heard he was in town. No, he hasn't been here. Not yet, that is, Judge. Yes, I hear. No, I won't, of course. Certainly not. I will, I will. I hear perfectly, I understand. Yes, sir. Good-bye, Judge."

Joe had begun to write his name in the register. "My trunk is still at the station," he said. "I'll give you my check to send down for it."

"Excuse me," said the clerk. "We have no rooms."

"What!" cried Joe, innocently. "Why, I never knew more than eight people to stay here at the same time in my life."

"We have no rooms," repeated the clerk, curtly.

"Is there a convention here?"

"We have no rooms, I say!"

Joe looked up into the condensed eyes of Mr. Brown. "Oh," he said, "I see."

Deathly silence followed him to the door, but, as it closed behind him, he heard the outbreak of the sages like a tidal wave striking a dump-heap of tin cans.

Two hours later he descended from an evil ark of a cab at the corral attached to Beaver Beach, and followed the path through the marsh to the crumbling pier. A red-bearded man was seated on a plank by the water edge, fishing.

"Mike," said Joe, "have you got room for me? Can you take me in for a few days until I find a place in town where they'll let me stay?"

The red-bearded man rose slowly, pushed back his hat, and stared hard at the wanderer; then he uttered a howl of joy and seized the other's hands in his and shook them wildly.

"Glory be on high!" he shouted. "It's Joe Louden come back! We never knew how we missed ye till ye'd gone! Place fer ye! Can I find it? There ain't a imp o' perdition in town, includin' myself, that wouldn't kill me if I couldn't! Ye'll have old Maggie's room, my own aunt's; ye remember how she used to dance! Ha, ha! She's been burnin' below these four years! And we'll have the celebration of yer return this night. There'll be many of 'em will come when they hear ye're back in Canaan! Praise God, we'll all hope ye're goin' to stay a while!"

IX

"OUTER DARKNESS"

F any echo of doubt concerning his undesirable conspicuousness sounded faintly in Joe's mind, it was silenced eftsoons. Canaan had not forgotten him—far from it!—so far that it began pointing him out to strangers on the street the very day of his return. His course of action, likewise that of his friends, permitted him little obscurity, and when the rumors of his finally obtaining lodging at Beaver Beach, and of the celebration of his installation there, were presently confirmed, he stood in the lime-light indeed, as a Mephistopheles upsprung through the trap-door.

The welcoming festivities had not been so discreetly conducted as to accord with the general policy of Beaver Beach. An unfortunate incident caused the arrest of one of the celebrators and the ambulancing to the hospital of another on the homeward way, the ensuing proceedings in court bringing to the whole affair a publicity devoutly unsought for. Mr. Happy Fear (such was the habitual name of the imprisoned gentleman) had to bear a great amount of harsh criticism for injuring a companion within the city limits after daylight, and for failing to observe that three policemen were not too distant from the scene of operations to engage therein.

"Happy, if ye had it in mind to harm him," said the red-bearded man to Mr. Fear, upon the latter's return to society, "why didn't ye do it out here at the Beach?"

"Because," returned the indiscreet, "he didn't say what he was goin' to say till we got in town."

Extraordinary probing on the part of the prosecutor had developed at the trial that the obnoxious speech had referred to the guest of the evening. The assaulted party, one "Nashville" Cory, was not of Canaan, but a bit of drift-wood haply touching shore for the moment at Beaver Beach; and— strange is this world—he had been introduced to the coterie of Mike's Place by Happy Fear himself, who had enjoyed a brief acquaintance with him on a day when both had chanced to travel incognito by the same freight. Naturally, Happy had felt responsible for the proper behavior of his protégé —was, in fact, bound to enforce it; additionally, Happy had once been saved from a term of imprisonment (at a time when it would have been

more than ordinarily inconvenient) by help and
advice from Joe, and he was not one to forget.
Therefore he was grieved to observe that his
own guest seemed to be somewhat jealous of the
hero of the occasion and disposed to look coldly upon him. The stranger, however, contented
himself with innuendo (mere expressions of the
face and other manner of things for which one
could not squarely lay hands upon him) until
such time as he and his sponsor had come to Main
Street in the clear dawn on their way to Happy's
apartment — a variable abode. It may be that
the stranger perceived what Happy did not; the
three bluecoats in the perspective; at all events,
he now put into words of simple strength the un-
favorable conception he had formed of Joe. The
result was mediævally immediate, and the period
of Mr. Cory's convalescence in the hospital was
almost half that of his sponsor's detention in the
county jail.

It needed nothing to finish Joe with the good
people of Canaan; had it needed anything, the
trial of Happy Fear would have overspilled the
necessity. An item of the testimony was that
Joseph Louden had helped to carry one of the
ladies present—a Miss Le Roy, who had fainted—
to the open air, and had jostled the stranger in
passing. After this, the oldest woman in Canaan

would not have dared to speak to Joe on the street (even if she wanted to), unless she happened to be very poor or very wicked. The *Tocsin* printed an adequate account (for there was "a large public interest"), recording in conclusion that Mr. Louden paid the culprit's fine—which was the largest in the power of the presiding judge in his mercy to bestow. Editorially, the *Tocsin* leaned to the facetious: "Mr. Louden has but recently 'returned to our midst.' We fervently hope that the distinguished Happy Fear will appreciate his patron's superb generosity. We say 'his patron,' but perhaps we err in this. Were it not better to figure Mr. Louden as the lady in distress, Mr. Fear as the champion in the lists? In the present case, however, contrary to the rules of romance, the champion falls in duress and passes to the dungeon. We merely suggest, *en passant*, that some of our best citizens might deem it a wonderful and beauteous thing if, in addition to paying the fine, Mr. Louden could serve for the loyal Happy his six months in the Bastile!"

"*En passant*," if nothing else, would have revealed to Joe, in this imitation of a better trick, the hand of Eugene. And, little doubt, he would have agreed with Squire Buckalew in the Squire's answer to the easily expected comment of Mr. Arp.

"Sometimes," said Eskew, "I think that 'Gene

Bantry is jest a leetle bit spiderier than he is lazy. That's the first thing he's written in the *Tocsin* this month—one of the boys over there told me. He wrote it out of spite against Joe; but he'd ought to of done better. If his spite hadn't run away with what mind he's got, he'd of said that both Joe Louden and that tramp Fear ought to of had ten years!"

"'Gene Bantry didn't write that out of spite," answered Buckalew. "He only thought he saw a chance to be kind of funny and please Judge Pike. The Judge has always thought Joe was a no-account—"

"Ain't he right?" cried Mr. Arp.

"*I* don't say he ain't." Squire Buckalew cast a glance at Mr. Brown, the clerk, and, perceiving that he was listening, added, "The Judge always *is* right!"

"Yes, sir!" said Colonel Flitcroft.

"I can't stand up for Joe Louden to any extent, but I don't think he done wrong," Buckalew went on, recovering, "when he paid this man Fear's fine."

"You don't!" exclaimed Mr. Arp. "Why, haven't you got gumption enough to see—"

"Look here, Eskew," interposed his antagonist. "How many friends have you got that hate to hear folks talk bad about you?"

"Not a one!" For once Eskew's guard was down, and his consistency led him to destruction. "Not a one! It ain't in human nature. They're bound to enjoy it!"

"Got any friends that would *fight* for you?"

Eskew walked straight into this hideous trap. "No! There ain't a dozen men ever *lived* that had! Cæsar was a popular man, but he didn't have a soul to help him when the crowd lit on him, and I'll bet old Mark Antony was mighty glad they got him out in the yard before it happened,— *he* wouldn't have lifted a finger without a gang behind him! Why, all Peter himself could do was to cut off an ear that wasn't no use to anybody. What are you tryin' to get *at?*"

The Squire had him; and paused, and stroked his chin, to make the ruin complete. "Then I reckon you'll have to admit," he murmured, "that, while I ain't defendin' Joe Louden's character, it *was* kind of proper for him to stand by a feller that wouldn't hear nothin' against him, and fought for him as soon as he *did* hear it!"

Eskew Arp rose from his chair and left the hotel. It was the only morning in all the days of the conclave when he was the first to leave.

Squire Buckalew looked after the retreating figure, total triumph shining brazenly from his spectacles. "I expect," he explained, modestly, to the others,—"I expect I don't think any more of Joe Louden than he does, and I'll be glad when Canaan sees the last of him for good; but sometimes the temptation to argue with Eskew does lead me on to kind of git the better of him."

When Happy Fear had suffered—with a give-and-take simplicity of patience—his allotment of months in durance, and was released and sent into the streets and sunshine once more, he knew that his first duty lay in the direction of a general apology to Joe. But the young man was no longer at Beaver Beach; the red-bearded proprietor dwelt alone there, and, receiving Happy with scorn and pity, directed him to retrace his footsteps to the town.

"Ye must have been in the black hole of incarceration indeed, if ye haven't heard that Mr. Louden has his law-office on the Square, and his livin'-room behind the office. It's in that little brick buildin' straight acrost from the sheriff's door o' the jail—ye've been neighbors this long time! A hard time the boy had, persuadin' any one to rent to him, but by payin' double the price he got a place at last. He's a practisin' lawyer now, praise the Lord! And all the boys and girls of our acquaintance go to him with their troubles. Ye'll see him with a murder case to try before long, as sure as ye're not worth yer salt! But I expect ye can still call him by his name of Joe, all the same!"

It was a bleak and meagre little office into which Mr. Fear ushered himself to offer his amends. The cracked plaster of the walls was bare (save for dust); there were no shelves; the fat brown volumes, most of them fairly new, were piled in regular columns upon a cheap pine table; there was but one window, small-paned and shadeless; an inner door of this sad chamber stood half ajar, permitting the visitor unreserved acquaintance with the domestic economy of the tenant; for it disclosed a second room, smaller than the office, and dependent upon the window of the latter for air and light. Behind a canvas camp-cot, dimly visible in the obscurity of the inner apartment, stood a small gas-stove, surmounted by a stew-pan, from which projected the handle of a big tin spoon, so that it needed no ghost from the dead to whisper that Joseph Louden, attorney-at-law, did his own cooking. Indeed, he looked it!

Upon the threshold of the second room reposed a small, worn, light-brown scrub-brush of a dog, so cosmopolitan in ancestry that his species was almost as undeterminable as the cast-iron dogs of the Pike Mansion. He greeted Mr. Fear hospitably, having been so lately an offcast of the streets himself that his adoption had taught him to lose only his old tremors, not his hopefulness. At the same time Joe rose quickly from the deal table, where he had been working with one hand in his hair, the other splattering ink from a bad pen.

"Good for you, Happy!" he cried, cheerfully. "I hoped you'd come to see me to-day. I've been thinking about a job for you."

"What kind of a job?" asked the visitor, as they shook hands. "I need one bad enough, but you know there ain't nobody in Canaan would gimme one, Joe."

Joe pushed him into one of the two chairs which completed the furniture of his office. "Yes, there is. I've got an idea—"

"First," broke in Mr. Fear, fingering his shapeless hat and fixing his eyes upon it with embarrassment,—"first lemme say what I come here to say. I—well—" His embarrassment increased and he paused, rubbing the hat between his hands.

"About this job," Joe began. "We can fix it so—"

"No," said Happy. "You lemme go on. I didn't mean fer to cause you no trouble when I lit on that loud-mouth, 'Nashville'; I never thought they'd git me, or you'd be dragged in. But I jest couldn't stand him no longer. He had me all wore out—all evening long a-hintin' and sniffin' and wearin' that kind of a high-smile 'cause they made so much fuss over you. And then when we got clear in town he come out with it! Said you was too quiet to suit *him*—said he couldn't see nothin' *to* you! 'Well,' I says to myself, 'jest let him go on, jest one more,' I says, 'then he gits it.' And he did. Said you tromped on his foot on purpose, said he knowed it,—when the Lord-a'mightiest fool on earth knows you never tromped on no one! Said you was one of the po'rest young sports he ever see around a place like the Beach. You see, he thought you was jest one of them fool 'Bloods' that come around raisin' a rumpus, and didn't know you was our friend and belonged out there, the same as me or Mike hisself. 'Go on,' I says to myself, 'jest one more!' '*He* better go home to his mamma,' he says; 'he'll git in trouble if he don't. Somebody 'll soak him if he hangs around in *my* company. *I* don't like his *ways*.' Then I *had* to do it. There jest wasn't nothin' *left*—but I wouldn't of done you no harm by it—"

"You didn't do me any harm, Happy."

"I mean your repitation."

"I didn't have one—so nothing in the world could harm it. About your getting some work, now—"

"I'll listen," said Happy, rather suspiciously.

"You see," Joe went on, growing red, "I need a sort of janitor here—"

"What fer?" Mr. Fear interrupted, with some shortness.

"To look after the place."

"You mean these two rooms?"

"There's a stairway, too," Joe put forth, quickly. "It wouldn't be any sinecure, Happy. You'd earn your money, don't be afraid of that!"

Mr. Fear straightened up, his burden of embarrassment gone from him, transferred to the other's shoulders.

"There always was a yellow streak in you, Joe," he said, firmly. "You're no good as a liar except when you're jokin'. A lot you need a janitor! You had no business to pay my fine; you'd ort of let me worked it out. Do you think my eyes ain't good enough to see how much you needed the money, most of all right now when you're tryin' to git started? If I ever take a cent from you, I hope the hand I hold out fer it 'll rot off."

"Now don't say that, Happy."

"I don't want a job, nohow!" said Mr. Fear, going to the door; "I don't want to work. There's plenty ways fer me to git along without that. But I've said what I come here to say, and I'll say one thing more. Don't you worry about gittin' law practice. Mike says you're goin' to git all you want—and if there ain't no other way, why, a few of us 'll go out and *make* some fer ye!"

These prophecies and promises, over which Joe chuckled at first, with his head cocked to one side, grew very soon, to his amazement, to wear a supernatural similarity to actual fulfilment. His friends brought him their own friends, such as had sinned against the laws of Canaan, those under the ban of the sheriff, those who had struck in anger, those who had stolen at night, those who owed and could not pay, those who lived by the dice, and to his other titles to notoriety was added that of defender of the poor and wicked. He found his hands full, especially after winning his first important case—on which occasion Canaan thought the jury mad, and was indignant with the puzzled Judge, who could not see just how it had happened.

Joe did not stop at that. He kept on winning cases, clearing the innocent and lightening the burdens of the guilty; he became the most dangerous attorney for the defence in Canaan; his honorable brethren, accepting the popular view of him, held him in personal contempt but feared him professionally; for he proved that he knew more law than they thought existed; nor could any trick him—failing which, many tempers were lost, but never Joe's. His practice was not all criminal, as shown by the peevish outburst of the eminent Buckalew (the Squire's nephew, esteemed the foremost lawyer in Canaan), "Before long, there won't be any

use trying to foreclose a mortgage or collect a note
—unless this shyster gets himself in jail!"

The wrath of Judge Martin Pike was august—
there was a kind of sublimity in its immenseness—
on a day when it befell that the shyster stood
betwixt him and money.

That was a monstrous task—to stand between
these two and separate them, to hold back the
hand of Martin Pike from what it had reached out
to grasp. It was in the matter of some tax-titles
which the magnate had acquired, and, in court,
Joe treated the case with such horrifying simplicity that it seemed almost credible that the
great man had counted upon the ignorance and
besottedness of Joe's client—a hard-drinking, disreputable old farmer—to get his land away from
him without paying for it. Now, as every one
knew such a thing to be ludicrously impossible,
it was at once noised abroad in Canaan that Joe
had helped to swindle Judge Pike out of a large
sum of money—it was notorious that the shyster
could bamboozle court and jury with his tricks;
and it was felt that Joe Louden was getting into
very deep waters indeed. *This* was serious: if
the young man did not *look out*, he might find himself in the penitentiary.

The *Tocsin* paragraphed him with a fine regular-
ity after this, usually opening with a Walrus-and-

the-Carpenter gravity: "The time has come when we must speak of a certain matter frankly," or, "At last the time has arrived when the demoralization of the bar caused by a certain criminal lawyer must be dealt with as it is and without gloves." Once when Joe had saved a half-witted negro from "the extreme penalty" for murder, the *Tocsin* had declared, with great originality: "This is just the kind of thing that causes mobs and justifies them. If we are to continue to permit the worst class of malefactors to escape the consequences of their crimes through the unwholesome dexterities and the shifty manipulations and technicalities of a certain criminal lawyer, the time will come when an outraged citizenry may take the enforcement of the law in its own hands. Let us call a spade a spade. If Canaan's streets ever echo with the tread of a mob, the fault lies upon the head of Joseph Louden, who has once more brought about a miscarriage of justice. . . ."

Joe did not move into a larger office; he remained in the little room with its one window and its fine view of the jail; his clients were nearly all poor, and many of his fees quite literally nominal. Tatters and rags came up the narrow stairway to his door —tatters and rags and pitiful fineries: the bleared, the sodden, the flaunting and rouged, the furtive and wary, some in rags, some in tags, and some—

the sorriest — in velvet gowns. With these, the distressed, the wrong-doers, the drunken, the dirty, and the very poor, his work lay and his days and nights were spent.

Ariel had told Roger Tabor that in time Joe might come to be what the town thought him, if it gave him no other chance. Only its dinginess and evil surrounded him; no respectable house was open to him; the barrooms—except that of the "National House"—welcomed him gratefully and admiringly. Once he went to church, on a pleasant morning when nice girls wear pretty spring dresses; it gave him a thrill of delight to see them, to be near clean, good people once more. Inadvertently, he took a seat by his step-mother, who rose with a slight rustle of silk and moved to another pew; and it happened, additionally, that this was the morning that the minister, fired by the *Tocsin's* warnings, had chosen to preach on the subject of Joe himself.

The outcast returned to his own kind. No lady spoke to him upon the street. Mamie Pike had passed him with averted eyes since her first meeting with him, but the shunning and snubbing of a young man by a pretty girl have never yet, if done in a certain way, prevented him from continuing to be in love with her. Mamie did it in the certain way. Joe did not wince, therefore it hurt all the more, for blows from which one cringes lose much of their force.

The town dog had been given a bad name, painted solid black from head to heel. He was a storm centre of scandal; the entrance to his dingy stairway was in square view of the "National House," and the result is imaginable. How many of Joe's clients, especially those sorriest of the velvet gowns, were conjectured to ascend his stairs for reasons more convivial than legal! Yes, he lived with his own kind, and, so far as the rest of Canaan was concerned, might as well have worn the scarlet letter on his breast or branded on his forehead.

When he went about the streets he was made to feel his condition by the elaborate avoidance, yet furtive attention, of every respectable person he met; and when he came home to his small rooms and shut the door behind him, he was as one who has been hissed and shamed in public and runs to bury his hot face in his pillow. He petted his mongrel extravagantly (well he might!), and would sit with him in his rooms at night, holding long converse with him, the two alone together. The dog was not his only confidant. There came to be another, a more and more frequent partner to their conversations, at last a familiar spirit. This third came from a brown jug which Joe kept on a shelf in his bedroom, a vessel too frequently replenished. When the day's work was done he shut himself up, drank alone and drank hard. Sometimes when the jug ran low and the night was late he would go out for a walk with his dog, and would awake in his room the next morning not remembering where he had gone or how he had come home. Once, after such a lapse of memory, he woke amazed to find himself at Beaver Beach, whither, he learned from the red - bearded man, Happy Fear had brought him, having found him wandering dazedly in a field near by. These lapses grew more frequent, until there occurred that which was one of the strange things of his life.

It was a June night, a little more than two years after his return to Canaan, and the *Tocsin* had that day announced the approaching marriage of Eugene Bantry and his employer's daughter. Joe ate nothing during the day, and went through his work clumsily, visiting the bedroom shelf at intervals. At ten in the evening he went out to have the jug refilled, but from the moment he left his door and the fresh air struck his face, he had no clear knowledge of what he did or of what went on about him until he woke in his bed the next morning.

And yet, whatever little part of the soul of him remained, that night, still undulled, not numbed, but alive, was in some strange manner lifted out of its pain towards a strange delight. His body was an automaton, his mind in bondage, yet there was a still, small consciousness in him which knew that in his wandering something incredible and unexpected was happening. What this was he did not know, could not see, though his eyes were open, could not have told himself any more than a baby could tell why it laughs, but it seemed something so beautiful and wonderful that the night became a night of perfume, its breezes bearing the music of harps and violins, while nightingales sang from the maples that bordered the streets of Canaan.

X

THE TRYST

E woke to the light of morning amazed and full of a strange wonder because he did not know what had amazed him. For a little while after his eyes opened, he lay quite motionless; then he lifted his head slightly and shook it with some caution. This had come to be custom. The operation assured him of the worst; the room swam round him, and, with a faint groan, he let his head fall back upon the pillow. But he could not sleep again; pain stung its way through his heart as memory began to come back to him, not of the preceding night—that was all blank,—but realization that the girl of whom he had dreamed so long was to be married. That his dreams had been quite hopeless was no balm to his hurt.

A chime of bells sounded from a church steeple across the Square, ringing out in assured righteousness, summoning the good people who maintained them to come and sit beneath them or be taken to

task; and they fell so dismally upon Joe's ear that
he bestirred himself and rose, to the delight of his
mongrel, who leaped upon him joyfully. An hour
later, or thereabout, the pair emerged from the narrow stairway and stood for a moment, blinking in
the fair sunshine, apparently undecided which way
to go. The church bells were silent; there was no
breeze; the air trembled a little with the deep
pipings of the organ across the Square, and, save for
that, the town was very quiet. The paths which
crossed the Court - house yard were flecked with
steady shadow, the strong young foliage of the
maples not moving, having the air of observing the
Sabbath with propriety. There were benches here
and there along the walks, and to one of these Joe
crossed, and sat down. The mongrel, at his master's
feet, rolled on his back in morning ecstasy, ceased
abruptly to roll and began to scratch his ear with
a hind foot intently. A tiny hand stretched to pat
his head, and the dog licked it appreciatively. It
belonged to a hard-washed young lady of six (in
starchy, white frills and new, pink ribbons), who
had run ahead of her mother, a belated church-goer;
and the mongrel charmed her.

"Will you give me this dog?" she asked, without
any tedious formalities.

Involuntarily, she departed before receiving a
reply. The mother, a red-faced matron whom Joe

recognized as a sister of Mrs. Louden's, consequently his step-aunt, swooped at the child with a rush and rustle of silk, and bore her on violently to her duty. When they had gone a little way the matron's voice was heard in sharp reproof; the child, held by one wrist and hurried along on tiptoe, staring back over one shoulder at Joe, her eyes wide, and her mouth the shape of the "O" she was ejaculating.

The dog looked up with wistful inquiry at his master, who cocked an eyebrow at him in return, wearing much the same expression. The mother and child disappeared within the church doors and left the Square to the two. Even the hotel showed no signs of life, for the wise men were not allowed to foregather on Sundays. The organ had ceased to stir the air and all was in quiet, yet a quiet which, for Louden, was not peace. He looked at his watch and, without intending it, spoke the hour aloud: "A quarter past eleven." The sound of his own voice gave him a little shock; he rose without knowing why, and, as he did so, it seemed to him that he heard close to his ear another voice, a woman's, troubled and insistent, but clear and sweet, saying:

"*Remember! Across Main Street bridge at noon!*"

It was so distinct that he started and looked round. Then he laughed. "I'll be seeing circus parades next!" His laughter fled, for, louder than the ringing in his ears, unmistakably came the strains of a far-away brass band which had no existence on land or sea or in the waters under the earth.

"Here!" he said to the mongrel. "We need a walk, I think. Let's you and me move on before the camels turn the corner!"

The music followed him to the street, where he turned westward toward the river, and presently, as he walked on, fanning himself with his straw hat, it faded and was gone. But the voice he had heard returned.

"*Remember! Across Main Street bridge at noon!*" it said again, close to his ear.

This time he did not start. "All right," he answered, wiping his forehead; "if you'll let me alone, I'll be there."

At a dingy saloon corner, near the river, a shabby little man greeted him heartily and petted the mongrel. "I'm mighty glad you didn't go, after all, Joe," he added, with a brightening face.

"Go where, Happy?"

Mr. Fear looked grave. "Don't you rec'lect meetin' me last night?"

Louden shook his head. "No. Did I?"

The other's jaw fell and his brow corrugated with self-reproach. "Well, if that don't show what a thick-head I am! I thought ye was all right er I'd gone on with ye. Nobody c'd 'a' walked straighter ner talked straighter. Said ye was goin' to leave Canaan fer good and didn't want nobody to know it. Said ye was goin' to take the 'leven-o'clock through train fer the West, and told me I couldn't come to the deepo with ye. Said ye'd had enough o' Canaan, and of everything! I follered ye part way to the deepo, but ye turned and made a motion fer me to go back, and I done it, because ye seemed to be kind of in trouble, and I thought ye'd ruther be by yerself. Well, sir, it's one on me!"

"Not at all," said Joe. "I was all right."

"Was ye?" returned the other. "*Do* remember, do ye?"

"Almost," Joe smiled, faintly.

"*Almost*," echoed Happy, shaking his head seriously. "I tell ye, Joe, ef I was *you*—" he began slowly, then paused and shook his head again. He seemed on the point of delivering some advice, but evidently perceiving the snobbishness of such a proceeding, or else convinced by his own experience of the futility of it, he swerved to cheerfulness:

"I hear the boys is all goin' to work hard fer the primaries. Mike says ye got some chances ye don't know about; *he* swears ye'll be the next Mayor of Canaan."

"Nonsense! Folly and nonsense, Happy! That's

the kind of thing I used to think when I was a boy. But now—pshaw!" Joe broke off with a tired laugh. "Tell them not to waste their time! Are you going out to the Beach this afternoon?"

The little man lowered his eyes moodily. "I'll be *near* there," he said, scraping his patched shoe up and down the curbstone. "That feller's in town agin."

"What fellow?"

"'Nashville' they call him; Ed's the name he give the hospital: Cory—him that I soaked the night you come back to Canaan. He's after Claudine to git his evens with me. He's made a raise somewheres, and plays the spender. And her—well, I reckon she's tired waitin' table at the 'National House'; tired o' me, too. I got a hint that they're goin' out to the Beach together this afternoon."

Joe passed his hand wearily over his aching forehead. "I understand," he said, "and you'd better try to. Cory's laying for you, of course. You say he's after your wife? He must have set about it pretty openly if they're going to the Beach to-day, for there is always a crowd there on Sundays. Is it hard for you to see why he's doing it? It's because he wants to make you jealous. What for? So that you'll tackle him again. And why does he want that? Because he's *ready* for you!"

THE TRYST

The other's eyes suddenly became bloodshot, his nostrils expanding incredibly. "*Ready*, is he? He *better* be ready. I—"

"That's enough!" Joe interrupted, swiftly. "We'll have no talk like that. I'll settle this for you, myself. You send word to Claudine that I want to see her at my office to-morrow morning, and you—you stay away from the Beach to-day. Give me your word."

Mr. Fear's expression softened. "All right, Joe," he said. "I'll do whatever you tell me to. Any of us 'll do that; we sure know who's our friend."

"Keep out of trouble, Happy." Joe turned to go and they shook hands. "Good day, and—keep out of trouble!"

When he had gone, Mr. Fear's countenance again gloomed ominously, and, shaking his head, he ruminatively entered an adjacent bar through the alley door.

The Main Street bridge was an old-fashioned, wooden, covered one, dust-colored and very narrow, squarely framing the fair, open country beyond; for the town had never crossed the river. Joe found the cool shadow in the bridge gracious to his hot brow, and through the slender chinks of the worn flooring he caught bright glimpses of running water. When he came out of the other end he felt enough refreshed to light a cigar.

"Well, here I am," he said. "Across Main Street bridge—and it must be getting on toward noon!" He spoke almost with the aspect of daring, and immediately stood still, listening. "'Remember,'" he ventured to repeat, again daring, "'Remember! Across Main Street bridge at noon!'" And again he listened. Then he chuckled faintly with relief, for the voice did not return. "Thank God, I've got rid of that!" he whispered. "And of the circus band too!"

A dust road turned to the right, following the river and shaded by big sycamores on the bank; the mongrel, intensely preoccupied with this road, scampered away, his nose to the ground. "Good enough," said the master. "Lead on and I'll come after you."

But he had not far to follow. The chase led him to a half-hollow log which lay on a low, grass-grown levee above the stream, where the dog's interest in the pursuit became vivid; temporarily, however, for after a few minutes of agitated investigation, he was seized with indifference to the whole world; panted briefly; slept. Joe sat upon the log, which was in the shade, and smoked.

"'Remember!'" He tried it once more. "'Across Main Street bridge at noon!'" Safety still; the voice came not. But the sound of his own repetition of the words brought him an eerie tremor;

for the mist of a memory came with it; nothing tangible, nothing definite, but something very far away and shadowy, yet just poignant enough to give him a queer feeling that he was really keeping an appointment here. Was it with some water-sprite that would rise from the river? Was it with a dryad of the sycamores? He knew too well that he might expect strange fancies to get hold of him this morning, and, as this one grew uncannily stronger, he moved his head briskly as if to shake it off. The result surprised him; the fancy remained, but his headache and dizziness had left him.

A breeze wandered up the river and touched the leaves and grass to life. Sparrows hopped and chirped in the branches, absurdly surprised; without doubt having concluded in the Sunday stillness that the world would drowse forever; and the mongrel lifted his head, blinked at them, hopelessly wishing they would alight near him, scratched his ear with the manner of one who has neglected such matters overlong; reversed his position; slept again. The young corn, deep green in the bottom land, moved with a staccato flurry, and the dust ghost of a mad whirling dervish sped up the main road to vanish at the bridge in a climax of lunacy. The stirring air brought a smell of blossoms; the distance took on faint lavender hazes which blended the outlines of the fields, lying like square coverlets upon the long slope of rising ground beyond the bottom-land, and empurpled the blue woodland shadows of the groves.

For the first time, it struck Joe that it was a beautiful day, and it came to him that a beautiful day was a thing which nothing except death, sickness, or imprisonment could take from him—not even the ban of Canaan! Unforewarned, music sounded in his ears again; but he did not shrink from it now; this was not the circus band he had heard as he left the Square, but a melody like a far-away serenade at night, as of "the horns of elf-land faintly blowing"; and he closed his eyes with the sweetness of it.

"Go ahead!" he whispered. "Do that all you want to. If you'll keep it up like this awhile, I'll follow with 'Little Brown Jug, How I Love Thee!' It seems to pay, after all!"

The welcome strains, however, were but the prelude to a harsher sound which interrupted and annihilated them: the Court-house bell clanging out twelve. "All right," said Joe. "It's noon and I'm 'across Main Street bridge.'"

He opened his eyes and looked about him whimsically. Then he shook his head again.

A lady had just emerged from the bridge and was coming toward him.

THE TRYST

It would be hard to get at Joe's first impressions of her. We can find conveyance for only the broadest and heaviest. Ancient and modern instances multiply the case of the sleeper who dreams out a long story in accurate color and fine detail, a tale of years, in the opening and shutting of a door. So with Joseph, in the brief space of the lady's approach. And with him, as with the sleeper, it must have been—in fact it was, in his recollections, later—a blur of emotion.

At first sight of her, perhaps it was pre-eminently the shock of seeing anything so exquisite where he had expected to see nothing at all. For she was exquisite—horrid as have been the uses of the word, its best and truest belong to her; she was that and much more, from the ivory ferrule of the parasol she carried, to the light and slender footprint she left in the dust of the road. Joe knew at once that nothing like her had ever before been seen in Canaan.

He had little knowledge of the millinery arts, and he needed none to see the harmony—harmony like that of the day he had discovered a little while ago. Her dress and hat and gloves and parasol showed a pale lavender overtint like that which he had seen overspreading the western slope. (Afterward, he discovered that the gloves she wore that day were gray, and that her hat was

for the most part white.) The charm of fabric
and tint belonging to what she wore was no shame
to her, not being of primal importance beyond herself; it was but the expression of her daintiness and
the adjunct of it. She was tall, but if Joe could
have spoken or thought of her as "slender," he
would have been capable of calling her lips "red,"
in which case he would not have been Joe, and
would have been as far from the truth as her lips
were from red, or as her supreme delicateness was
from mere slenderness.

Under the summer hat her very dark hair swept
back over her temples with something near trimness in the extent to which it was withheld from
being fluffy. It may be that this approach to
trimness, which was, after all, only a sort of co-
quetry with trimness, is the true key to the mystery of the vision of the lady who appeared to Joe.
Let us say that she suppressed everything that
went beyond grace; that the hint of floridity was
abhorrent to her. "Trim" is as clumsy as "slender"; she had escaped from the trimness of girlhood as wholly as she had gone through its colt-
ishness. "Exquisite." Let us go back to Joe's
own blurred first thought of her and be content
with that!

She was to pass him—so he thought—and as
she drew nearer, his breath came faster

THE TRYST

" Remember!   Across Main Street bridge at noon!"

Was *this* the fay of whom the voice had warned him? With that, there befell him the mystery of last night. He did not remember, but it was as if he lived again, dimly, the highest hour of happiness in a life a thousand years ago; perfume and music, roses, nightingales and plucked harp-strings. Yes; something wonderful was happening to him.

She had stopped directly in front of him; stopped and stood looking at him with her clear eyes. He did not lift his own to hers; he had long experience of the averted gaze of women; but it was not only that; a great shyness beset him. He had risen and removed his hat, trying (ineffectually) not to clear his throat; his every-day sense urging upon him that she was a stranger in Canaan who had lost her way—the preposterousness of any one's losing the way in Canaan not just now appealing to his every-day sense.

"Can I—can I—" he stammered, blushing miserably, meaning to finish with "direct you," or "show you the way."

Then he looked at her again and saw what seemed to him the strangest sight of his life. The lady's eyes had filled with tears—filled and over-filled.

" I'll sit here on the log with you," she said. And

her voice was the voice which he had heard saying, "*Remember! Across Main Street bridge at noon!*"

"*What!*" he gasped.

"You don't need to dust it!" she went on, tremulously. And even then he did not know who she was.

XI

WHEN HALF-GODS GO

THERE was a silence, for if the dazzled young man could have spoken at all, he could have found nothing to say; and, perhaps, the lady would not trust her own voice just then. His eyes had fallen again; he was too dazed, and, in truth, too panic-stricken, now, to look at her, though if he had been quite sure that she was part of a wonderful dream he might have dared. She was seated beside him, and had handed him her parasol in a little way which seemed to imply that of course he had reached for it, so that it was to be seen how used she was to have all tiny things done for her, though this was not then of his tremulous observing. He did perceive, however, that he was to furl the dainty thing; he pressed the catch, and let down the top timidly, as if fearing to break or tear it; and, as it closed, held near his face, he caught a very faint, sweet, spicy emanation from it like wild roses and cinnamon.

He did not know her; but his timidity and a strange little choke in his throat, the sudden fright which had seized upon him, were not caused by embarrassment. He had no thought that she was one he had known but could not, for the moment, recall; there was nothing of the awkwardness of that; no, he was overpowered by the miracle of this meeting. And yet, white with marvelling, he felt it to be so much more touchingly a great happiness than he had ever known that at first it was inexpressibly sad.

At last he heard her voice again, shaking a little, as she said:

"I am glad you remembered."

"Remembered what?" he faltered.

"Then you don't?" she cried. "And yet you came."

"Came here, do you mean?"

"Yes—now, at noon."

"Ah!" he half whispered, unable to speak aloud. "Was it you who said—who said, 'Remember! Across—across—'"

"'Across Main Street bridge at noon!'" she finished for him, gently. "Yes."

He took a deep breath in the wonder of it. "Where was it you said that?" he asked, slowly. "Was it last night?"

"Don't you even know that you came to meet me?"

"*I*—came to—to meet—you!"

She gave a little pitying cry, very near a sob, seeing his utter bewilderment.

"It was like the strangest dream in the world," she said. "You were at the station when I came, last night. You don't remember at all?"

His eyes downcast, his face burning hotly, he could only shake his head.

"Yes," she continued. "I thought no one would be there, for I had not written to say what train I should take, but when I stepped down from the platform, you were standing there; though you didn't see me at first, not until I had called your name and ran to you. You said, 'I've come to meet you,' but you said it queerly, I thought. And then you called a carriage for me; but you seemed so strange—you couldn't tell how you knew that I was coming, and—and then I—I understood you weren't yourself. You were very quiet, but I knew, I knew! So I made you get into the carriage—and—and—"

She faltered to a stop, and with that, shame itself brought him courage; he turned and faced her. She had lifted her handkerchief to her eyes, but at his movement she dropped it, and it was not so much the delicate loveliness of her face that he saw then as the tears upon her cheeks.

"Ah, poor boy!" she cried. "I knew! I knew!"

" You—you took me home?"

" You told me where you lived," she answered. "Yes, I took you home."

" I don't understand," he stammered, huskily. "I don't understand!"

She leaned toward him slightly, looking at him with great intentness.

" You didn't know me last night," she said. "Do you know me now?"

For answer he could only stare at her, dumfounded. He lifted an unsteady hand toward her appealingly. But the manner of the lady, as she saw the truth, underwent an April change. She drew back lightly; he was favored with the most delicious, low laugh he had ever heard, and, by some magic whisk which she accomplished, there was no sign of tears about her.

"Ah! I'm glad you're the same, Joe!" she said. "You never would or could pretend very well. I'm glad you're the same, and I'm glad I've changed, though that isn't why you have forgotten me. You've forgotten me because you never thought of me. Perhaps I should not have known you if you had changed a great deal—as I have!"

He started, leaning back from her.

"Ah!" she laughed. "That's it! That funny little twist of the head you always had, like a—

like a—well, you know I must have told you a
thousand times that it was like a nice friendly
puppy; so why shouldn't I say so now? And your
eyebrows! When you look like that, nobody could
ever forget you, Joe!"

He rose from the log, and the mongrel leaped
upon him uproariously, thinking they were to go
home, belike to food.

The lady laughed again. "Don't let him spoil
my parasol. And I must warn you now: Never,
never *tread on my skirt!* I'm very irritable about
such things!"

He had taken three or four uncertain backward
steps from her. She sat before him, radiant with
laughter, the loveliest creature he had ever seen;
but between him and this charming vision there
swept, through the warm, scented June air, a veil
of snow like a driven fog, and, half obscured in the
heart of it, a young girl stood, knee-deep in a drift
piled against an old picket gate, her black water-
proof and shabby skirt flapping in the blizzard
like torn sails, one of her hands out-stretched toward him, her startled eyes fixed on his.

"And, oh, how like you," said the lady; "how
like you and nobody else in the world, Joe, to have
a yellow dog!"

"*Ariel Tabor!*"

His lips formed the words without sound.

"Isn't it about time?" she said. "Are strange ladies in the *habit* of descending from trains to take you home?"

Once, upon a white morning long ago, the sensational progress of a certain youth up Main Street had stirred Canaan. But that day was as nothing to this. Mr. Bantry had left temporary paralysis in his wake; but in the case of the two young people who passed slowly along the street to-day it was petrifaction, which seemingly threatened in several instances (most notably that of Mr. Arp) to become permanent.

The lower portion of the street, lined with three and four story buildings of brick and stone, rather grim and hot façades under the mid-day sun, afforded little shade to the church-comers, who were working homeward in processional little groups and clumps, none walking fast, though none with the appearance of great leisure, since neither rate of progress would have been esteemed befitting the day. The growth of Canaan, steady, though never startling, had left almost all of the churches down-town, and Main Street the principal avenue of communication between them and the "residence section." So, to-day, the intermittent procession stretched along the new cement sidewalks from a little below the Square to Upper

Main Street, where maples lined the thoroughfare and the mansions of the affluent stood among pleasant lawns and shrubberies. It was late; for this had been a communion Sunday, and those far in advance, who had already reached the pretty and shady part of the street, were members of the churches where services had been shortest; though few in the long parade looked as if they had been attending anything very short, and many heads of families were crisp in their replies to the theological inquiries of their offspring. The men imparted largely a gloom to the itinerant concourse, most of them wearing hot, long black coats and having wilted their collars; the ladies relieving this gloom somewhat by the lighter tints of their garments; the spick-and-span little girls relieving it greatly by their white dresses and their faces, the latter bright with the hope of Sunday ice-cream; while the boys, experiencing some solace in that they were finally out where a person could at least scratch himself if he had to, yet oppressed by the decorous necessities of the day, marched along, furtively planning, behind imperturbably secretive countenances, various means for the later dispersal of an odious monotony.

Usually the conversation of this long string of the homeward-bound was not too frivolous or worldly; nay, it properly inclined to discussion of the sermon;

that is, praise of the sermon, with here and there a mild " I-didn't-like-his-saying" or so; and its lighter aspects were apt to concern the next "Social," or various pleasurable schemes for the raising of funds to help the heathen, the quite worthy poor, or the church.

This was the serious and seemly parade, the propriety of whose behavior was to-day almost disintegrated when the lady of the bridge walked up the street in the shadow of a lacy, lavender parasol carried by Joseph Louden. The congregation of the church across the Square, that to which Joe's step-aunt had been late, was just debouching, almost in mass, upon Main Street, when these two went by. It is not quite the truth to say that all except the children came to a dead halt, but it is not very far from it. The air was thick with subdued exclamations and whisperings.

Here is no mystery. Joe was probably the only person of respectable derivation in Canaan who had not known for weeks that Ariel Tabor was on her way home. And the news that she had arrived the night before had been widely disseminated on the way to church, entering church, *in* church (even so!), and coming out of church. An account of her house in the Avenue Henri Martin, and of her portrait in the Salon—a mysterious business to many, and not lacking in grandeur for that!—had occupied two

columns in the *Tocsin*, on a day, some months before, when Joe had found himself inimically head-
lined on the first page, and had dropped the paper
without reading further. Ariel's name had been
in the mouth of Canaan for a long time; unfort-
unately for Joe, however, not in the mouth of that
Canaan which held converse with him.

Joe had not known her. The women recognized
her, infallibly, at first glance; even those who had
quite forgotten her. And the women told their
men. Hence the un-Sunday-like demeanor of the
procession, for few towns hold it more unseemly to
stand and stare at passers-by, especially on the
Sabbath.—*But* Ariel Tabor returned—and walking
with—*with Joe Louden!* . . .

A low but increasing murmur followed the two
as they proceeded. It ran up the street ahead of
them; people turned to look back and paused, so
that they had to walk round one or two groups.
They had, also, to walk round Norbert Flitcroft,
which was very like walking round a group. He
was one of the few (he was waddling home alone)
who did not identify Miss Tabor, and her effect upon
him was extraordinary. His mouth opened and he
gazed stodgily, his widening eyes like sun-dogs
coming out of a fog. He did not recognize her escort; did not see him at all until they had passed,
after which Mr. Flitcroft experienced a few mo-

ments of trance; came out of it stricken through and through; felt nervously of his tie; resolutely fell in behind the heeling mongrel and followed, at a distance of some forty paces, determined to learn what household this heavenly visitor honored, and thrilling with the intention to please that same household with his own presence as soon and as often as possible.

Ariel flushed a little when she perceived the extent of their conspicuousness; but it was not the blush that Joe remembered had reddened the tanned skin of old; for her brownness had gone long ago, though it had not left her merely pink and white. This was a delicate rosiness rising from her cheeks to her temples as the earliest dawn rises. If there had been many words left in Joe, he would have called it a divine blush; it fascinated him, and if anything could have deepened the glamour about her, it would have been this blush. He did not understand it, but when he saw it he stumbled.

Those who gaped and stared were for him only blurs in the background; truly, he saw "men as trees walking"; and when it became necessary to step out to the curb in passing some clump of people, it was to him as if Ariel and he, enchantedly alone, were working their way through underbrush in the woods.

He kept trying to realize that this lady of wonder

was Ariel Tabor, but he could not; he could not connect the shabby Ariel, whom he had treated as one boy treats another, with this young woman of the world. He had always been embarrassed, himself, and ashamed of her, when anything she did made him remember that, after all, she was a girl; as, on the day he ran away, when she kissed a lock of his hair escaping from the bandage. With that recollection, even his ears grew red: it did not seem probable that it would ever happen again! The next instant he heard himself calling her "Miss Tabor."

At this she seemed amused. "You ought to have called me that, years ago," she said, "for all you knew me!"

"I did know her—*you*, I mean!" he answered. "I used to know nearly everything you were going to say before you said it. It seems strange now—"

"Yes," she interrupted. "It does seem strange now!"

"Somehow," he went on, "I doubt if now I'd know."

"Somehow," she echoed, with fine gravity, "I doubt it, too."

Although he had so dim a perception of the staring and whispering which greeted and followed them, Ariel, of course, was thoroughly aware of it, though the only sign she gave was the slight blush, which very soon disappeared. That people turned to look at her may have been not altogether a novelty: a girl who had learned to appear unconscious of the Continental stare, the following gaze of the boulevards, the frank glasses of the Costanza in Rome, was not ill equipped to face Main Street, Canaan, even as it was to-day.

Under the sycamores, before they started, they had not talked a great deal; there had been long silences: almost all her questions concerning the period of his runaway absence; she appeared to know and to understand everything which had happened since his return to the town. He had not, in his turn, reached the point where he would begin to question her; he was too breathless in his consciousness of the marvellous present hour. She had told him of the death of Roger Tabor, the year before. "Poor man," she said, gently, "he lived to see 'how the other fellows did it' at last, and everybody liked him. He was very happy over there."

After a little while she had said that it was growing close upon lunch-time; she must be going back.

"Then—then—good-bye," he replied, ruefully.

"Why?"

"I'm afraid you don't understand. It wouldn't do for you to be seen with me. Perhaps, though, you do understand. Wasn't that why you asked me to meet you out here beyond the bridge?"

In answer she looked at him full and straight for three seconds, then threw back her head and closed her eyes tight with laughter. Without a word she took the parasol from him, opened it herself, placed the smooth white coral handle of it in his hand, and lightly took his arm. There was no further demur on the part of the young man. He did not know where she was going; he did not ask.

Soon after Norbert turned to follow them, they came to the shady part of the street, where the town in summer was like a grove. Detachments from the procession had already, here and there, turned in at the various gates. Nobody, however, appeared to have gone in-doors, except for fans, armed with which immediately to return to rockers upon the shaded verandas. As Miss Tabor and Joe went by, the rocking-chairs stopped; the fans poised, motionless; and perpsiring old gentlemen, wiping their necks, paused in arrested attitudes.

Once Ariel smiled politely, not at Mr. Louden, and inclined her head twice, with the result that the latter, after thinking for a time of how gracefully she did it and how pretty the top of her hat was, became gradually conscious of a meaning in her action: that she had bowed to some one across the street. He lifted his hat, about four minutes late, and discovered Mamie Pike and Eugene, upon the opposite pavement, walking home from church together. Joe changed color.

There, just over the way, was she who had been, in his first youth, the fairy child, the little princess playing in the palace yard, and always afterward his lady of dreams, his fair unreachable moon! And Joe, seeing her to-day, changed color; that was all! He had passed Mamie in the street only a week before, and she had seemed all that she had always seemed; to-day an incomprehensible and subtle change had befallen her—a change so mystifying to him that for a moment he almost doubted that she was Mamie Pike. It came to him with a breath-taking shock that her face lacked a certain vivacity of meaning; that its sweetness was perhaps too placid; that there would have been a deeper good-ness in it had there been any hint of daring. As-tonishing questions assailed him, startled him: could it be true that, after all, there might be some day too much of her? Was her amber hair a little too—*fluffy?* Was something the matter with her dress? Everything she wore had always seemed so beautiful. Where had the exquisiteness of it gone? For there was surely no exquisiteness about it now! It was incredible that any one could so greatly alter in the few days elapsed since he had seen her.

Strange matters! Mamie had never looked prettier.

At the sound of Ariel's voice he emerged from the profundities of his psychic enigma with a leap.

"She is lovelier than ever, isn't she?"

"Yes, indeed," he answered, blankly.

"Would you still risk—" she began, smiling, but, apparently thinking better of it, changed her question: "What is the name of your dog, Mr. Louden? You haven't told me."

"Oh, he's just a yellow dog," he evaded, unskilfully.

"*Young man!*" she said, sharply.

"Well," he admitted, reluctantly, "I call him Speck for short."

"And what for long? I want to know his real name."

"It's mighty inappropriate, because we're fond of each other," said Joe, "but when I picked him up he was so yellow, and so thin, and so creeping, and so scared that I christened him 'Respectability.'"

She broke into light laughter, stopped short in the midst of it, and became grave. "Ah, you've grown bitter," she said, gently.

"No, no," he protested. "I told you I liked him."

She did not answer.

They were now opposite the Pike Mansion, and to his surprise she turned, indicating the way by a touch upon his sleeve, and crossed the street toward the gate, which Mamie and Eugene had entered. Mamie, after exchanging a word with Eugene upon the steps, was already hurrying into the house.

Ariel paused at the gate, as if waiting for Joe to open it.

He cocked his head, his higher eyebrow rose, and the distorted smile appeared. "I don't believe we'd better stop here," he said. "The last time I tried it I was expunged from the face of the universe."

"Don't you know?" she cried. "I'm staying here. Judge Pike has charge of all my property; he was the administrator, or something." Then seeing him chopfallen and aghast, she went on: "Of course you don't know! You don't know anything about me. You haven't even asked!"

"You're going to live *here*?" he gasped.

"Will you come to see me?" she laughed. "Will you come this afternoon?"

He grew white. "You know I can't," he said.

"You came here once. You risked a good deal then, just to see Mamie dance by a window. Don't you dare a little for an old friend?"

"All right," he gulped. "I'll try."

Mr. Bantry had come down to the gate and was holding it open, his eyes fixed upon Ariel, within them a rising glow. An impression came to Joe afterward that his step-brother had looked very handsome.

"Possibly you remember me, Miss Tabor?" said Eugene, in a deep and impressive voice, lifting his hat. "We were neighbors, I believe, in the old days."

She gave him her hand in a fashion somewhat mannerly, favoring him with a bright, negligent smile. "Oh, quite," she answered, turning again to Joe as she entered the gate. "Then I shall expect you?"

"I'll try," said Joe. "I'll try."

He stumbled away; Respectability and he, together, interfering alarmingly with the comfort of Mr. Flitcroft, who had stopped in the middle of the pavement to stare glassily at Ariel. Eugene accompanied the latter into the house, and Joe, looking back, understood: Mamie had sent his step-brother to bring Ariel in—and to keep him from following.

"This afternoon!" The thought took away his breath, and he became paler.

The Pike brougham rolled by him, and Sam Warden, from the box, favored his old friend upon the pavement with a liberal display of the whites of his eyes. The Judge, evidently, had been detained after services—without doubt a meeting of the church officials. Mrs. Pike, blinking and frightened, sat at her husband's side, agreeing feebly with the bull-bass which rumbled out of the open window of the brougham: "I want orthodox preaching in *my* church, and, by God, madam, I'll have it! That fellow has got to go!"

Joe took off his hat and wiped his brow.

XII

TO REMAIN ON THE FIELD OF BATTLE IS NOT
ALWAYS A VICTORY

AMIE, waiting just inside the door as Ariel and Eugene entered, gave the visitor a pale greeting, and, a moment later, hearing the wheels of the brougham crunch the gravel of the carriage-drive, hurried away, down the broad hall, and disappeared. Ariel dropped her parasol upon a marble-topped table near the door, and, removing her gloves, drifted into a room at the left, where a grand piano found shelter beneath crimson plush. After a moment of contemplation, she pushed back the coverlet, and, seating herself upon the plush-covered piano-stool (to match), let her fingers run up and down the key-board once and fall listlessly in her lap, as she gazed with deep interest at three life-sized colored photographs (in carved gilt frames) upon the wall she was facing: Judge Pike, Mamie, and Mrs. Pike with her rubies.

"Please don't stop playing, Miss Tabor," said a

voice behind her. She had not observed that
Eugene had followed her into the room.

"Very well, if you like," she answered, looking
up to smile absently at him. And she began to
play a rakish little air which, composed by some
rattle-brain at a café table, had lately skipped out
of the *Moulin Rouge* to disport itself over Paris.
She played it slowly, in the minor, with elfish
pathos; while he leaned upon the piano, his eyes
fixed upon her fingers, which bore few rings, none,
he observed with an unreasonable pleasure, upon
the third finger of the left hand.

"It's one of those simpler Grieg things, isn't
it?" he said, sighing gently. "I care for Grieg."

"Would you mind its being Chaminade?" she
returned, dropping her eyes to cloak the sin.

"Ah no; I recognize it now," replied Eugene.
"He appeals to me even more than Grieg."

At this she glanced quickly up at him, but more
quickly down again, and hastened the time emphatically, swinging the little air into the major.

"Do you play the 'Pilgrim's Chorus'?"

She shook her head.

"Vous name pas Wagner?" inquired Eugene,
leaning toward her.

"Oh yes," she answered, bending her head far
over, so that her face was concealed from him,
except the chin, which, he saw with a thrill of in-

explicable emotion, was trembling slightly. There were some small white flowers upon her hat, and these shook too.

She stopped playing abruptly, rose from the stool and crossed the room to a large mahogany chair, upholstered in red velvet and of hybrid construction, possessing both rockers and legs. She had moved in a way which prevented him from seeing her face, but he was certain of her agitation, and strangely glad, while curious, tremulous half-thoughts, edged with prophecy, bubbled to the surface of his consciousness.

When she turned to him, he was surprised to see that she looked astonishingly happy, almost as if she had been struggling with joy, instead of pain.

"This chair," she said, sinking into it, "makes me feel at home."

Naturally he could not understand.

"Because," she explained, "I once thought I was going to live in it. It has been reupholstered, but I should know it if I met in anywhere in the world!"

"How very odd!" exclaimed Eugene, staring.

"I settled here in pioneer days," she went on, tapping the arms lightly with her finger-tips. "It was the last dance I went to in Canaan."

"I fear the town was very provincial at that

time," he returned, having completely forgotten
the occasion she mentioned, therefore wishing to
shift the subject. "I fear you may still find it
so. There is not much here that one is in sympathy with, intellectually — few people really of
the world."

"Few people, I suppose you mean," she said,
softly, with a look that went deep enough into his
eyes, "few people who really understand one?"

Eugene had seated himself on the sill of an open
window close by. "There has been," he answered,
with the ghost of a sigh, "no one."

She turned her head slightly away from him, apparently occupied with a loose thread in her sleeve.
There were no loose threads; it was an old habit of
hers which she retained. "I suppose," she murmured, in a voice as low as his had been, "that a
man of your sort might find Canaan rather lonely
and sad."

"It *has* been!" Whereupon she made him a
laughing little bow.

"You are sure you complain of Canaan?"

"Yes!" he exclaimed. "You don't know what
it is to live here—"

"I think I do. I lived here seventeen years."

"Oh yes," he began to object, "as a child, but—"

"Have you any recollection," she interrupted,
"of the day before your brother ran away? Of

coming home for vacation—I think it was your first year in college — and intervening between your brother and me in a snow-fight?"

For a moment he was genuinely perplexed; then his face cleared. "Certainly," he said: "I found him bullying you and gave him a good punishing for it."

"Is that all you remember?"

"Yes," he replied, honestly. "Wasn't that all?"

"Quite!" she smiled, her eyes half closed. "Except that I went home immediately afterward."

"Naturally," said Eugene. "My step - brother wasn't very much *chevalier sans peur et sans reproche!* Ah, I should like to polish up my French a little. Would you mind my asking you to read a bit with me, some little thing of Daudet's if you care for him, in the original? An hour, now and then, perhaps—"

Mamie appeared in the doorway and Eugene rose swiftly. "I have been trying to persuade Miss Tabor," he explained, with something too much of laughter, "to play again. You heard that little thing of Chaminade's—"

Mamie did not appear to hear him; she entered breathlessly, and there was no color in her cheeks. "Ariel," she exclaimed, "I don't want you to think I'm a tale-bearer—"

"Oh, my dear!" Ariel said, with a gesture of deprecation.

"No," Miss Pike went on, all in one breath, "but I'm afraid you will think it, because papa knows and he wants to see you."

"What is it that he knows?"

"That you were walking with Joseph Louden!" (This was as if she had said, "That you poisoned your mother.") "I *didn't* tell him, but when we saw you with him I was troubled, and asked Eugene what I'd better do, because Eugene always knows what is best." (Mr. Bantry's expression, despite this tribute, was not happy.) "And he advised me to tell mamma about it and leave it in her hands. But she always tells papa everything—"

"Certainly; that is understood," said Ariel, slowly, turning to smile at Eugene.

"And she told him this right away," Mamie finished.

"Why shouldn't she, if it is of the slightest interest to him?"

The daughter of the house exhibited signs of consternation. "He wants to see you," she repeated, falteringly. "He's in the library."

Having thus discharged her errand, she hastened to the front-door, which had been left open, and out to the steps, evidently with the intention of removing herself as soon and as far as possible from the vicinity of the library.

Eugene, visibly perturbed, followed her to the doorway of the room, and paused.

"Do you know the way?" he inquired, with a note of solemnity.

"Where?" Ariel had not risen.

"To the library."

"Of course," she said, beaming upon him. "I was about to ask you if you wouldn't speak to the Judge for me. This is such a comfortable old friend, this chair."

"Speak to him for you?" repeated the non-plussed Eugene.

She nodded cheerfully. "If I may trouble you. Tell him, certainly, I shall be glad to see him."

He threw a piteous glance after Mamie, who was now, as he saw through the open door, out upon the lawn and beyond easy hailing distance. When he turned again to look at Ariel he discovered that she had shifted the position of her chair slightly, and was gazing out of the window with every appearance of cheerful meditation. She assumed so unmistakably that he had of course gone on her mission that, dismayed and his soul quaking, he could find neither an alternative nor words to explain to this dazzling lady that not he nor any other could bear such a message to Martin Pike.

Eugene went. There was nothing else to do; and he wished with every step that the distance to the portals of the library might have been greater.

In whatever guise he delivered the summons, it was perfectly efficacious. A door slammed, a heavy and rapid tread was heard in the hall, and Ariel, without otherwise moving, turned her head and offered a brilliant smile of greeting.

"It was good of you," she said, as the doorway filled with red, imperial wrath, "to wish to have a little chat with me. I'm anxious, of course, to go over my affairs with you, and last night, after my journey, I was too tired. But now we might begin; not in detail, of course, just yet. That will do for later, when I've learned more about business."

The great one had stopped on the threshold.

"Madam," he began, coldly, "when I say my library, I mean my—"

"Oh yes," she interrupted, with amiable weariness. "I know. You mean you keep all the papers and books of the estate in there, but I think we'd better put them off for a few days—"

"I'm not talking about the estate!" he exclaimed. "What I want to talk to you about is being seen with Joseph Louden!"

"Yes," she nodded, brightly. "That's along the line we must take up first."

"Yes, it is!" He hurled his bull-bass at her.

"You knew everything about him and his standing in this community! I know you did, because Mrs. Pike told me you asked all about him from Mamie after you came last night, and, see here, don't you—"

"Oh, but I knew before that," she laughed. "I had a correspondent in Canaan, one who has always taken a great interest in Mr. Louden. I asked Miss Pike only to get her own point of view."

"I want to tell you, madam," he shouted, coming toward her, "that no member of my household—"

"That's another point we must take up to-day. I'm glad you remind me of it," she said, thoughtfully, yet with so magically compelling an intonation that he stopped his shouting in the middle of a word; stopped with an apoplectic splutter. "We must arrange to put the old house in order at once."

"We'll arrange nothing of the sort," he responded, after a moment of angry silence. "You're going to stay right here."

"Ah, I know your hospitality," she bowed, graciously. "But of course I must not tax it too far. And about Mr. Louden? As I said, I want to speak to you about him."

"Yes," he intervened, harshly. "So do I, and I'm going to do it quick! You'll find—"

Again she mysteriously baffled him. "He's a

dear old friend of mine, you know, and I have made up my mind that we both need his help, you and I."

"What!"

"Yes," she continued, calmly, "in a business way I mean. I know you have great interests in a hundred directions, all more important than mine; it isn't fair that you should bear the whole burden of my affairs, and I think it will be best to retain Mr. Louden as my man of business. He could take all the cares of the estate off your shoulders."

Martin Pike spoke no word, but he looked at her strangely; and she watched him with sudden keenness, leaning forward in her chair, her gaze alert but quiet, fixed on the dilating pupils of his eyes. He seemed to become dizzy, and the choleric scarlet which had overspread his broad face and big neck faded splotchily.

Still keeping her eyes upon him, she went on: "I haven't asked him yet, and so I don't know whether or not he'll consent, but I think it possible that he may come to see me this afternoon, and if he does we can propose it to him together and go over things a little."

Judge Pike recovered his voice. "He'll get a warm welcome," he promised, huskily, "if he sets foot on my premises!"

"You mean you prefer I shouldn't receive him here?" She nodded pleasantly. "Then certainly

I shall not. Such things are much better for offices; you are quite right."

"You'll not see him at all!"

"Ah, Judge Pike," she lifted her hand with gentle deprecation, "don't you understand that we can't quite arrange that? You see, Mr. Louden is even an older friend of mine than you are, and so I must trust his advice about such things more than yours. Of course, if he too should think it better for me not to see him—"

The Judge advanced toward her. "I'm tired of this," he began, in a loud voice. "I'm—"

She moved as if to rise, but he had come very close, leaning above her, one arm out-stretched and at the end of it a heavy forefinger which he was shaking at her, so that it was difficult to get out of her chair without pushing him away—a feat apparently impossible. Ariel Tabor, in rising, placed her hand upon his out-stretched arm, quite as if he had offered it to assist her; he fell back a step in complete astonishment; she rose quickly, and released his arm.

"Thank you," she said, beamingly. "It's quite all my fault that you're tired. I've been thoughtless to keep you so long, and you have been standing, too!" She swept lightly and quickly to the door, where she paused, gathering her skirts. "I shall not detain you another instant! And if Mr.

Louden comes, this afternoon, I'll remember. I'll not let him come in, of course. It will be perhaps pleasanter to talk over my proposition as we walk!"

There was a very faint, spicy odor like wild roses and cinnamon left in the room where Martin Pike stood alone, staring whitely at the open doorway.

XIII

THE WATCHER AND THE WARDEN

THERE was a custom of Canaan, time-worn and seldom honored in the breach, which put Ariel, that afternoon, in easy possession of a coign of vantage commanding the front gate. The heavy Sunday dinner was finished in silence (on the part of Judge Pike, deafening) about three o'clock, and, soon after, Mamie tossed a number of cushions out upon the stoop between the cast-iron dogs,—Sam Warden having previously covered the steps with a rug and placed several garden chairs near by on the grass. These simple preparations concluded, Eugene sprawled comfortably upon the rug, and Mamie seated herself near him, while Ariel wandered with apparent aimlessness about the lawn, followed by the gaze of Mr. Bantry, until Miss Pike begged her, a little petulantly, to join them.

She came, looking about her dreamily, and touching to her lips, now and then, with an absent air, a clover blossom she had found in the longer grass against the fence. She stopped to pat the neck of one of the cast-iron deer, and with grave eyes proffered the clover-top first for inspection, then as food. There were those in the world who, seeing her, might have wondered that the deer did not play Galatea and come to life.

"No?" she said, aloud, to the steadfast head. "You won't? What a mistake to be made of cast-iron!" She smiled and nodded to a clump of lilac-bushes near a cedar-tree, and to nothing else — so far as Eugene and Mamie could see,—then walked thoughtfully to the steps.

"Who in the world were you speaking to?" asked Mamie, curiously.

"That deer."

"But you bowed to some one."

"Oh, that," Ariel lifted her eyebrows, — "that was your father. Didn't you see him?"

"No."

"I believe you can't from here, after all," said Ariel, slowly. "He is sitting upon a rustic bench between the bushes and the cedar-tree, quite near the gate. No, you couldn't see him from here; you'd have to go as far as the deer, at least, and even then you might not notice him, unless you looked for him. He has a book—a Bible, I think— but I don't think he is reading."

"He usually takes a nap on Sunday afternoons," said Mamie.

"I don't think he will, to-day." Ariel looked at Eugene, who avoided her clear gaze. "He has the air of having settled himself to stay for a long time, perhaps until evening."

She had put on her hat after dinner, and Mamie now inquired if she would not prefer to remove it, offering to carry it in-doors for her, to Ariel's room, to insure its safety. "You look so sort of temporary, wearing it," she urged, "as if you were only here for a little while. It's the loveliest hat I ever saw, and so fragile, too, but I'll take care—"

Ariel laughed, leaned over, and touched the other's hand lightly. "It isn't that, dear."

"What is it, then?" Mamie beamed out into a joyful smile. She had felt sure that she could not understand Ariel; was, indeed, afraid of her; and she found herself astonishingly pleased to be called "dear," and delighted with the little familiarity of the hand-tap. Her feeling toward the visitor (who was, so her father had announced, to become a permanent member of the household) had been, until now, undefined. She had been on her guard, watching for some sign of conscious "superiority" in this lady who had been so long over-seas, not knowing what to make of her; though thrown, by the contents of her trunks, into a wistfulness which would have had something of rapture in it had she been sure that she was going to like Ariel. She had gone to the latter's room before church, and had perceived uneasily that it had become, even by the process of unpacking, the prettiest room she had ever seen. Mrs. Warden, wife of Sam, and handmaiden of the mansion, was assisting, alternately faint and vociferous with marvelling. Mamie feared that Ariel might be a little overpowering.

With the word "dear" (that is, of course, with the way it was spoken), and with the touch upon the hand, it was all suddenly settled; she would not understand Ariel always—that was clear—but they would like each other.

"I am wearing my hat," answered Ariel, "because at any moment I may decide to go for a long walk!"

"Oh, I hope not," said Mamie. "There are sure to be people: a few still come, even though I'm an engaged girl. I expect that's just to console me, though," she added, smiling over this worn quip of the betrothed, and shaking her head at Eugene, who grew red and coughed. "There'll be plenty to-day, but they won't be here to see *me*. It's you, Ariel, and they'd be terribly disappointed if you weren't here. I shouldn't wonder if the whole town came; it's curious enough about you!"

Canaan (at least that part of it which Mamie meant when she said "the whole town") already offered testimony to her truthfulness. Two gentlemen, aged nine and eleven, and clad in white "sailor suits," were at that moment grooving their cheeks between the round pickets of the gate. They had come from the house across the street, evidently stimulated by the conversation at their own recent dinner-table (they wore a few deposits such as are left by chocolate-cake), and the motive of their conduct became obvious when, upon being joined by a person from next door (a starched and frilled person of the opposite sex but sympathetic age), one of them waggled a forefinger through the gate at Ariel, and a voice was heard in explanation:

"*That's her.*"

There was a rustle in the lilac-bushes near the cedar-tree; the three small heads turned simultaneously in that direction; something terrific was evidently seen, and with a horrified "*Oooh!*" the trio skedaddled headlong.

They were but the gay vanguard of the life which the street, quite dead through the Sunday dinner - hour, presently took on. Young couples with their progeny began to appear, returning from the weekly reunion Sunday dinner with relatives; young people meditative (until they reached the Pike Mansion), the wives fanning themselves or shooing the tots-able-to-walk ahead of them, while the husbands, wearing long coats, satin ties, and showing dust upon their blazing shoes, invariably pushed the perambulators. Most of these passers-by exchanged greetings with Mamie and Eugene, and all of them looked hard at Ariel as long as it was possible.

And now the young men of the town, laboriously arranged as to apparel, began to appear on the street in small squads, making their Sunday rounds; the youngest working in phalanxes of threes and fours, those somewhat older inclining to move in pairs; the eldest, such as were now beginning to be considered middle-aged beaux, or (by the extremely youthful) "old bachelors," evidently considered it advantageous to travel alone. Of all these, there were few who did not, before evening fell, turn in at the gate of the Pike Mansion. Consciously, shyly or confidently, according to the condition of their souls, they made their way between the cast-iron deer to be presented to the visitor.

Ariel sat at the top of the steps, and, looking amiably over their heads, talked with such as could get near her. There were many who could not, and Mamie, occupying the bench below, was surrounded by the overflow. The difficulty of reaching and maintaining a position near Miss

"I've seen him there myself." Page 196.

—*The Conquest of Canaan.*

Tabor was increased by the attitude and behavior of Mr. Flitcroft, who that day cooled the feeling of friendship which several of his fellow-townsmen had hitherto entertained for him. He had been the first to arrive, coming alone, though that was not his custom, and he established himself at Ariel's right, upon the step just below her, so disposing the great body and the ponderous arms and legs the gods had given him, that no one could mount above him to sit beside her, or approach her from that direction within conversational distance. Once established, he was not to be dislodged, and the only satisfaction for those in this manner debarred from the society of the beautiful stranger was obtained when they were presented to her and when they took their departure. On these occasions it was necessary by custom for them to shake her hand, a ceremony they accomplished by leaning across Mr. Flitcroft, which was a long way to lean, and the fat back and shoulders were sore that night because of what had been surreptitiously done to them by revengeful elbows and knees.

Norbert, not ordinarily talkative, had nothing to say; he seemed to find sufficient occupation in keeping the place he had gained; and from this close vantage he fastened his small eyes immovably upon Ariel's profile. Eugene, also apparently determined not to move, sat throughout the afternoon at her left, but as he was thin, others, who came and went, were able to approach upon that side and hold speech with her.

She was a stranger to these young people, most of whom had grown up together in a nickname intimacy. Few of them had more than a very imperfect recollection of her as she was before Roger Tabor and she had departed out of Canaan. She had lived her girlhood only upon their borderland, with no intimates save her grandfather and Joe; and she returned to her native town "a revelation and a dream," as young Mr. Bradbury told his incredulous grandmother that night.

The conversation of the gallants consisted, for the greater part, of witticisms at one another's expense, which, though evoked for Ariel's benefit (all eyes furtively reverting to her as each shaft was loosed), she found more or less enigmatical. The young men, however, laughed at each other loudly, and seemed content if now and then she smiled. "You must be frightfully *ennuied* with all this," Eugene said to her. "You see how provincial we still are."

She did not answer; she had not heard him. The shadows were stretching themselves over the grass, long and attenuated; the sunlight upon the trees and houses was like a thin, rosy pigment; blackbirds were calling each other home to beech and elm; and Ariel's eyes were fixed upon the western distance of the street where gold-dust was beginning to quiver in the air. She did not hear Eugene, but she started, a moment later, when the name "Joe Louden" was pronounced by a young man, the poetic Bradbury, on the step below Eugene. Some one immediately said "'Sh!'" But she leaned over and addressed Mr. Bradbury, who, shut out, not only from the group about her, but from the other centring upon Miss Pike, as well, was holding a private conversation with a friend in like misfortune.

"What were you saying of Mr. Louden?" she asked, smiling down upon the young man. (It was this smile which inspired his description of her as "a revelation and a dream.")

"Oh, nothing particular," was his embarrassed reply. "I only mentioned I'd heard there was some talk among the—" He paused awkwardly, remembering that Ariel had walked with Joseph Louden in the face of Canaan that very day. "That is, I mean to say, there's some talk of his running for Mayor."

"*What?*"

There was a general exclamation, followed by an uncomfortable moment or two of silence. No one present was unaware of that noon walk, though there was prevalent a pleasing notion that it would not happen again, founded on the idea that Ariel, having only arrived the previous evening, had probably met Joe on the street by accident, and, remembering him as a playmate of her childhood and uninformed as to his reputation, had, naturally enough, permitted him to walk home with her.

Mr. Flitcroft broke the silence, rushing into words with a derisive laugh: "Yes, he's 'talked of' for Mayor—by the saloon people and the niggers! I expect the Beaver Beach crowd would be for him, and if tramps could vote he might—"

"What is Beaver Beach?" asked Ariel, not turning.

"What is Beaver Beach?" he repeated, and cast his eyes to the sky, shaking his head awesomely. "It's a Place," he said, with abysmal solemnity, —"a Place I shouldn't have mentioned in your presence, Miss Tabor."

"What has it to do with Mr. Louden?"

The predestined Norbert conceived the present to be a heaven-sent opportunity to enlighten her concerning Joe's character, since the Pikes appeared to have been derelict in the performance of this kindness.

"He goes there!" he proceeded heavily. "He lived there for a while when he first came back from running away, and he's a friend of Mike

Sheehan's that runs it; he's a friend of all the riff-raff that hang around there."

"How do you know he goes there?"

"Why, it was in the paper the day after he came back!" He appealed for corroboration. "Wasn't it, Eugene?"

"No, no!" she persisted. "Newspapers are sometimes mistaken, aren't they?" Laughing a little, she swept across the bulbous face beside her a swift regard that was like a search-light. "How do you *know*, Mr. Flitcroft," she went on very rapidly, raising her voice, — "how do you *know* that Mr. Louden is familiar with this place? The newspapers may have been falsely informed; you must admit that? Then how do you *know?* Have you ever *met* any one who has seen him there?"

"I've seen him there myself!" The words skipped out of Norbert's mouth like so many little devils, the instant he opened it. She had spoken so quickly and with such vehemence, looking him full in the eye, that he had forgotten everything in the world except making the point to which her insistence had led him.

Mamie looked horrified; there was a sound of smothered laughter, and Norbert, overwhelmed by the treachery of his own mouth, sat gasping.

"It can't be such a terrific place, then, after all,"

said Ariel, gently, and turning to Eugene, "Have you ever been there, Mr. Bantry?" she asked.

He changed color, but answered with enough glibness: "No."

Several of the young men rose; the wretched Flitcroft, however, evading Mamie's eye—in which there was a distinct hint,—sat where he was until all of them, except Eugene, had taken a reluctant departure, one group after another, leaving in the order of their arrival.

The rosy pigment which had colored the trees faded; the gold-dust of the western distance danced itself pale and departed; dusk stalked into the town from the east; and still the watcher upon the steps and the warden of the gate (he of the lilac-bushes and the Bible) held their places and waited —waited, alas! in vain. . . . Ah! Joe, is *this* the mettle of your daring? Did you not say you would "try"? Was your courage so frail a vessel that it could not carry you even to the gate yonder? Surely you knew that if you had striven so far, there you would have been met! Perhaps you foresaw that not one, but two, would meet you at the gate, both the warden and the watcher. What of that? What of that, O faint heart? What was there to fear? Listen! The gate clicks. Ah, have you come at last?

Ariel started to her feet, but the bent figure,

coming up the walk in the darkness, was that of Eskew Arp. He bowed gloomily to Mamie, and in response to her inquiry if he wished to see her father, answered no; he had come to talk with the granddaughter of his old friend Roger Tabor.

"Mr. Arp!" called Ariel. "I am so very glad!" She ran down to him and gave him her hand. "We'll sit here on the bench, sha'n't we?"

Mamie had risen, and skirting Norbert frostily, touched Eugene upon the shoulder as she went up the steps. He understood that he was to follow her in-doors, and, after a deep look at the bench where Ariel had seated herself beside Mr. Arp, he obeyed. Norbert was left a lonely ruin between the cold, twin dogs. He had wrought desolation this afternoon, and that sweet verdure, his good name, so long in the planting, so carefully tended, was now a dreary waste; yet he contemplated this not so much as his present aspect of splendid isolation. Frozen by the daughter of the house, forgotten by the visitor, whose conversation with Mr. Arp was carried on in tones so low that he could not understand it, the fat one, though heart-breakingly loath to take himself away, began to comprehend that his hour had struck. He rose, descended the steps to the bench, and seated himself unexpectedly upon the cement walk at Ariel's feet.

"Leg's gone to sleep," he explained, in response

to her startled exclamation; but, like a great soul, ignoring the accident of his position as well as the presence of Mr. Arp, he immediately proceeded: "Will you go riding with me to-morrow afternoon?"

"Aren't you very good-natured, Mr. Flitcroft?" she asked, with an odd intonation.

"I'm imposed on, often enough," he replied, rubbing his leg, "by people who think I am! Why?"

"It is only that your sitting so abruptly upon the ground reminded me of something that happened long ago, before I left Canaan, the last time I met you."

"I don't think I knew you before you went away. You haven't said if you'll go riding with me to-morrow. Please—"

"Get up," interrupted Mr. Arp, acidly. "Somebody 'll fall over you if you stay there."

Such a catastrophe in truth loomed imminent. Judge Pike was rapidly approaching on his way to the house, Bible in hand—far better in hand than was his temper, for it is an enraging thing to wait five hours in ambush for a man who does not come. In the darkness a desecration occurred, and Norbert perfected to the last detail whatever had been left incomplete of his own destruction. He began lumberingly to rise, talking at the same time, urging upon Ariel the charms of the roadside; wild flowers were in blossom, he said, recounting the benefits she might derive through acceptance of his invitation; and having, thus busily, risen to his knees, became aware that some one was passing near him. This some one Mr. Flitcroft, absorbed in artful persuasions, may have been betrayed by the darkness to mistake for Eugene. Reaching out for assistance, he mechanically seized upon the skirts of a coat, which he put to the uses of a rope, coming up hand-over-hand with such noble weight and energy that he brought himself to his feet and the owner of the coat to the ground simultaneously. The latter, hideously astonished, went down with an objurgation so outrageous in venom that Mr. Arp jumped with the shock. Judge Pike got to his feet quickly, but not so quickly as the piteous Flitcroft betook himself into the deep shadows of the street. Only a word, hoarse and horror-stricken, was left quivering on the night breeze by this accursed, whom the gods, intent upon his ruin, had early in the day, at his first sight of Ariel, in good truth, made mad: "*Murder!*"

"Can I help you brush off, Judge?" asked Eskew, rising painfully.

Either Martin Pike was beyond words, or the courtesy proposed by the feeble old fellow (for Eskew was now very far along in years, and looked his age) emphasized too bitterly the indignity which had been put upon him: whatever the case, he went his way in-doors, leaving the cynic's offer unacknowledged. Eskew sank back upon the bench, with the little rusty sounds, suggestions of creaks and sighs, which accompany the movement of antiques. "I've always thought," he said, "that the Judge had spells when he was hard of hearing."

Oblongs of light abruptly dropped from the windows confronting them, one, falling across the bench, appropriately touching with lemon the acrid, withered face and trembling hands of the veteran. "You are younger than you were nine years ago, Mr. Arp," said Ariel, gayly. "I caught a glimpse of you upon the street, to-day, and I thought so then. Now I see that I was right."

"*Me—younger!*" he groaned. "No, ma'am! I'm mighty near through with this fool world—and I'd be glad of it, if I didn't expect that if there *is* another one afterwards, it would be jest as ornery!"

She laughed, leaning forward, resting her elbows on her knee, and her chin in her hand, so that the shadow of her hat shielded her eyes from the light. "I thought you looked surprised when you saw me to-day."

"I reckon I did!" he exclaimed. "Who wouldn't of been?"

"Why?"

"Why?" he repeated, confounded by her simplicity. "Why?"

"Yes," she laughed. "That's what I'm anxious to know."

"Wasn't the whole town the same way?" he demanded. "Did you meet anybody that didn't look surprised?"

"But why should they?"

"Good Lord A'mighty!" he broke out. "Ain't you got any lookin'-glasses?"

"I think almost all I have are still in the customs warehouse."

"Then use Mamie Pike's," responded the old man. "The town never dreamed you were goin' to turn out pretty at all, let alone the *way* you've turned out pretty! The *Tocsin* had a good deal about your looks and so forth in it once, in a letter from Paris, but the folks that remembered you kind of set that down to the way papers talk about anybody with money, and nobody was prepared for it when they saw you. You don't need to drop no curtseys to *me*." He set his mouth grimly, in response to the bow she made him. "*I* think female beauty is like all other human furbelows, and as holler as heaven will be if only the good people are let in! But yet I did stop to look at you when you went past me to-day, and I kept on lookin', long as you were in sight. I reckon I always will, when I git the chance, too—only shows what human nature *is!* But that wasn't all that folks were starin' at to-day. It was your walkin' with Joe Louden that really finished 'em, and I can say it upset me more than anything I've seen for a good many years."

"Upset you, Mr. Arp?" she cried. "I don't quite see."

The old man shook his head deploringly. "After what I'd written you about that boy—"

"Ah," she said, softly, touching his sleeve with her fingers, "I haven't thanked you for that."

"You needn't," he returned, sharply. "It was a pleasure. Do you remember how easy and quick I promised you?"

"I remember that you were very kind."

"Kind!" He gave forth an acid and chilling laugh. "It was about two months after Louden ran away, and before you and Roger left Canaan, and you asked me to promise to write to you whenever word of that outcast came—"

"I didn't put it so, Mr. Arp."

"No, but you'd ought of! You asked me to write you whatever news of him should come, and if he came back to tell you how and when and all about it. And I did it, and kept you sharp on his record ever since he landed here again. Do you know why I've done it? Do you know why I promised so quick and easy I *would* do it?"

"Out of the kindness of your heart, I think."

The acid laugh was repeated. "*No*, ma'am! You couldn't of guessed colder. I promised, and I kept my promise, because I knew there would never be anything good to tell! *And there never was!*"

"Nothing at all?" she insisted, gravely.

"Never! I leave it to you if I've written one good word of him."

"You've written of the treatment he has received here," she began, "and I've been able to see what he has borne—and bears!"

"But have I written one word to show that he didn't deserve it all? Haven't I told you everything, of his associates, his—"

"Indeed you have!"

"Then do you wonder that I was more surprised than most when I saw you walking with him to-day? Because I knew you did it in cold blood and knowledge aforethought! Other folks thought it was because you hadn't been here long enough to hear his reputation, but I *knew!*"

"Tell me," she said, "if you were disappointed when you saw me with him."

"Yes," he snapped. "I was!"

"I thought so. I saw the consternation in your face! You *approved*, didn't you?"

"I don't know what you're talking about!"

"Yes, you do! I know it bothers you to have

me read you between the lines, but for this once you must let me. You are so consistent that you are never disappointed when things turn out badly, or people are wicked or foolish, are you?"

"No, certainly not. I expect it."

"And you were disappointed in me to-day. Therefore, it must be that I was doing something you knew was right and good. You see?" She leaned a little closer to him, smiling angelically. "Ah, Mr. Arp," she cried, "I know your secret: you *admire* me!"

He rose, confused and incoherent, as full of denial as a detected pickpocket. "I *don't!* Me *admire? What?* It's an ornery world," he protested. "I don't admire any human that ever lived!"

"Yes, you do," she persisted. "I've just proved it! But that is the least of your secret; the great thing is this: *you admire Mr. Louden!*"

"I never heard such nonsense," he continued to protest, at the same time moving down the walk toward the gate, leaning heavily on his stick. "Nothin' of the kind. There ain't any *logic* to that kind of an argument, nor no *reason!*"

"You see, I understand you," she called after him. "I'm sorry you go away in the bitterness of being found out."

"Found out!" His stick ceased for a moment to tap the cement. "Pooh!" he ejaculated, uneasily. There was a pause, followed by a malevolent chuckle. "At any rate," he said, with joy in the afterthought, "you'll never go walkin' with him *again!*"

He waited for the answer, which came, after a time, sadly. "Perhaps you are right. Perhaps I shall not."

"Ha, I thought so! Good-night."

"Good-night, Mr. Arp."

She turned toward the lighted house. Through the windows nearest her she could see Mamie, seated in the familiar chair, following with happy and tender eyes the figure of Eugene, who was pacing up and down the room. The town was deadly quiet: Ariel could hear the sound of footsteps perhaps a block away. She went to the gate and gazed a long time into the empty street, watching the yellow grains of light, sieved through the maples from the arc lights on the corner, moving to and fro in the deep shadow as the lamp swung slightly in the night air. Somewhere, not far away, the peace was broken by the screams of a "parlor organ," which honked and wailed in pious agonies (the intention was hymnal), interminably protracting each spasm. Presently a woman's voice outdid the organ, a voice which made vivid the picture of the woman who owned it, and the ploughed forehead of her, above the nose-glasses, when the "grace-notes" were proudly given birth. "Rescue the Perishing" was the startlingly appropriate selection, rendered with inconceivable lingering upon each syllable: "Roos-cyoo the Poor-oosh-oong!" At unexpected intervals two male voices, evidently belonging to men who had contracted the habit of holding tin in their mouths, joined the lady in a thorough search for the Lost Chord.

That was the last of silence in Canaan for an hour or so. The organ was merely inaugural: across the street a piano sounded; firm, emphatic, determined, vocal competition with the instrument here also; "Rock of Ages" the incentive. Another piano presently followed suit, in a neighboring house: "Precious Jewels." More distant, a second organ was heard; other pianos, other organs, took up other themes; and as a wakeful puppy's barking will go over a village at night, stirring first the nearer dogs to give voice, these in turn stimulating those farther away to join, one passing the excitement on to another, until hounds in farm-yards far beyond the town contribute to the long-distance conversation, even so did "Rescue the Perishing" enliven the greater part of Canaan.

It was this that made Ariel realize a thing of which hitherto she had not been able to convince

"Think! What's happened lately to make him bite so hard?" Page 208.

—*The Conquest of Canaan.*

herself: that she was actually once more in the town where she had spent her long-ago girlhood, now grown to seem the girlhood of some other person. It was true: her foot was on her native heath and her name was Ariel Tabor—the very name of the girl who had shared the town's disapproval with Joe Louden! "Rescue the Perishing" brought it all back to her; and she listened to these sharply familiar rites of the Canaanite Sabbath evening with a shiver of pain.

She turned from the gate to go into the house, heard Eugene's voice at the door, and paused. He was saying good-night to Mamie.

"And please say '*au revoir*' to Miss Tabor for me," he added, peering out under his hand. "I don't know where she can have gone."

"Probably she came in and went to her room," said Mamie.

"Don't forget to tell her '*au revoir*.'"

"I won't, dear. Good-night."

"Good-night." She lifted her face and he kissed her perfunctorily. Then he came down the steps and went slowly toward the gate, looking about him into the darkness as if searching for something; but Ariel had fled away from the path of light that led from the open door.

She skimmed noiselessly across the lawn and paused at the side of the house, leaning against the veranda, where, on a night long past, a boy had hid and a girl had wept. A small creaking sound fell upon her ear, and she made out an ungainly figure approaching, wheeling something of curious shape.

" Is that you, Sam?" she said.

Mr. Warden stopped, close by. "Yes'm," he replied. "I'm a-gittin' out de hose to lay de dus' yonnah." He stretched an arm along the crossbar of the reel, relaxing himself, apparently, for conversation. "Y'all done change consid'able, Miss Airil," he continued, with the directness of one sure of privilege.

" You think so, Sam?"

" Yes'm. Ev'ybody think so, *I* reckon. Be'n a tai'ble lot o' talkum 'bout you to-day. Dun'no' how all dem oth' young ladies goin' take it!" He laughed with immoderate delight, yet, as to the volume of mere sound, discreetly, with an eye to open windows. "You got 'em all beat, Miss Airil! Dey ain' be'n no one 'roun' dis town evah got in a thousum mile o' you! Fer looks, an' de way you walk an' ca'y yo'self; an' as fer de clo'es—name o' de good lan', honey, dey ain' nevah *see* style befo'! My ole woman say you got mo' fixin's in a minute dan de whole res' of 'em got in a yeah. She say when she helpin' you onpack she must 'a' see mo'n a hunerd paihs o' slippahs alone! An' de good

Man knows I 'membuh w'en you runnin' roun' de back-yods an' up de alley rompin' 'ith Joe Louden, same you's a boy!"

"Do you ever see Mr. Louden, nowadays?" she asked.

His laugh was repeated with the same discreet violence. "Ain' I seen him dis ve'y day, fur up de street at de gate yonnah, stan'in' 'ith you, w'en I drivin' de Judge?"

"You—you didn't happen to see him anywhere this—this afternoon?"

"No'm, I ain' *see* him." Sam's laughter vanished and his lowered voice became serious. "I ain' *see* him, but I hearn about him."

"What did you hear?"

"Dey be'n consid'able stir on de aidge o' town, I reckon," he answered, gravely, "an' dey be'n havin' some trouble out at de Beach—"

"Beaver Beach, do you mean?"

"Yes'm. Dey be'n some shootin' goin' on out dat way."

She sprang forward and caught at his arm without speaking.

"Joe Louden all right," he said, reassuringly. "Ain' nuffum happen to him! Nigh as I kin mek out f'm de *talk*, dat Happy Fear gone on de ram-*page* ag'in, an' dey hatta sent fer Mist' Louden to come in a hurry."

XIV

WHITE ROSES IN A LAW-OFFICE

S upon a world canopied with storm, hung with mourning purple and habited in black, did Mr. Flitcroft turn his morning face at eight o'clock antemeridian Monday, as he hied himself to his daily duty at the Washington National Bank. Yet more than the merely funereal gloomed out from the hillocky area of his countenance. Was there not, i'faith, a glow, a Vesuvian shimmer, beneath the murk of that darkling eye? Was here one, think you, to turn the other cheek? Little has he learned of Norbert Flitcroft who conceives that this fiery spirit was easily to be quenched! Look upon the jowl of him, and let him who dares maintain that people—even the very Pikes themselves—were to grind beneath their brougham wheels a prostrate Norbert and ride on scatheless! In this his own metaphor is nearly touched: "I guess not! They don't run over *me!* Martin Pike better look out how he tries it!"

WHITE ROSES IN A LAW-OFFICE

So Mother Nature at her kindly tasks, good Norbert, uses for her unguent our own perfect inconsistency: and often when we are stabbed deep in the breast she distracts us by thin scratches in other parts, that in the itch of these we may forget the greater hurt till it be healed. Thus, the remembrance of last night, when you undisguisedly ran from the wrath of a Pike, with a pretty girl looking on (to say nothing of the acrid Arp, who will fling the legend on a thousand winds), might well agonize you now, as, in less hasty moments and at a safe distance, you brood upon the piteous figure you cut. On the contrary, behold: you see no blood crimsoning the edges of the horrid gash in your panoply of self-esteem: you but smart and scratch the scratches, forgetting your wound in the hot itch for vengeance. It is an itch which will last (for in such matters your temper shall be steadfast), and let the great Goliath in the mean time beware of you! You ran, last night. You ran—of course you ran. Why not? You ran to fight another day!

A bank clerk sometimes has opportunities.

The stricken fat one could not understand how it came about that he had blurted out the damning confession that he had visited Beaver Beach. When he tried to solve the puzzle, his mind refused the strain, became foggy and the terrors of his position acute. Was he, like Joe Louden, to endure the ban of Canaan, and like him stand excommunicate beyond the pale because of Martin Pike's displeasure? For Norbert saw with perfect clearness to-day what the Judge had done for Joe. Now that he stood in danger of a fate identical, this came home to him. How many others, he wondered, would do as Mamie had done and write notes such as he had received by the hand of Sam Warden, late last night?

"DEAR SIR." (This from Mamie, who, in the Canaanitish way, had been wont to address him as "Norb"!)— "My father wishes me to state that after your remark yesterday afternoon on the steps which was overheard by my mother who happened to be standing in the hall behind you and your *behavior* to himself later on—he considers it impossible to allow you to call any more or to speak to any member of his household.

"Yours respectfully,
"MAMIE PIKE."

Erasures and restorations bore witness to a considerable doubt in Mamie's mind concerning "Yours respectfully," but she had finally let it stand, evidently convinced that the plain signature, without preface, savored of an intimacy denied by the context.

"'*Dear sir*'!" repeated Norbert, between set teeth. "'*Impossible to allow you to call* any more'!" These and other terms of his dismissal recurred to him during the morning, and ever and anon he looked up from his desk, his lips moving to the tune of those horrid phrases, and stared out at the street. Basilisk glaring this, with no Christian softness in it, not even when it fell upon his own grandfather, sitting among the sages within easy eye-shot from the big window at Norbert's elbow. However, Colonel Flitcroft was not disturbed by the gaze of his descendant, being, in fact, quite unaware of it. The aged men were having a busy morning.

The conclave was not what it had been. [*See Arp and all his works.*] There had come, as the years went by, a few recruits; but faces were missing: the two Tabors had gone, and Uncle Joe Davey could no longer lay claim to the patriarchship; he had laid it down with a half-sigh and gone his way. Eskew himself was now the oldest of the conscript fathers, the Colonel and Squire Buckalew pressing him closely, with Peter Bradbury no great time behind.

To-day they did not plant their feet upon the brass rail inside the hotel windows, but courted the genial weather out-doors, and, as their summer custom was, tilted back their chairs in the shade of the western wall of the building.

"And who could of dreamed," Mr. Bradbury was saying, with a side-glance of expectancy at Eskew.

"that Jonas Tabor would ever turn out to have a niece like that!"

Mr. Arp ceased to fan himself with his wide straw hat and said grimly:

"I don't see as Jonas *has* 'turned out'—not in particular! If he's turned at all, lately, I reckon it's in his grave, and I'll bet he *has* if he had any way of hearin' how much she must of spent for clothes!"

"I believe," Squire Buckalew began, "that young folks' memories are short."

"They're lucky!" interjected Eskew. The shorter your memory the less meanness you know."

"I meant young folks don't remember as well as older people do," continued the Squire. "I don't see what's so remarkable in her comin' back and walkin' up-street with Joe Louden. She used to go kitin' round with him all the time, before she left here. And yet everybody talks as if they never *heard* of sech a thing!"

"It seems to me," said Colonel Flitcroft, hesitatingly, "that she did right. I know it sounds kind of a queer thing to say, and I stirred up a good deal of opposition at home, yesterday evening, by sort of mentioning something of the kind. Nobody seemed to agree with me, except Norbert, and he didn't *say* much, but—"

He was interrupted by an uncontrollable cackle

which issued from the mouth of Mr. Arp. The Colonel turned upon him with a frown, inquiring the cause of his mirth.

"It put me in mind," Mr. Arp began promptly, "of something that happened last night."

"What was it?"

Eskew's mouth was open to tell, but he remembered, just in time, that the grandfather of Norbert was not the audience properly to be selected for this recital, choked a half-born word, coughed loudly, realizing that he must withhold the story of the felling of Martin Pike until the Colonel had taken his departure, and replied:

"Nothin' to speak of. Go on with your argument."

"I've finished," said the Colonel. "I only wanted to say that it seems to me a good action for a young lady like that to come back here and stick to her old friend and playmate."

"*Stick* to him!" echoed Mr. Arp. "She walked up Main Street with him yesterday. Do you call that stickin' to him? She's been away a good while; she's forgotten what Canaan *is*. You wait till she sees for herself jest what his standing in this com—"

"I agree with Eskew for once," interrupted Peter Bradbury. "I agree because—"

"Then you better wait," cried Eskew, allowing

him to proceed no farther, "till you hear what you're agreein' to! I say: you take a young lady like that, pretty and rich and all cultured up, and it stands to reason that she won't—"

"No, it don't," exclaimed Buckalew, impatiently. "Nothing of the sort! I tell you—"

Eskew rose to his feet and pounded the pavement with his stick. "It stands to reason that she won't stick to a man no other decent woman will speak to, a feller that's been the mark for every stone throwed in the town, ever since he was a boy, an outcast with a reputation as black as a preacher's shoes on Sunday! I don't care if he's her oldest friend on *earth*, she won't stick to him! She walked with him yesterday, but you can mark my words: his goose is cooked!" The old man's voice rose, shrill and high. "It ain't in human nature fer her to do it! You hear what I say: you'll never see her with Joe Louden again in this livin' world, and she as good as told me so, herself, last night. You can take your oath she's quit him already! Don't—"

Eskew paused abruptly, his eyes widening behind his spectacles; his jaw fell; his stick, raised to hammer the pavement, remained suspended in the air. A sudden color rushed over his face, and he dropped speechless in his chair. The others, after staring at him in momentary alarm, followed the direction of his gaze.

WHITE ROSES IN A LAW-OFFICE

Just across Main Street, and in plain view, was the entrance to the stairway which led to Joe's office. Ariel Tabor, all in cool gray, carrying a big bunch of white roses in her white-gloved hands, had just crossed the sidewalk from a carriage and was ascending the dark stairway. A moment later she came down again, empty-handed, got into the carriage, and drove away.

"She missed him," said Squire Buckalew. "I saw him go out half an hour ago. *But*," he added, and, exercising a self-restraint close upon the saintly, did not even glance toward the heap which was Mr. Arp, "I notice she left her flowers!"

Ariel was not the only one who climbed the dingy stairs that day and read the pencilled script upon Joe's door: "Will not return until evening. J. Louden." Many others came, all exceedingly unlike the first visitor: some were quick and watchful, dodging into the narrow entrance furtively; some smiled contemptuously as long as they were in view of the street, drooping wanly as they reached the stairs: some were brazen and amused; and some were thin and troubled. Not all of them read the message, for not all could read, but all looked curiously through the half-opened door at the many roses which lifted their heads delicately from a water-pitcher on Joe's desk to scent that dusty place with their cool breath.

Most of these clients, after a grunt of disappointment, turned and went away; though there were a few, either unable to read the message or so pressed by anxiety that they disregarded it, who entered the room and sat down to wait for the absentee. [There were plenty of chairs in the office now, bookcases also, and a big steel safe.] But when evening came and the final gray of twilight had vanished from the window-panes, all had gone except one, a woman who sat patiently, her eyes upon the floor, and her hands folded in her lap, until the footsteps of the last of the others to depart had ceased to sound upon the pavement below. Then, with a wordless exclamation, she sprang to her feet, pulled the window-shade carefully down to the sill, and, when she had done that, struck a match on the heel of her shoe—a soiled white canvas shoe, not a small one—and applied the flame to a gas jet. The yellow light flared up; and she began to pace the room haggardly.

The court-house bell rang nine, and as the tremors following the last stroke pulsed themselves into silence, she heard a footfall on the stairs and immediately relapsed into a chair, folding her hands again in her lap, her expression composing itself to passivity, for the step was very much lighter than Joe's.

A lady beautifully dressed in white dimity appeared in the doorway. She hesitated at the threshold, not, apparently, because of any timidity (her expression being too thoughtfully assured for that), but almost immediately she came in and seated herself near the desk, acknowledging the other's presence by a slight inclination of the head.

This grave courtesy caused a strong, deep flush to spread itself under the rouge which unevenly covered the woman's cheeks, as she bowed elaborately in return. Then, furtively, during a protracted silence, she took stock of the new-comer, from the tip of her white suède shoes to the filmy lace and pink roses upon her wide white hat; and the sidelong gaze lingered marvellingly upon the quiet, delicate hands, slender and finely expressive, in their white gloves.

Her own hands, unlike the lady's, began to fidget confusedly, and, the silence continuing, she coughed several times, to effect the preface required by her sense of fitness, before she felt it proper to observe, with a polite titter:

"Mr. Louden seems to be a good while comin'."

"Have you been waiting very long?" asked the lady.

"Ever since six o'clock!"

"Yes," said the other. "That is very long."

"Yes, ma'am, it cert'nly is." The ice thus broken, she felt free to use her eyes more directly, and, after a long, frank stare, exclaimed:

"Why, you must be Miss Ariel Tabor, ain't you?"

"Yes." Ariel touched one of the roses upon Joe's desk with her finger-tips. "I am Miss Tabor."

"Well, excuse me fer asking; I'm sure it ain't any business of mine," said the other, remembering the manners due one lady from another. "But I thought it must be. I expect," she added, with loud, inconsequent laughter, "there's not many in Canaan ain't heard you've come back." She paused, laughed again, nervously, and again, less loudly, to take off the edge of her abruptness: gradually tittering herself down to a pause, to fill which she put forth: "Right nice weather we be'n havin'."

"Yes," said Ariel.

"It was rainy, first of last week, though. *I* don't mind rain so much"—this with more laughter,— "I stay in the house when it rains. Some people don't know enough to, they say! You've heard that saying, ain't you, Miss Tabor?"

"Yes."

"Well, I tell *you*," she exclaimed, noisily,

"there's plenty ladies and gen'lemen in this town that's like that!"

Her laughter did not cease; it became louder and shriller. It had been, until now, a mere lubrication of the conversation, helping to make her easier in Miss Tabor's presence, but as it increased in shrillness, she seemed to be losing control of herself, as if her laughter were getting away with her; she was not far from hysteria, when it stopped with a gasp, and she sat up straight in her chair, white and rigid.

"*There!*" she said, listening intently. "Ain't that him?" Steps sounded upon the pavement below; paused for a second at the foot of the stairs; there was the snap of a match; then the steps sounded again, retreating. She sank back in her chair limply. "It was only some one stoppin' to light his cigar in the entry. It wasn't Joe Louden's step, anyway."

"You know his step?" Ariel's eyes were bent upon the woman wonderingly.

"I'd know it to-night," was the answer, delivered with a sharp and painful giggle. "I got plenty reason to!"

Ariel did not respond. She leaned a little closer to the roses upon the desk, letting them touch her face, and breathing deeply of their fragrance to neutralize a perfume which pervaded the room;

an odor as heavy and cheap-sweet as the face of the woman who had saturated her handkerchief with it, a scent which went with her perfectly and made her unhappily definite; suited to her clumsily dyed hair, to her soiled white shoes, to the hot red hat smothered in plumage, to the restless stub-fingered hands, to the fat, plated rings, of which she wore a great quantity, though, surprisingly enough, the large diamonds in her ears were pure, and of a very clear water.

It was she who broke the silence once more. "Well," she drawled, coughing genteelly at the same time, "better late than never, as the saying is. I wonder who it is gits up all them comical sayings?" Apparently she had no genuine desire for light upon this mystery, as she continued, immediately: "I have a gen'leman friend that's always gittin' 'em off. 'Well,' he says, 'the best of friends must part,' and, 'Thou strikest me to the heart'—all kinds of cracks like that. He's real comical. And yet," she went on in an altered voice, "I don't like him much. I'd be glad if I'd never seen him."

The change of tone was so marked that Ariel looked at her keenly, to find herself surprised into pitying this strange client of Joe's; for tears had sprung to the woman's eyes and slid along the lids, where she tried vainly to restrain them. Her face had altered too, like her voice, haggard lines suddenly appearing about the eyes and mouth as if they had just been pencilled there: the truth issuing from beneath her pinchbeck simulations, like a tragic mask revealed by the displacement of a tawdry covering.

"I expect you think I'm real foolish," she said, "but I be'n waitin' so awful long—and I got a good deal of worry on my mind till I see Mr. Louden."

"I am sorry," Ariel turned from the roses, and faced her and the heavy perfume. "I hope he will come soon."

"I hope so," said the other. "It's something to do with me that keeps him away, and the longer he is the more it scares me." She shivered and set her teeth together. "It's kind of hard, waitin'. I cert'nly got my share of troubles."

"Don't you think that Mr. Louden will be able to take care of them for you?"

"Oh, I *hope* so, Miss Tabor! If he can't, nobody can." She was crying openly now, wiping her eyes with her musk-soaked handkerchief. "We had to send fer him yesterday afternoon—"

"To come to Beaver Beach, do you mean?" asked Ariel, leaning forward.

"Yes, ma'am. It all begun out there,—leastways it begun before that with me. It was all my fault. I deserve all that's comin' to me, I guess. I done wrong—I done wrong! I'd oughtn't never to of went out there yesterday."

She checked herself sharply, but, after a moment's pause, continued, encouraged by the grave kindliness of the delicate face in the shadow of the wide white hat. "I'd oughtn't to of went," she repeated. "Oh, I reckon I'll never, never learn enough to keep out o' trouble, even when I see it comin'! But that gen'leman friend of mine—Mr. Nashville Cory's his name—he kind o' coaxed me into it, and he's right comical when he's with ladies, and he's good company—and he says, 'Claudine, we'll dance the light fantastic,' he says, and I kind o' wanted something cheerful—I'd be'n workin' steady quite a spell, and it looked like he wanted to show me a good time, so I went, and that's what started it." Now that she had begun, she babbled on with her story, at times incoherently; full of excuses, made to herself more than to Ariel, pitifully endeavoring to convince herself that the responsibility for the muddle she had made was not hers. "Mr. Cory told me my husband was drinkin' and wouldn't know about it, and, 'Besides,' he says, 'what's the odds?' Of course I knowed there was trouble between him and Mr. Fear—that's my husband—a good while ago, when Mr. Fear up and laid him out. That was before me and Mr. Fear got married; I hadn't even be'n to Canaan then.

I was on the stage. I was on the stage quite a while in Chicago before I got acquainted with my husband."

"You were on the stage?" Ariel exclaimed, involuntarily.

"Yes, ma'am. Livin' pitchers at Goldberg's Rat'skeller, and amunchoor nights I nearly always done a sketch with a gen'leman friend. That's the way I met Mr. Fear; he seemed to be real struck with me right away, and soon as I got through my turn he ast me to order whatever I wanted. He's always gen'lemanlike when he ain't had too much, and even then he vurry, vurry seldom acks rough unless he's jealous. That was the trouble yesterday. I never would of gone to the Beach if I'd dreamed what was comin'! When we got there I saw Mike — that's the gen'leman that runs the Beach—lookin' at my company and me kind of anxious, and pretty soon he got me away from Mr. Cory and told me what's what. Seems this Cory only wanted me to go with him to make my husband mad, and he'd took good care that Mr. Fear heard I'd be there with him! And he'd be'n hangin' around me, every time he struck town, jest to make Mr. Fear mad—the fresh thing! You see he wanted to make my husband start something again, this Mr. Cory did, and he was fixed for it."

"I don't understand," said Ariel.

"It's this way: if Mr. Fear attacted Mr. Cory, why, Mr. Cory could shoot him down and claim self-defence. You see, it would be easy for Mr. Cory, because Mr. Fear nearly killed him when they had their first trouble, and that would give Mr. Cory a good excuse to shoot if Mr. Fear jest only pushed him. That's the way it is with the law. Mr. Cory could wipe out their old score and git off scot-free."

"Surely not!"

"Yes, ma'am, that's the way it would be. And when Mike told me that Mr. Cory had got me out there jest to provoke my husband I went straight up to him and begun to give him a piece of my mind. I didn't talk loud, because I never was one to make a disturbance and start trouble the way *some* do; and right while I was talkin' we both see my husband pass the window. Mr. Cory give a kind of yelling laugh and put his arm round me jest as Mr. Fear come in the door. And then it all happened so quick that you could hardly tell what *was* goin' on. Mr. Fear, we found afterwards, had promised Mr. Louden that he wouldn't come out there, but he took too much—you could see that by the look of him—and fergot his promise; fergot everything but me and Cory, I guess.

"He come right up to us, where I was tryin' to git away from Cory's arm—it was the left one he had around me, and the other behind his back—and neither of 'em said a word. Cory kept on laughin' loud as he could, and Mr. Fear struck him in the mouth. He's little, but he can hit awful hard, and Mr. Cory let out a screech, and I see his gun go off— right in Mr. Fear's face, I thought, but it wasn't; it only scorched him. Most of the other gen'lemen had run, but Mike made a dive and managed to knock the gun to one side, jest barely in time. Then Mike and three or four others that come out from behind things separated 'em—both of 'em fightin' to git at each other. They locked Mr. Cory up in Mike's room, and took Mr. Fear over to where they hitch the horses. Then Mike sent fer Mr. Louden to come out to talk to my husband and take care of him—he's the only one can do anything with him when he's like that—but before Mr. Louden could git there, Mr. Fear broke loose and run through a corn-field and got away; at least they couldn't find him. And Mr. Cory jumped through a window and slid down into one of Mike's boats, so they'd both gone. When Mr. Louden come, he only stayed long enough to hear what had happened and started out to find Happy—that's my husband. He's bound to keep them apart, but he hasn't found Mr. Fear yet or he'd be here."

Ariel had sunk back in her chair. "Why should your husband hide?" she asked, in a low voice.

"Waitin' fer his chance at Cory," the woman

answered, huskily. "I expect he's afraid the cops are after him, too, on account of the trouble, and he doesn't want to git locked up till he's met Cory again. They ain't after him, but he may not know it. They haven't heard of the trouble, I reckon, or they'd of run Cory in. *He's* around town to-day, drinkin' heavy, and I guess he's lookin' fer Mr. Fear about as hard as Mr. Louden is." She rose to her feet, lifted her coarse hands, and dropped them despairingly. "Oh, I'm scared!" she said. "Mr. Fear's be'n mighty good to me."

A slow and tired footstep was heard upon the stairs, and Joe's dog ran into the room droopingly, wagged his tail with no energy, and crept under the desk. Mrs. Fear wheeled toward the door and stood, rigid, her hands clenched tight, her whole body still, except her breast, which rose and fell with her tumultuous breathing. She could not wait till the laggard step reached the landing.

"*Mr. Louden!*" she called, suddenly.

Joe's voice came from the stairway. "It's all right, Claudine. It's all fixed up. Don't worry."

Mrs. Fear gave a thick cry of relief and sank back in her chair as Joe entered the room. He came in shamblingly, with his hand over his eyes as if they were very tired and the light hurt them, so that, for a moment or two, he did not perceive the second visitor. Then he let his hand fall, revealing a face very white and worn.

"It's all right, Claudine," he repeated. "It's all right."

He was moving to lay his hat on the desk when his eye caught first the roses, then fell upon Ariel, and he stopped stock-still with one arm outstretched, remaining for perhaps ten seconds in that attitude, while she, her lips parted, her eyes lustrous, returned his gaze with a look that was as inscrutable as it was kind.

"Yes," she said, as if in answer to a question, "I have come here twice to-day." She nodded slightly toward Mrs. Fear. "I can wait. I am very glad you bring good news."

Joe turned dazedly toward the other. "Claudine," he said, "you've been telling Miss Tabor."

"I cert'nly have!" Mrs. Fear's expression had cleared and her tone was cheerful. "I don't see no harm in that! I'm sure she's a good friend of *yours*, Mr. Louden."

Joe glanced at Ariel with a faint, troubled smile, and turned again to Mrs. Fear. "I've had a long talk with Happy."

"I'm awful glad. Is he ready to listen to reason? she asked, with a titter.

"He's waiting for you."

"Where?" She rose quickly.

"Stop," said Joe, sharply. "You must be very careful with him—"

"Don't you s'pose I'm goin' to be?" she interrupted, with a catch in her voice. "Don't you s'pose I've had trouble enough?"

"No," said Joe, deliberately and impersonally, "I don't. Unless you keep remembering to be careful all the time, you'll follow the first impulse you have, as you did yesterday, and your excuse will be that you never thought any harm would come of it. He's in a queer mood; but he will forgive you if you ask him—"

"Well, ain't that what I *want* to do!" she exclaimed.

"I know, I know," he said, dropping into the desk-chair and passing his hand over his eyes with a gesture of infinite weariness. "But you must be very careful. I hunted for him most of the night and all day. He was trying to keep out of my way because he didn't want me to find him until he had met this fellow Nashville. Happy is a hard man to come at when he doesn't care to be found, and he kept shifting from place to place until I ran him down. Then I got him in a corner and told him that you hadn't meant any harm—which is always true of you, poor woman!—and I didn't leave him till he had promised me to forgive you if you would come and ask him. And you must keep him out of

Cory's way until I can arrange to have him—Cory, I mean—sent out of town. Will you?"

"Why, cert'nly," she answered, smiling. "That Nashville's the vurry last person I ever want to see again—the fresh thing!" Mrs. Fear's burden had fallen; her relief was perfect and she beamed vapidly; but Joe marked her renewed irresponsibility with an anxious eye.

"You mustn't make any mistakes," he said, rising stiffly with fatigue.

"Not *me! I* don't take no more chances," she responded, tittering happily. "Not after yesterday. *My!* but it's a load off my shoulders! I do hate it to have gen'lemen quarrelling over me, especially Mr. Fear. I never *did* like to *start* anything; I like to see people laugh and be friendly, and I'm mighty glad it's all blown over. I kind o' thought it would, all along. *Psho!*" She burst into genuine, noisy laughter. "I don't expect either of 'em meant no real harm to each other, after they got cooled off a little! If they'd met to-day, they'd probably both run! Now, Mr. Louden, where's Happy?"

Joe went to the door with her. He waited a moment, perplexed, then his brow cleared and he said in a low voice: "You know the alley beyond Vent Miller's pool-room? Go down the alley till you come to the second gate. Go in, and you'll see a basement door opening into a little room under Miller's bar. The door won't be locked, and Happy's in there waiting for you. But remember—"

"Oh, don't you worry," she cut him off, loudly. "I know *him!* Inside of an hour I'll have him *laughin'* over all this. You'll see!"

When she had gone, he stood upon the landing looking thoughtfully after her. "Perhaps, after all, that is the best mood to let her meet him in," he murmured.

Then, with a deep breath, he turned. The heavy perfume had gone; the air was clear and sweet, and Ariel was pressing her face into the roses again. As he saw how like them she was, he was shaken with a profound and mysterious sigh, like that which moves in the breast of one who listens in the dark to his dearest music.

XV

HAPPY FEAR GIVES HIMSELF UP

"I KNOW how tired you are," said Ariel, as he came back into the room. "I shall not keep you long."

"Ah, please do!" he returned, quickly, beginning to fumble with the shade of a student-lamp at one end of the desk.

"Let me do that," she said. "Sit down." He obeyed at once, and watched her as she lit the lamp, and, stretching upon tiptoe, turned out the gas. "No," she continued, seated again and looking across the desk at him, "I wanted to see you at the first possible opportunity, but what I have to say—"

"Wait," he interrupted. "Let me tell you why I did not come yesterday."

"You need not tell me. I know." She glanced at the chair which had been occupied by Mrs. Fear. "I knew last night that they had sent for you."

"You did?" he exclaimed. "Ah, I understand Sam Warden must have told you."

"Yes," she said. "It was he; and I have been wondering ever since how he heard of it. He knew last night, but there was nothing in the papers this morning; and until I came here I heard no one else speak of it; yet Canaan is not large."

Joe laughed. "It wouldn't seem strange if you lived with the Canaan that I do. Sam had been down-town during the afternoon and had met friends; the colored people are a good deal like a freemasonry, you know. A great many knew last night all about what had happened, and had their theories about what might happen to-day in case the two men met. Still, you see, those who knew, also knew just what people not to tell. The *Tocsin* is the only newspaper worth the name here; but even if the *Tocsin* had known of the trouble, it wouldn't have been likely to mention it. That's a thing I don't understand." He frowned and rubbed the back of his head. "There's something underneath it. For more than a year the *Tocsin* hasn't spoken of Beaver Beach. I'd like to know why."

"Joe," she said, slowly, "tell me something truly. A man said to me yesterday that he found life here insufferable. Do you find it so?"

"Why, no!" he answered, surprised.

"Do you hate Canaan?"

"Certainly not."

"You don't find it dull, provincial, unsympathetic?"

He laughed cheerily. "Well, there's this," he explained: "I have an advantage over your friend. I see a more interesting side of things probably. The people I live among are pretty thorough cosmopolites in a way, and the life I lead—"

"I think I begin to understand a little about the life you lead," she interrupted. "Then you don't complain of Canaan?"

"Of course not."

She threw him a quick, bright, happy look, then glanced again at the chair in which Mrs. Fear had sat. "Joe," she said, "last night I heard the people singing in the houses, the old Sunday-evening way. It 'took me back so'!"

"Yes, it would. And something else: there's one hymn they sing more than any other; it's Canaan's favorite. Do you know what it is?"

"Is it 'Rescue the Perishing'?"

"That's it. 'Rescue the Perishing'!" he cried, and repeating the words again, gave forth a peal of laughter so hearty that it brought tears to his eyes. "'*Rescue the Perishing*'!"

At first she did not understand his laughter, but, after a moment, she did, and joined her own to it, though with a certain tremulousness.

"It *is* funny, isn't it?" said Joe, wiping the moisture from his eyes. Then all trace of mirth left him. "Is it really *you*, sitting here and laughing with me, Ariel?"

"It seems to be," she answered, in a low voice. "I'm not at all sure."

"You didn't think, yesterday afternoon," he began, almost in a whisper,—"you didn't think that I had failed to come because I—" He grew very red, and shifted the sentence awkwardly: "I was afraid you might think that I was—that I didn't come because I might have been the same way again that I was when—when I met you at the station?"

"Oh no!" she answered, gently. "No. I knew better."

"And do you know," he faltered, "that that is all over? That it can never happen again?"

"Yes, I know it," she returned, quickly.

"Then you know a little of what I owe you."

"No, no," she protested.

"Yes," he said. "You've made that change in me already. It wasn't hard—it won't be—though it might have been if—if you hadn't come soon."

"Tell me something," she demanded. "If these people had not sent for you yesterday, would you have come to Judge Pike's house to see me? You said you would try." She laughed a little, and

238

looked away from him   "I want to know if you would have come."

There was a silence, and in spite of her averted glance she knew that he was looking at her steadily. Finally, "Don't you know?" he said.

She shook her head and blushed faintly.

"Don't you know?" he repeated.

She looked up and met his eyes, and thereupon both became very grave. "Yes, I do," she answered. "You would have come. When you left me at the gate and went away, you were afraid. But you would have come."

"Yes,—I'd have come. You are right: I was afraid at first; but I knew," he went on, rapidly, "that you would have come to the gate to meet me."

"You understood that?" she cried, her eyes sparkling and her face flushing happily.

"Yes. I knew that you wouldn't have asked me to come," he said, with a catch in his voice which was half chuckle, half groan, "if you hadn't meant to take care of me! And it came to me that you would know how to do it."

She leaned back in her chair, and again they laughed together, but only for a moment, becoming serious and very quiet almost instantly.

"I haven't thanked you for the roses," he said.

"Oh yes, you did. When you first looked at them!"

"So I did," he whispered. "I'm glad you saw. To find them here took my breath away—and to find you with them—"

"I brought them this morning, you know."

"Would you have come if you had not understood why I failed yesterday?"

"Oh yes, I think so," she returned, the fine edge of a smile upon her lips. "For a time last evening, before I heard what had happened, I thought you were too frightened a friend to bother about."

He made a little ejaculation, partly joyful, partly sad.

"And yet," she went on, "I think that I should have come this morning, after all, even if you had a poorer excuse for your absence, because, you see, I came on business."

"You did?"

"That's why I've come again. That makes it respectable for me to be here now, doesn't it?—for me to have come out alone after dark without their knowing it? I'm here as your client, Joe."

"Why?" he asked.

She did not answer at once, but picked up a pen from beneath her hand on the desk, and turning it, meditatively felt its point with her forefinger before she said slowly, "Are most men careful of other people's—well, of other people's money?"

"You mean Martin Pike?" he asked.

"Yes. I want you to take charge of everything I have for me."

He bent a frowning regard upon the lamp-shade. "You ought to look after your own property," he said. "You surely have plenty of time."

"You mean—you mean you won't help me?" she returned, with intentional pathos.

"Ariel!" he laughed, shortly, in answer; then asked, "What makes you think Judge Pike isn't trustworthy?"

"Nothing very definite perhaps, unless it was his look when I told him that I meant to ask you to take charge of things for me."

"He's been rather hard pressed this year, I think," said Joe. "You might be right — if he could have found a way. I hope he hasn't."

"I'm afraid," she began, gayly, "that I know very little of my own affairs. He sent me a draft every three months, with receipts and other things to sign and return to him. I haven't the faintest notion of what I own—except the old house and some money from the income that I hadn't used and brought with me. Judge Pike has all the papers—everything."

Joe looked troubled. "And Roger Tabor, did he—"

"The dear man!" She shook her head. "He was just the same. To him poor Uncle Jonas's money seemed to come from heaven through the hands of Judge Pike—"

"And there's a handsome roundabout way!" said Joe.

"Wasn't it!" she agreed, cheerfully. "And he trusted the Judge absolutely. I don't, you see."

He gave her a thoughtful look and nodded. "No, he isn't a good man," he said, "not even according to his lights; but I doubt if he could have managed to get away with anything of consequence after he became the administrator. He wouldn't have tried it, probably, unless he was more desperately pushed than I think he has been. It would have been too dangerous. Suppose you wait a week or so and think it over."

"But there's something I want you to do for me immediately, Joe."

"What's that?"

"I want the old house put in order. I'm going to live there."

"Alone?"

"I'm almost twenty-seven, and that's being enough of an old maid for me to risk Canaan's thinking me eccentric, isn't it?"

"It will think anything you do is all right."

"And once," she cried, "it thought everything I did all wrong!"

"Yes. That's the difference."

"You mean it will commend me because I'm thought rich?"

"No, no," he said, meditatively, "it isn't that. It's because everybody will be in love with you."

"Quite everybody!" she asked.

"Certainly," he replied. "Anybody who didn't would be absurd."

"Ah, Joe!" she laughed. "You always *were* the nicest boy in the world, my dear!"

At that he turned toward her with a sudden movement and his lips parted, but not to speak. She had rested one arm upon the desk, and her cheek upon her hand; the pen she had picked up, still absently held in her fingers, touching her lips; and it was given to him to know that he would always keep that pen, though he would never write with it again. The soft lamplight fell across the lower part of her face, leaving her eyes, which were lowered thoughtfully, in the shadow of her hat. The room was blotted out in darkness behind her. Like the background of an antique portrait, the office, with its dusty corners and shelves and hideous safe, had vanished, leaving the charming and thoughtful face revealed against an even, spacious brownness. Only Ariel and the roses and the lamp were clear; and a strange, small pain moved from Joe's heart to his throat, as he thought that this ugly office, always before so harsh and grim and lonely — loneliest for him when it had been most crowded, — was now transfigured into something very, very different from an office; that this place where he sat, with a lamp and flowers on a desk between him and a woman who called him "my dear," must be like—like something that people called "home."

And then he leaned across the desk toward her, as he said again what he had said a little while before,—and his voice trembled:

"Ariel, it *is* you?"

She looked at him and smiled.

"You'll be here always, won't you? You're not going away from Canaan again?"

For a moment it seemed that she had not heard him. Then her bright glance at him wavered and fell. She rose, turning slightly away from him, but not so far that he could not see the sudden agitation in her face.

"Ah!" he cried, rising too, "I don't want you to think I don't understand, or that I meant *I* should ever ask you to stay here! I couldn't mean that; you know I couldn't, don't you? You know I

understand that it's all just your beautiful friendliness, don't you?"

"It isn't beautiful; it's just *me*, Joe," she said.
"It couldn't be any other way."

"It's enough that you should be here now," he
went on, bravely, his voice steady, though his hand
shook. "Nothing so wonderful as your staying
could ever actually happen. It's just a light
coming into a dark room and out again. One day,
long ago—I never forgot it—some apple-blossoms
blew by me as I passed an orchard; and it's
like that, too. But, oh, my dear, when you go
you'll leave a fragrance in my heart that will
last!"

She turned toward him, her face suffused with
a rosy light. "You'd rather have died than have
said that to me once," she cried. "I'm glad you're
weak enough now to confess it!"

He sank down again into his chair and his arms
fell heavily on the desk. "Confess it!" he cried,
despairingly. "And you don't deny that you're
going away again—so it's true! I wish I hadn't
realized it so soon. I think I'd rather have tried
to fool myself about it a little longer!"

"Joe," she cried, in a voice of great pain, "you
mustn't feel like that! How do you know I'm
going away again? Why should I want the old
house put in order unless I mean to stay? And if

I went, you know that I could never change; you know how I've always cared for you—"

"Yes," he said, "I do know how. It was always the same and it always will be, won't it?"

"I've shown that," she returned, quickly.

"Yes. You say I know how you've cared for me—and I do. I know *how*. It's just in one certain way—Jonathan and David—"

"Isn't that a pretty good way, Joe?"

"Never fear that I don't understand!" He got to his feet again and looked at her steadily.

"Thank you, Joe." She wiped sudden tears from her eyes.

"Don't you be sorry for me," he said. "Do you think that 'passing the love of women' isn't enough for me?"

"No," she answered, humbly.

"I'll have people at work on the old house to-morrow," he began. "And for the—"

"I've kept you so long!" she interrupted, helped to a meek sort of gayety by his matter-of-fact tone. "Good-night, Joe." She gave him her hand. "I don't want you to come with me. It isn't very late and this is Canaan."

"I want to come with you, however," he said, picking up his hat. "You can't go alone."

"But you are so tired, you—"

She was interrupted. There were muffled, flying footsteps on the stairs, and a shabby little man ran furtively into the room, shut the door behind him, and set his back against it. His face was mottled like a colored map, thick lines of perspiration shining across the splotches.

"Joe," he panted, "I've got Nashville good, and he's got me good, too;—I got to clear out. He's fixed me good, damn him! but he won't trouble nobody—"

Joe was across the room like a flying shadow.

"*Quiet!*" His voice rang like a shot, and on the instant his hand fell sharply across the speaker's mouth. "In *there*, Happy!"

He threw an arm across the little man's shoulders and swung him toward the door of the other room.

Happy Fear looked up from beneath the downbent brim of his black slouch hat; his eyes followed an imperious gesture toward Ariel, gave her a brief, ghastly stare, and stumbled into the inner chamber.

"Wait!" Joe said, cavalierly, to Ariel. He went in quickly after Mr. Fear and closed the door.

This was Joseph Louden, Attorney-at-Law; and to Ariel it was like a new face seen in a flash-light —not at all the face of Joe. The sense of his strangeness, his unfamiliarity in this electrical aspect, overcame her. She was possessed by astonishment: Did she know him so well, after

all? The strange client had burst in, shaken beyond belief with some passion unknown to her,
but Joe, alert, and masterful beyond denial, had
controlled him instantly; had swept him into the
other room as with a broom. Could it be that
Joe sometimes did other things in the same sweeping fashion?

She heard a match struck in the next room, and
the voices of the two men: Joe's, then the other's,
the latter at first broken and protestive, but soon
rising shrilly. She could hear only fragments.
Once she heard the client cry, almost scream:
"By God! Joe, I thought Claudine had chased him
around there to *do* me!" And, instantly, followed
Louden's voice:

"*Steady, Happy, steady!*"

The name "Claudine" startled her; and although
she had had no comprehension of the argot of
Happy Fear, the sense of a mysterious catastrophe
oppressed her; she was sure that something horrible had happened. She went to the window;
touched the shade, which disappeared upward
immediately, and lifted the sash. The front of a
square building in the Court-house Square was
bright with lights; and figures were passing in and
out of the Main Street doors. She remembered
that this was the jail.

"Claudine!" The voice of the husband of

Claudine was like the voice of one lamenting over Jerusalem.

"*Steady, Happy, steady!*"

"But, Joe, if they git me, what 'll she do? She can't hold her job no longer—not after this. . . ."

The door opened, and the two men came out, Joe with his hand on the other's shoulder. The splotches had gone from Happy's face, leaving it an even, deathly white. He did not glance toward Ariel; he gazed far beyond all that was about him; and suddenly she was aware of a great tragedy. The little man's chin trembled and he swallowed painfully; nevertheless he bore himself upright and dauntlessly as the two walked slowly to the door, like men taking part in some fateful ceremony. Joe stopped upon the landing at the head of the stairs, but Happy Fear went on, clumping heavily down the steps.

"It's all right, Happy," said Joe. "It's better for you to go alone. Don't you worry. I'll see you through. It will be all right."

"Just as *you* say, Joe," a breaking voice came back from the foot of the steps,—"just as *you* say!"

The lawyer turned from the landing and went rapidly to the window beside Ariel. Together they watched the shabby little figure cross the street below; and she felt an infinite pathos gathering about it as it paused for a moment, hesitating, underneath the arc-lamp at the corner. They saw the white face lifted as Happy Fear gave one last look about him; then he set his shoulders sturdily, and steadfastly entered the door of the jail.

Joe took a deep breath. "Now we'll go," he said. "I must be quick."

"What was it?" she asked, tremulously, as they reached the street. "Can you tell me?"

"Nothing—just an old story."

He had not offered her his arm, but walked on hurriedly, a pace ahead of her, though she came as rapidly as she could. She put her hand rather timidly on his sleeve, and without need of more words from her he understood her insistence.

"That was the husband of the woman who told you her story," he said. "Perhaps it would shock you less if I tell you now than if you heard it to-morrow, as you will. He's just shot the other man."

"Killed him!" she gasped.

"Yes," he answered. "He wanted to run away, but I wouldn't let him. He has my word that I'll clear him, and I made him give himself up."

XVI

WHEN Joe left Ariel at Judge Pike's gate she lingered there, her elbows upon the uppermost cross-bar, like a village girl at twilight, watching his thin figure vanish into the heavy shadow of the maples, then emerge momentarily, ghost-gray and rapid, at the lighted crossing down the street, to disappear again under the trees beyond, followed a second later by a brownish streak as the mongrel heeled after him. When they had passed the second corner she could no longer be certain of them, although the street was straight, with flat, draughtsmanlike Western directness: both figures and Joe's quick footsteps merging with the night. Still she did not turn to go; did not alter her position, nor cease to gaze down the dim street. Few lights shone; almost all the windows of the houses were darkened, and, save for the summer murmurs, the faint creak of upper branches, and the infinitesimal voices of insects in

251

the grass, there was silence: the pleasant and som-
nolent hush, swathed in which that part of Canaan
crosses to the far side of the eleventh hour.

But Ariel, not soothed by this balm, sought beyond it, to see that unquiet Canaan whither her
old friend bent his steps and found his labor and
his dwelling: that other Canaan where peace did
not fall comfortably with the coming of night; a
place as alien in habit, in thought, and almost in
speech as if it had been upon another continent.
And yet—so strange is the duality of towns—it lay
but a few blocks distant.

Here, about Ariel, as she stood at the gate of the
Pike Mansion, the houses of the good (secure of
salvation and daily bread) were closed and quiet,
as safely shut and sound asleep as the churches;
but deeper in the town there was light and life
and merry, evil industry,—screened, but strong to
last until morning; there were haunts of haggard
merriment in plenty: surreptitious chambers where
roulette - wheels swam beneath dizzied eyes; ill-
favored bars, reached by devious ways, where
quavering voices offered song and were harshly
checked; and through the burdened air of this
Canaan wandered heavy smells of musk like that
upon Happy Fear's wife, who must now be so pale
beneath her rouge. And above all this, and for
all this, and because of all this, was that one re-

sort to which Joe now made his way; that haven whose lights burn all night long, whose doors are never closed, but are open from dawn until dawn —the jail.

There, in that desolate refuge, lay Happy Fear, surrendered sturdily by himself at Joe's word. The picture of the little man was clear and fresh in Ariel's eyes, and though she had seen him when he was newly come from a thing so terrible that she could not realize it as a fact, she felt only an overwhelming pity for him. She was not even horror-stricken, though she had shuddered. The pathos of the shabby little figure crossing the street toward the lighted doors had touched her. Something about him had appealed to her, for he had not seemed wicked; his face was not cruel, though it was desperate. Perhaps it was partly his very desperation which had moved her. She had understood Joe, when he told her, that this man was his friend; and comprehended his great fear when he said: "I've got to clear him! I promised him."

Over and over Joe had reiterated: "I've got to save him! I've got to!" She had answered gently, "Yes, Joe," hurrying to keep up with him. "He's a good man," he said. "I've known few better, given his chances. And none of this would have happened except for his old-time friendship for me. It was his loyalty—oh, the rarest and

absurdest loyalty!—that made the first trouble between him and the man he shot. I've got to clear
him!"

"Will it be hard?"

"They may make it so. I can only see part of
it surely. When his wife left the office, she met
Cory on the street. You saw what a pitiful kind of
fool she was, irresponsible and helpless and feather-
brained. There are thousands of women like that
everywhere—some of them are 'Court Beauties,'
I dare say—and they always mix things up; but
they are most dangerous when they're like Claudine, because then they live among men of action
like Cory and Fear. Cory was artful: he spent the
day about town telling people that he had always
liked Happy; that his ill feeling of yesterday was
all gone; he wanted to find him and shake his hand,
bury past troubles and be friends. I think he
told Claudine the same thing when they met, and
convinced the tiny brainlet of his sincerity. Cory
was a man who 'had a way with him,' and I can
see Claudine flattered at the idea of being peacemaker between 'two such nice gen'lemen as Mr.
Cory and Mr. Fear.' Her commonest asseveration—
quite genuine, too—is that she doesn't like to have
the gen'lemen making trouble about her! So the
poor imbecile led him to where her husband was
waiting. All that Happy knew of this was in her

cry afterwards. He was sitting alone, when Cory threw open the door and said, 'I've got you this time, Happy!' His pistol was raised but never fired. He waited too long, meaning to establish his case of 'self-defence,' and Fear is the quickest man I know. Cory fell just inside the door. Claudine stumbled upon him as she came running after him, crying out to her husband that she 'never meant no trouble,' that Cory had sworn to her that he only wanted to shake hands and 'make up.' Other people heard the shot and broke into the room, but they did not try to stop Fear; he warned them off and walked out without hindrance, and came to me. I've got to clear him."

Ariel knew what he meant: she realized the actual thing as it was, and, though possessed by a strange feeling that it must all be medieval and not possibly of to-day, understood that he would have to fight to keep his friend from being killed; that the unhappy creature who had run into the office out of the dark stood in high danger of having his neck broken, unless Joe could help him. He made it clear to her that the State would kill Happy if it could; that it would be a point of pride with certain deliberate men holding office to take the life of the little man; that if they did secure his death it would be set down to their efficiency, and was even competent as campaign material. "I wish to point out," Joe had heard a candidate for re-election vehemently orate, "that in addition to the other successful convictions I have named, I and my assistants have achieved the sending of three men to the gallows during my term of office!"

"I can't tell yet," said Joe, at parting. "It may be hard. I'm so sorry you saw all this. I—"

"Oh *no!*" she cried. "I want to *understand!*"

She was still there, at the gate, her elbows resting upon the cross-bar, when, a long time after Joe had gone, there came from the alley behind the big back yard the minor chordings of a quartette of those dark strollers who never seem to go to bed, who play by night and playfully pretend to work by day:

> "You know my soul is a-full o' them-a-trub-bils,
> Ev-ry mawn!
> I cain' a-walk withouten I stum-bils!
> Then le'ss go on—
> Keep walkin' on!
> These times is sow'owful, an' I am pow'owful
> Sick an' fo'lawn!"

She heard a step upon the path behind her, and, turning, saw a white-wrapped figure coming toward her.

"Mamie?" she called.

"Hush!" Mamie lifted a warning hand. "The windows are open," she whispered. "They might hear you!"

"Why haven't you gone to bed?"

"Oh, don't you see?" Mamie answered, in deep distress,—"I've been sitting up for you. We all thought you were writing letters in your room, but after papa and mamma had gone to bed I went in to tell you good night, and you weren't there, nor anywhere else; so I knew you must have gone out. I've been sitting by the front window, waiting to let you in, but I went to sleep until a little while ago, when the telephone-bell rang and he got up and answered it. He kept talking a long time; it was something about the *Tocsin*, and I'm afraid there's been a murder down-town. When he went back to bed I fell asleep again, and then those darkies woke me up. How on earth did you expect to get in? Don't you know he always locks up the house?"

"I could have rung," said Ariel.

"Oh—oh!" gasped Miss Pike; and, after she had recovered somewhat, asked: "Do you mind telling me where you've been? I won't tell him—nor mamma, either. I think, after all, I was wrong yesterday to follow Eugene's advice. He meant for the best, but I—"

"Don't think that. You weren't wrong." Ariel

put her arm round the other's waist. "I went to talk over some things with Mr. Louden."

"I think," whispered Mamie, trembling, "that you are the bravest girl I ever knew—and—and—I could almost believe there's some good in him, since you like him so. I know there is. And I—I think he's had a hard time. I want you to know I won't even tell Eugene!"

"You can tell everybody in the world," said Ariel, and kissed her.

XVII

MR. SHEEHAN'S HINTS

"NEVER," said the *Tocsin* on the morrow, "has this community been stirred to deeper indignation than by the cold-blooded and unmitigated brutality of the deliberate murder committed almost under the very shadow of the Courthouse cupola last night. The victim was not a man of good repute, it is true, but at the moment of his death he was in the act of performing a noble and generous action which showed that he might have become, if he lived, a good and law-fearing citizen. In brief, he went to forgive his enemy and was stretching forth the hand of fellowship when that enemy shot him down. Not half an hour before his death, Cory had repeated within the hearing of a dozen men what he had been saying all day, as many can testify: 'I want to find my old friend Fear and shake hands with him. I want to tell him that I forgive him and that I am ashamed of whatever has been my part in the trouble between us.' He went with that intention to his death. The wife of the murderer has confessed that this was the substance of what he said to her, and that she was convinced of his peaceful intentions. When they reached the room where her husband was waiting for her, Cory entered first. The woman claims now that as they neared the vicinity he hastened forward at a pace which she could not equal. Naturally, her testimony on all points favoring her husband is practically worthless. She followed and heard the murdered man speak, though what his words were she declares she does not know, and of course the murderer, after consultation with his lawyer, claims that their nature was threatening. Such a statement, in determining the truth, is worse than valueless. It is known and readily proved that Fear repeatedly threatened the deceased's life yesterday, and there is no question in the mind of any man, woman, or child, who reads these words, of the cold-blooded nature of the crime. The slayer, who had formerly made a murderous attack upon his victim, lately quarrelled with him and uttered threats, as we have stated, upon his life. The dead man came to him with protestations of friendship and was struck down a corpse. It is understood that the defence will in desperation set up the theory of self-defence, based on an unsubstantiated claim that

Cory entered the room with a drawn pistol. No pistol was found in the room. The weapon with which the deed was accomplished was found upon the person of the murderer when he was seized by the police, one chamber discharged. Another revolver was discovered upon the person of the woman, when she was arrested on the scene of the crime. This, upon being strictly interrogated, she said she had picked up from the floor in the confusion, thinking it was her husband's and hoping to conceal it. The chambers were full and undischarged, and we have heard it surmised that the defence means to claim that it was Cory's. Cory doubtless went on his errand of forgiveness unarmed, and beyond doubt the second weapon belonged to the woman herself, who has an unenviable record.

"The point of it all is plainly this: here is an unquestionable murder in the first degree, and the people of this city and county are outraged and incensed that such a crime should have been committed in their law-abiding and respectable community. With whom does the fault lie? On whose head is this murder? Not with the authorities, for they do not countenance crime. Has it come to the pass that, counting on juggleries of the law, criminals believe that they may kill, maim, burn, and slay as they list without punishment? Is this to be another instance of the law's delays and immunity for a hideous crime, compassed by a cunning and cynical trickster of legal technicalities? The people of Canaan cry out for a speedy trial, speedy conviction, and speedy punishment of this cold-blooded and murderous monster. If he is not dealt with quickly according to his deserts, the climax is upon us and the limit of Canaan's patience has been reached.

"One last word, and we shall be glad to have its significance noted: J. Louden, Esq., has been retained for the defence! The murderer, before being apprehended by the authorities, *went straight from the scene of his crime to place his retainer in his attorney's pocket!* How LONG IS THIS TO LAST?"

The *Tocsin* was quoted on street corners that morning, in shop and store and office, wherever people talked of the Cory murder; and that was everywhere, for the people of Canaan and of the country roundabout talked of nothing else. Women chattered of it in parlor and kitchen; men gathered in small groups on the street and shook their heads ominously over it; farmers, meeting on the road, halted their teams and loudly damned the little man in the Canaan jail; milkmen lingered on back porches over their cans to agree with cooks that it was an awful thing, and that if ever any man deserved hanging, that there Fear deserved it —his lawyer along with him! Tipsy men hammered bars with fists and beer-glasses, inquiring if there was no rope to be had in the town; and Joe Louden, returning to his office from the little restaurant where he sometimes ate his breakfast, heard hisses following him along Main Street. A clerk, a fat-shouldered, blue-aproned, pimple-cheeked youth, stood in the open doors of a grocery, and as he passed, stared him in the face and said "Yah!" with supreme disgust.

Joe stopped. "Why?" he asked, mildly.

The clerk put two fingers in his mouth and whistled shrilly in derision. "You'd ort to be run out o' town!" he exclaimed.

"I believe," said Joe, "that we have never met before."

"Go on, you shyster!"

Joe looked at him gravely. "My dear sir," he returned, "you speak to me with the familiarity of an old friend."

The clerk did not recover so far as to be capable of repartee until Joe had entered his own stairway. Then, with a bitter sneer, he seized a bad potato from an open barrel and threw it at the mongrel, who had paused to examine the landscape. The missile failed, and Respectability, after bestowing a

THE CONQUEST OF CANAAN

slightly injured look upon the clerk, followed his master.

In the office the red-bearded man sat waiting. Not so red-bearded as of yore, however, was Mr. Sheehan, but grizzled and gray, and, this morning, gray of face, too, as he sat, perspiring and anxious, wiping a troubled brow with a black silk handkerchief.

"Here's the devil and all to pay at last, Joe," he said, uneasily, on the other's entrance. "This is the worst I ever knew; and I hate to say it, but I doubt yer pullin' it off."

"I've got to, Mike."

"I hope on my soul there's a chanst of it! I like the little man, Joe."

"So do I."

"I know ye do, my boy. But here's this *Tocsin* kickin' up the public sentiment; and if there ever was a follerin' sheep on earth, it's that same public sentiment!"

"If it weren't for that"—Joe flung himself heavily in a chair—"there'd not be so much trouble. It's a clear enough case."

"But don't ye see," interrupted Sheehan, "the *Tocsin's* tried it and convicted him aforehand? And that if things keep goin' the way they've started to-day, the gran' jury's bound to indict him, and the trial jury to convict him? They

wouldn't dare not to! What's more, they'll
to! And they'll rush the trial, summer
summer, and—"

"I know, I know."

"I'll tell ye one thing," said the other, wiping his
forehead with the black handkerchief, "and that's
this, my boy: last night's business has just about
put the cap on the Beach fer me. I'm sick of it
and I'm tired of it! I'm ready to quit, sir!"

Joe looked at him sharply. "Don't you think
my old notion of what might be done could be
made to pay?"

Sheehan laughed. "Whoo! You and yer hints,
Joe! How long past have ye come around me
with 'em! 'I b'lieve ye c'd make more money,
Mike'—that's the way ye'd put it,—'if ye altered
the Beach a bit. Make a little country-side restaurant of it,' ye'd say, 'and have good cookin',
and keep the boys and girls from raisin' so much
hell out there. Soon ye'd have other people
comin' beside the regular crowd. Make a little
garden on the shore, and let 'em eat at tables
under trees an' grape-arbors—'"

"Well, why not?" asked Joe.

"Haven't I been tellin' ye I'm thinkin' of it?
It's only yer way of hintin' that's funny to me,—yer
way of sayin' I'd make more money, because ye're
afraid of preachin' at any of us: partly because ye

know the little good it 'd be, and partly because ye have humor. Well, I'm thinkin' ye'll git yer way. *I'm* willin' to go into the missionary business with ye!"

"Mike!" said Joe, angrily, but he grew very red and failed to meet the other's eye, "I'm not—"

"Yes, ye are!" cried Sheehan. "Yes, sir! It's a thing ye prob'ly haven't had the nerve to say to yerself since a boy, but that's yer notion inside: ye're little better than a missionary! It took me a long while to understand what was drivin' ye, but I do now. And ye've gone the right way about it, because we know ye'll stand fer us when we're in trouble and fight fer us till we git a square deal, as ye're goin' to fight for Happy now."

Joe looked deeply troubled. "Never mind," he said, crossly, and with visible embarrassment. "You think you couldn't make more at the Beach if you ran it on my plan?"

"I'm game to try," said Sheehan, slowly. "I'm too old to hold 'em down out there the way I yoosta could, and I'm sick of it—sick of it into the very bones of me!" He wiped his forehead. "Where's Claudine?"

"Held as a witness."

"I'm not sorry fer *her!*" said the red-bearded man, emphatically. "Women o' that kind are so light-headed it's a wonder they don't float. Think of her pickin' up Cory's gun from the floor and hidin' it in her clothes! Took it fer granted it was Happy's, and thought she'd help him by hidin' it! There's a hard point fer ye, Joe: to prove the gun belonged to Cory. There's nobody about here could swear to it. I couldn't myself, though I forced him to stick it back in his pocket yesterday. He was a wanderer, too; and ye'll have to send a keen one to trace him, I'm thinkin', to find where he got it, so's ye can show it in court."

"I'm going myself. I've found out that he came here from Denver."

"And from where before that?"

"I don't know, but I'll keep on travelling till I get what I want."

"That's right, my boy," exclaimed the other, heartily. "It may be a long trip, but ye're all the little man has to depend on. Did ye notice the *Tocsin* didn't even give him the credit fer givin' himself up?"

"Yes," said Joe. "It's part of their game."

"Did it strike ye now," Mr. Sheehan asked, earnestly, leaning forward in his chair, — "did it strike ye that the *Tocsin* was aimin' more to do Happy harm because of you than himself?"

"Yes." Joe looked sadly out of the window. "I've thought that over, and it seemed possible that I might do Happy more good by giving his case to some other lawyer."

"No, sir!" exclaimed the proprietor of Beaver Beach, loudly. "They've begun their attack; they're bound to keep it up, and they'd manage to turn it to the discredit of both of ye. Besides, Happy wouldn't have no other lawyer; he'd ruther be hung with you fightin' fer him than be cleared by anybody else. I b'lieve it,—on my soul I do! But look here," he went on, leaning still farther forward; "I want to know if it struck ye that this morning the *Tocsin* attacked ye in a way that was somehow vi'lenter than ever before?"

"Yes," replied Joe, "because it was aimed to strike where it would most count."

"It ain't only that," said the other, excitedly. "It ain't only that! I want ye to listen. Now see here: the *Tocsin* is Pike, and the town is Pike— I mean the town ye naturally belonged to. Ain't it?"

"In a way, I suppose—yes."

"In a way!" echoed the other, scornfully. "Ye know it is! Even as a boy Pike disliked ye and hated the kind of a boy ye was. Ye wasn't respectable and he was! Ye wasn't rich and he was! Ye had a grin on yer face when ye'd meet him on the street." The red-bearded man broke off at a gesture from Joe and exclaimed sharply: "Don't deny it! *I* know what ye was like! Ye wasn't impudent, but ye looked at him as if ye saw through him. Now listen and I'll lead ye somewhere! Ye run with riffraff, naggers, and even"—Mr. Sheehan lifted a forefinger solemnly and shook it at his auditor—"and even with the Irish! Now I ask ye this: ye've had one part of Canaan with ye from the start, *my* part, that is; but the other's against ye; that part's *Pike*, and it's the rulin' part—"

"Yes, Mike," said Joe, wearily. "In the spirit of things. I know."

"No, sir," cried the other. "That's the trouble: ye don't know. There's more in Canaan than ye've understood. Listen to this: Why was the *Tocsin's* attack harder this morning than ever before? On yer soul didn't it sound so bitter that it sounded desprit? Now why? It looked to me as if it had started to ruin ye, this time fer good and all! Why? What have ye had to do with Martin Pike lately? Has the old wolf *got* to injure ye?" Mr. Sheehan's voice rose and his eyes gleamed under bushy brows. "Think," he finished. "What's happened lately to make him bite so hard?"

There were some faded roses on the desk, and as Joe's haggard eyes fell upon them the answer came. "What makes you think Judge Pike isn't trustworthy?" he had asked Ariel, and her reply had been: "Nothing very definite, unless it was his look when I told him that I meant to ask you to take charge of things for me."

He got slowly and amazedly to his feet. "You've got it!" he said.

"Ye see?" cried Mike Sheehan, slapping his thigh with a big hand. "On my soul I have the penetration! Ye don't need to tell me one thing except this: I told ye I'd lead ye somewhere; haven't I kept me word?"

"Yes," said Joe.

"But I have the penetration!" exclaimed Mr. Sheehan. "Should I miss my guess if I said that ye think Pike may be scared ye'll stumble on his track in some queer performances? Should I miss it?"

"No," said Joe. "You wouldn't miss it."

"Just one thing more." The red-bearded man rose, mopping the inner band of his straw hat. "In the matter of yer runnin' fer Mayor, now—"

Joe, who had begun to pace up and down the room, made an impatient gesture. "Pshaw!" he interrupted; but his friend stopped him with a hand laid on his arm.

"Don't be treatin' it as clean out of all possibility, Joe Louden. If ye do, it shows ye haven't sense to know that nobody can say what way the wind's blowin' week after next. All the boys want ye:

Louie Farbach wants ye, and Louie has a big say. Who is it that doesn't want ye?"

"Canaan," said Joe.

"Hold up! It's Pike's Canaan ye mean. If ye git the nomination, ye'd be elected, wouldn't ye?"

"I couldn't be nominated."

"I ain't claimin' ye'd git Martin Pike's vote," returned Mr. Sheehan, sharply, "though I don't say it's impossible. Ye've got to beat him, that's all. Ye've got to do to him what he's done to *you*, and what he's tryin' to do now worse than ever before. Well—there may be ways to do it; and if he tempts me enough, I may fergit my troth and honor as a noble gentleman and help ye with a word ye'd never guess yerself."

"You've hinted at such mysteries before, Mike," Joe smiled. "I'd be glad to know what you mean, if there's anything in them."

"It may come to that," said the other, with some embarrassment. "It may come to that some day, if the old wolf presses me too hard in the matter o' tryin' to git the little man across the street hanged by the neck and yerself mobbed fer helpin' him! But to-day I'll say no more."

"Very well, Mike." Joe turned wearily to his desk. "I don't want you to break any promises."

Mr. Sheehan had gone to the door, but he paused on the threshold, and wiped his forehead again.

"And I don't want to break any," he said, "but if ever the time should come when I couldn't help it"—he lowered his voice to a hoarse but piercing whisper—"that will be the devourin' angel's day fer Martin Pike!"

XVIII

IN THE HEAT OF THE DAY

T was a morning of the warmest week of mid-July, and Canaan lay inert and helpless beneath a broiling sun. The few people who moved about the streets went languidly, keeping close to the wall on the shady side; the women in thin white fabrics; the men, often coatless, carrying palm-leaf fans, and replacing collars with handkerchiefs. In the Court-house yard the maple leaves, gray with blown dust and grown to great breadth, drooped heavily, depressing the long, motionless branches with their weight, so low that the four or five shabby idlers, upon the benches beneath, now and then flicked them sleepily with whittled sprigs. The doors and windows of the stores stood open, displaying limp wares of trade, but few tokens of life; the clerks hanging over dim counters as far as possible from the glare in front, gossiping fragmentarily, usually about the Cory murder, and, anon, upon a subject suggested by the sight of an occasional pedestrian passing perspiring by with scrooged eyelids and purpling skin. From street and sidewalk, transparent hot waves swam up and danced themselves into nothing; while from the river bank a half-mile away, came a sound hotter than even the locust's midsummer rasp: the drone of a planing-mill. A chance boy, lying prone in the grass of the Court-house yard, was annoyed by the relentless chant and lifted his head to mock it: "*Awr-eer-awr-eer! Shut up, can't you?*" The effort was exhausting: he relapsed and suffered with increasing malice but in silence.

Abruptly there was a violent outbreak on the "National House" corner, as when a quiet farmhouse is startled by some one's inadvertently bringing down all the tin from a shelf in the pantry. The loafers on the benches turned hopefully, saw what it was, then closed their eyes, and slumped back into their former positions. The outbreak subsided as suddenly as it had arisen: Colonel Flitcroft pulled Mr. Arp down into his chair again, and it was all over.

Greater heat than that of these blazing days could not have kept one of the sages from attending the conclave now. For the battle was on in Canaan: and here, upon the National House corner, under the shadow of the west wall, it waxed even keener. Perhaps we may find full justification for calling what was happening a battle in so far as we restrict the figure to apply to this one spot; elsewhere, in the Canaan of the *Tocsin*, the conflict was too one-sided. The *Tocsin* had indeed tried the case of Happy Fear in advance, had convicted and condemned, and every day grew more bitter. Nor was the urgent vigor of its attack without effect. Sleepy as Main Street seemed in the heat, the town was incensed and roused to a tensity of feeling it had not known since the civil war, when, on occasion, it had set out to hang half a dozen "Knights of the Golden Circle." Joe had been hissed on the street many times since the inimical clerk had whistled at him. Probably demonstrations of that sort would have continued had he remained in Canaan; but for almost a month he had been absent and his office closed, its threshold gray with dust. There were people who believed that he had run away again, this time never to return; among those who held to this opinion being Mrs. Louden and her sister, Joe's stepaunt. Upon only one point was everybody agreed: that twelve men could not be found in the county who could be so far persuaded and befuddled by Louden that they would dare to allow Happy Fear to escape. The women of Canaan, incensed by the terrible circumstance of the case, as the *Tocsin* colored it—a man shot down in the act of begging his enemy's forgiveness — clamored as loudly as the men: there was only the difference that the latter vociferated for the hanging of Happy; their good ladies used the word "punishment."

And yet, while the place rang with condemnation of the little man in the jail and his attorney, there were voices, here and there, uplifted on the other side. People existed, it astonishingly appeared, who *liked* Happy Fear. These were for the greater part obscure and even darkling in their lives, yet quite demonstrably human beings, able to smile, suffer, leap, run, and to entertain fancies; even to have, according to their degree, a certain rudimentary sense of right and wrong, in spite of which they strongly favored the prisoner's acquittal. Precisely on that account, it was argued, an acquittal would outrage Canaan and lay it open to untold danger: such people needed a lesson.

The *Tocsin* interviewed the town's great ones, printing their opinions of the heinousness of the crime and the character of the defendant's lawyer. . . . "The Hon. P. J. Parrott, who so ably represented this county in the Legislature some fourteen years ago, could scarcely restrain himself when approached by a reporter as to his sentiments anent the repulsive deed. 'I should like to know how long Canaan is going to put up with this sort of

business,' were his words. 'I am a law-abiding
citizen, and I have served faithfully, and with my
full endeavor and ability, to enact the laws and
statutes of my State, but there is a point in my
patience, I would state, which lawbreakers and
their lawyers may not safely pass. Of what use
are our most solemn enactments, I may even ask
of what use is the Legislature itself, chosen by the
will of the people, if they are to ruthlessly be set
aside by criminals and their shifty protectors?
The blame should be put upon the lawyers who by
tricks enable such rascals to escape the rigors of
the carefully enacted laws, the fruits of the Solon's
labor, more than upon the criminals themselves.
In this case, if there is any miscarriage of justice, I
will say here and now that in my opinion the
people of this county will be sorely tempted; and
while I do not believe in lynch-law, yet if that
should be the result it is my unalterable conviction that the vigilantes may well turn their attention to the lawyers—*or lawyer*—who bring about
such miscarriage. I am sick of it.'"

The *Tocsin* did not print the interview it obtained
from Louie Farbach—the same Louie Farbach who
long ago had owned a beer-saloon with a little room
behind the bar, where a shabby boy sometimes
played dominoes and "seven-up" with loafers:
not quite the same Louie Farbach, however, in

outward circumstance: for he was now the brewer of Farbach Beer and making Canaan famous. His rise had been Teutonic and sure; and he contributed one-twentieth of his income to the German Orphan Asylum and one-tenth to his party's campaign fund. The twentieth saved the orphans from the county, while the tithe gave the county to his party.

He occupied a kitchen chair, enjoying the society of some chickens in a wired enclosure behind the new Italian villa he had erected in that part of Canaan where he would be most uncomfortable, and he looked woodenly at the reporter when the latter put his question.

"Hef you any aguaintunce off Mitster Fear?" he inquired, in return, with no expression decipherable either upon his Gargantuan face or in his heavily enfolded eyes.

"No, sir," replied the reporter, grinning. "I never ran across him."

"Dot iss a goot t'ing fer you," said Mr. Farbach, stonily. "He iss not a man peobles bedder try to run across. It iss what Gory tried. Now Gory iss dead."

The reporter, slightly puzzled, lit a cigarette. "See here, Mr. Farbach," he urged, "I only want a word or two about this thing; and you might give me a brief expression concerning that man

Louden besides: just a hint of what you think of his influence here, you know, and of the kind of sharp work he practises. Something like that."

"I see," said the brewer, slowly. "Happy Fear I hef knowt for a goot many years. He is a goot frient of mine."

"What?"

"Choe Louten iss a bedder one," continued Mr. Farbach, turning again to stare at his chickens. "Git owit."

"What?"

"Git owit," repeated the otﾍer, without passion, without anger, without any expression whatsoever. "Git owit."

The reporter's prejudice against the German nation dated from that moment.

There were others, here and there, who were less self-contained than the brewer. A farm-hand struck a fellow laborer in the harvest-field for speaking ill of Joe; and the unravelling of a strange street fight, one day, disclosed as its cause a like resentment, on the part of a blind broom-maker, engendered by a like offence. The broom-maker's companion, reading the *Tocsin* as the two walked together, had begun the quarrel by remarking that Happy Fear ought to be hanged once for his own sake and twice more "to show up that shyster Louden." Warm words followed, leading to extremely material conflict, in which, in spite of his blindness, the broom-maker had so much the best of it that he was removed from the triumphant attitude he had assumed toward the person of his adversary, which was an admirable imitation of the dismounted St. George and the Dragon, and conveyed to the jail. Keenest investigation failed to reveal anything oblique in the man's record; to the astonishment of Canaan, there was nothing against him. He was blind and moderately poor; but a respectable, hard - working artisan, and a pride to the church in which he was what has been called an "active worker." It was discovered that his sensitiveness to his companion's attack on Joseph Louden arose from the fact that Joe had obtained the acquittal of an imbecile sister of the blind man, a two-thirds-witted woman who had been charged with bigamy.

The *Tocsin* made what it could of this, and so dexterously that the wrath of Canaan was one farther jot increased against the shyster. Ay, the town was hot, inside and out.

Let us consider the Forum. Was there ever before such a summer for the "National House" corner? How voices first thundered there, then cracked and piped, is not to be rendered in all the tales of the fathers. One who would make vivid the great doings must indeed "dip his brush in

earthquake and eclipse"; even then he could but
picture the credible, and must despair of this: the
silence of Eskew Arp. Not that Eskew held his
tongue, not that he was chary of speech — no!
O tempora, O mores! No! But that he refused the
subject in hand, that he eschewed expression upon
it and resolutely drove the argument in other directions, that he achieved such superbly un-Arplike
inconsistency; and with such rich material for his
sardonic humors, not at arm's length, not even so
far as his finger-tips, but beneath his very palms,
he rejected it: this was the impossible fact.

Eskew—there is no option but to declare—was
no longer Eskew. It is the truth; since the morning when Ariel Tabor came down from Joe's office,
leaving her offering of white roses in that dingy,
dusty, shady place, Eskew had not been himself.
His comrades observed it somewhat in a physical
difference, one of those alterations which may
come upon men of his years suddenly, like a "sea
change": his face was whiter, his walk slower, his
voice filed thinner; he creaked louder when he rose
or sat. Old always, from his boyhood, he had,
in the turn of a hand, become aged. But such
things come and such things go: after eighty there
are ups and downs; people fading away one week,
bloom out pleasantly the next, and resiliency is
not at all a patent belonging to youth alone. The

material change in Mr. Arp might have been thought little worth remarking. What caused Peter Bradbury, Squire Buckalew, and the Colonel to shake their heads secretly to one another and wonder if their good old friend's mind had not "begun to go" was something very different. To come straight down to it: he not only abstained from all argument upon the "Cory Murder" and the case of Happy Fear, refusing to discuss either in any terms or under any circumstances, but he also declined to speak of Ariel Tabor or of Joseph Louden; or of their affairs, singular or plural, masculine, feminine, or neuter, or in any declension. Not a word, committal or non-committal. None!

And his face, when he was silent, fell into sorrowful and troubled lines.

At first they merely marvelled. Then Squire Buckalew dared to tempt him. Eskew's faded eyes showed a blue gleam, but he withstood, speaking of Babylon to the disparagement of Chicago. They sought to lead him into what he evidently would not, employing many devices; but the old man was wily and often carried them far afield by secret ways of his own. This hot morning he had done that thing: they were close upon him, pressing him hard, when he roused that outburst which had stirred the idlers on the benches in the Court-house yard. Squire Buckalew (sidelong at the others but squarely at Eskew) had volunteered the information that Cory was a reformed priest. Stung by the mystery of Eskew's silence, the Squire's imagination had become magically gymnastic; and if anything under heaven could have lifted the veil, this was the thing. Mr. Arp's reply may be reverenced.

"I consider," he said, deliberately, "that James G. Blaine's furrin policy was childish, and, what's more, I never thought much of *him!*"

This outdefied Ajax, and every trace of the matter in hand went to the four winds. Eskew, like Rome, was saved by a cackle, in which he joined, and a few moments later, as the bench loafers saw, was pulled down into his seat by the Colonel.

The voices of the fathers fell to the pitch of ordinary discourse; the drowsy town was quiet again; the whine of the planing-mill boring its way through the sizzling air to every wakening ear. Far away, on a quiet street, it sounded faintly, like the hum of a bee across a creek, and was drowned in the noise of men at work on the old Tabor house. It seemed the only busy place in Canaan that day: the shade of the big beech-trees which surrounded it affording some shelter from the destroying sun to the dripping laborers who were sawing, hammering, painting, plumbing, papering, and ripping open old and new packing-boxes.

There were many changes in the old house—pleasantly in keeping with its simple character: airy enlargements now almost completed so that some of the rooms were already finished, and stood, furnished and immaculate, ready for tenancy.

In that which had been Roger Tabor's studio sat Ariel, alone. She had caused some chests and cases, stored there, to be opened, and had taken out of them a few of Roger's canvases and set them along the wall. Tears filled her eyes as she looked at them, seeing the tragedy of labor the old man had expended upon them; but she felt the recompense: hard, tight, literal as they were, he had had his moment of joy in each of them before he saw them coldly and knew the truth. And he had been given his years of Paris at last: and had seen "how the other fellows did it."

A heavy foot strode through the hall, coming abruptly to a halt in the doorway, and turning, she discovered Martin Pike, his big Henry-the-Eighth face flushed more with anger than with the heat. His hat was upon his head, and remained there, nor did he offer any token or word of greeting whatever, but demanded to know when the work upon the house had been begun.

"The second morning after my return," she answered.

"I want to know," he pursued, "why it was kept secret from me, and I want to know quick."

"Secret?" she echoed, with a wave of her hand to indicate the noise which the workmen were making.

"Upon whose authority was it begun?"

"Mine. Who else could give it?"

"Look here," he said, advancing toward her, "don't you try to fool me! You haven't done all this by yourself. Who hired these workmen?"

Remembering her first interview with him, she rose quickly before he could come near her. "Mr. Louden made most of the arrangements for me," she replied, quietly, "before he went away. He will take charge of everything when he returns. You haven't forgotten that I told you I intended to place my affairs in his hands?"

He had started forward, but at this he stopped and stared at her inarticulately.

"You remember?" she said, her hands resting negligently upon the back of the chair. "Surely you remember?"

She was not in the least afraid of him, but coolly watchful of him. This had been her habit with him since her return. She had seen little of him, except at table, when he was usually grimly laconic, though now and then she would hear him joking heavily with Sam Warden in the yard, or, with evidently humorous intent, groaning at Mamie over Eugene's health; but it had not escaped Ariel that he was, on his part, watchful of herself, and upon his guard with a wariness in which she was sometimes surprised to believe that she saw an almost haggard apprehension.

He did not answer her question, and it seemed to her, as she continued steadily to meet his hot eyes, that he was trying to hold himself under some measure of control; and a vain effort it proved.

"You go back to my house!" he burst out, shouting hoarsely. "You get back there! You stay there!"

"No," she said, moving between him and the door. "Mamie and I are going for a drive."

"You go back to my house!" He followed her, waving an arm fiercely at her. "Don't you come around here trying to run over me! You talk about your 'affairs'! All you've got on earth is this two-for-a-nickel old shack over your head and a bushel-basket of distillery stock that you can sell by the pound for old paper!" He threw the words in her face, the bull-bass voice seamed and cracked with falsetto. "Old paper, old rags, old iron, bottles, old clothes! You talk about your affairs! Who are you? Rothschild? You haven't *got* any affairs!"

Not a look, not a word, not a motion of his e--

caped her in all the fury of sound and gesture in which he seemed fairly to envelop himself; least of all did that shaking of his—the quivering of jaw and temple, the tumultuous agitation of his hands —evade her watchfulness.

"When did you find this out?" she said, very quickly. "After you became administrator?"

He struck the back of the chair she had vacated a vicious blow with his open hand. "No, you spendthrift! All there was *to* your grandfather when you buried him was a basket full of distillery stock, I tell you! Old paper! Can't you hear me? Old paper, old rags—"

"You have sent me the same income," she lifted her voice to interrupt; "you have made the same quarterly payments since his death that you made before. If you knew, why did you do that?"

He had been shouting at her with the frantic and incredulous exasperation of an intolerant man utterly unused to opposition; his face empurpled, his forehead dripping, and his hands ruthlessly pounding the back of the chair; but this straight question stripped him suddenly of gesture and left him standing limp and still before her, pale splotches beginning to show on his hot cheeks.

"If you knew, why did you do it?" she repeated. "You wrote me that my income was from dividends, and I knew and thought nothing about it;

but if the stock which came to me was worthless, how could it pay dividends?"

"It did not," he answered, huskily. "That distillery stock, I tell you, isn't worth the matches to burn it."

"But there has been no difference in my income," she persisted, steadily. "Why? Can you explain that to me?"

"Yes, I can," he replied, and it seemed to her that he spoke with a pallid and bitter desperation, like a man driven to the wall. "I can if you think you want to know."

"I do."

"I sent it."

"Do you mean from you own—"

"I mean it was my own money."

She had not taken her eyes from his, which met hers straightly and angrily; and at this she leaned forward, gazing at him with profound scrutiny.

"Why did you send it?" she asked.

"Charity," he answered, after palpable hesitation.

Her eyes widened and she leaned back against the lintel of the door, staring at him incredulously. "Charity!" she echoed, in a whisper.

Perhaps he mistook her amazement at his performance for dismay caused by the sense of her own position, for, as she seemed to weaken before him, the strength of his own habit of dominance came back to him. "Charity, madam!" he broke out, shouting intolerably. "Charity, d'ye hear? I was a friend of the man that made the money you and your grandfather squandered; I was a friend of Jonas Tabor, I say! That's why I was willing to support you for a year and over, rather than let a niece of his suffer,"

"'Suffer'!" she cried. "'Support'! You sent me a hundred thousand francs!"

The white splotches which had mottled Martin Pike's face disappeared as if they had been suddenly splashed with hot red. "You go back to my house," he said. "What I sent you only shows the extent of my—"

"Effrontery!" The word rang through the whole house, so loudly and clearly did she strike it, rang in his ears till it stung like a castigation. It was ominous, portentous of justice and of disaster. There was more than doubt of him in it: there was conviction.

He fell back from this word; and when he again advanced, Ariel had left the house. She had turned the next corner before he came out of the gate; and as he passed his own home on his way down-town, he saw her white dress mingling with his daughter's near the horse-block beside the fire, where the two, with their arms about each other, stood waiting for Sam Warden and the open summer carriage.

Judge Pike walked on, the white splotches re-appearing like a pale rash upon his face. A yellow butterfly zigzagged before him, knee-high, across the sidewalk. He raised his foot and half kicked at it.

XIX

ESKEW ARP

S the Judge continued his walk down Main Street, he wished profoundly that the butterfly (which exhibited no annoyance) had been of greater bulk and more approachable; and it was the evil fortune of Joe's mongrel to encounter him in the sinister humor of such a wish unfulfilled.

Respectability dwelt at Beaver Beach under the care of Mr. Sheehan until his master should return; and Sheehan was kind; but the small dog found the world lonely and time long without Joe. He had grown more and more restless, and at last, this hot morning, having managed to evade the eye of all concerned in his keeping, made off unobtrusively, partly by swimming, and reaching the road, cantered into town, his ears erect with anxiety. Bent upon reaching the familiar office, he passed the grocery from the doorway of which the pimply-cheeked clerk had thrown a bad potato at him a month before. The same clerk had just laid down the *Tocsin* as Respectability went by, and, inspired to great deeds in behalf of justice and his native city, he rushed to the door, lavishly seized, this time, a perfectly good potato, and hurled it with a result which ecstasized him, for it took the mongrel fairly aside the head, which it matched in size.

The luckless Respectability's purpose to reach Joe's stairway had been entirely definite, but upon this violence he forgot it momentarily. It is not easy to keep things in mind when one is violently smitten on mouth, nose, cheek, eye, and ear by a missile large enough to strike them simultaneously. Yelping and half blinded, he deflected to cross Main Street. Judge Pike had elected to cross in the opposite direction, and the two met in the middle of the street.

The encounter was miraculously fitted to the Judge's need: here was no butterfly, but a solid body, light withal, a wet, muddy, and dusty yellow dog, eminently kickable. The man was heavily built about the legs, and the vigor of what he did may have been additionally inspired by his recognition of the mongrel as Joe Louden's. The impact of his toe upon the little runner's side was momentous, and the latter rose into the air. The Judge hopped, as one hops who, unshod in the night, discovers an unexpected chair. Let us be reconciled to his pain and not reproach the gods with it,—for two of his unintending adversary's ribs were cracked.

The dog, thus again deflected, retraced his tracks, shrieking distractedly, and, by one of those ironical twists which Karma reserves for the tails of the fated, dived for blind safety into the store commanded by the ecstatic and inimical clerk. There were shouts; the sleepy Square beginning to wake up: the boy who had mocked the planing-mill got to his feet, calling upon his fellows; the bench loafers strolled to the street; the aged men stirred and rose from their chairs; faces appeared in the open windows of offices; sales ladies and gentlemen came to the doorways of the trading-places; so that when Respectability emerged from the grocery he had a notable audience for the scene he enacted with a brass dinner-bell tied to his tail.

Another potato, flung by the pimpled, uproarious, prodigal clerk, added to the impetus of his flight. A shower of pebbles from the hands of exhilarated boys dented the soft asphalt about him; the hideous clamor of the pursuing bell increased as he turned the next corner, running distractedly. The dead town had come to life, and its inhabitants gladly risked the dangerous heat in the interests of sport, whereby it was a merry chase the little dog led around the block. For thus some destructive instinct drove him; he could not stop with the unappeasable Terror clanging at his heels and the increasing crowd yelling in pursuit; but he turned to the left at each corner, and thus came back to pass Joe's stairway again, unable to pause there or anywhere, unable to do anything except to continue his hapless flight, poor meteor.

Round the block he went once more, and still no chance at that empty stairway where, perhaps, he thought, there might be succor and safety. Blood was upon his side where Martin Pike's boot had crashed, foam and blood hung upon his jaws and lolling tongue. He ran desperately, keeping to the middle of the street, and, not howling, set himself despairingly to outstrip the Terror. The mob, disdaining the sun superbly, pursued as closely as it could, throwing bricks and rocks at him, striking at him with clubs and sticks. Happy Fear, playing "tic-tac-toe," right hand against left, in his cell, heard the uproar, made out something of what was happening, and, though unaware that it was a friend whose life was sought, discovered a similarity to his own case, and prayed to his dim gods that the quarry might get away.

"*Mad dog!*" they yelled. "*Mad dog!*" And there were some who cried, "*Joe Louden's dog!*" that being equally as exciting and explanatory.

Three times round, and still the little fugitive

maintained a lead. A gray-helmeted policeman, a big fellow, had joined the pursuit. He had children at home who might be playing in the street, and the thought of what might happen to them if the mad dog should head that way resolved him to be cool and steady. He was falling behind, so he stopped on the corner, trusting that Respectability would come round again. He was right, and the flying brownish thing streaked along Main Street, passing the beloved stairway for the fourth time. The policeman lifted his revolver, fired twice, missed once, but caught him with the second shot in a forepaw, clipping off a fifth toe, one of the small claws that grow above the foot and are always in trouble. This did not stop him; but the policeman, afraid to risk another shot because of the crowd, waited for him to come again; and many others, seeing the hopeless circuit the mongrel followed, did likewise, armed with bricks and clubs. Among them was the pimply clerk, who had been inspired to commandeer a pitchfork from a hardware store.

When the fifth round came, Respectability's race was run. He turned into Main Street at a broken speed, limping, parched, voiceless, flecked with blood and foam, snapping feebly at the showering rocks, but still indomitably a little ahead of the hunt. There was no yelp left in him—he was too thoroughly winded for that,—but in his brilliant and despairing eyes shone the agony of a cry louder than the tongue of a dog could utter: "O master! O all the god I know! Where are you in my mortal need?"

Now indeed he had a gauntlet to run; for the street was lined with those who awaited him, while the pursuit grew closer behind. A number of the hardiest stood squarely in his path, and he hesitated for a second, which gave the opportunity for a surer aim, and many missiles struck him. "Let him have it now, officer," said Eugene Bantry, standing with Judge Pike at the policeman's elbow. "There's your chance."

But before the revolver could be discharged, Respectability had begun to run again, hobbling on three legs and dodging feebly. A heavy stone struck him on the shoulder and he turned across the street, making for the "National House" corner, where the joyful clerk brandished his pitchfork. Going slowly, he almost touched the pimply one as he passed, and the clerk, already rehearsing in his mind the honors which should follow the brave stroke, raised the tines above the little dog's head for the *coup de grâce*. They did not descend, and the daring youth failed of fame as the laurel almost embraced his brows. A hickory walking-stick was thrust between his legs; and he, expecting to strike, received a blow upon the temple sufficient for his present undoing and bedazzlement. He went over backwards, and the pitchfork (not the thing to hold poised on high when one is knocked down) fell with the force he had intended for Respectability upon his own shin.

A train had pulled into the station, and a tired, travel-worn young man, descending from a sleeper, walked rapidly up the street to learn the occasion of what appeared to be a riot. When he was close enough to understand its nature, he dropped his bag and came on at top speed, shouting loudly to the battered mongrel, who tried with his remaining strength to leap toward him through a cordon of kicking legs, while Eugene Bantry again called to the policeman to fire.

"If he does, damn you, I'll kill him!" Joe saw the revolver raised; and then, Eugene being in his way, he ran full-tilt into his stepbrother with all his force, sending him to earth, and went on literally over him as he lay prone upon the asphalt, that being the shortest way to Respectability. The next instant the mongrel was in his master's arms and weakly licking his hands.

But it was Eskew Arp who had saved the little dog; for it was his stick which had tripped the clerk, and his hand which had struck him down. All his bodily strength had departed in that effort, but he staggered out into the street toward Joe.

"Joe Louden!" called the veteran, in a loud voice. "Joe Louden!" and suddenly reeled. The Colonel and Squire Buckalew were making their way toward him, but Joe, holding the dog to his breast with one arm, threw the other about Eskew.

"It's a town—it's a town"—the old fellow flung himself free from the supporting arm — "it's a town you couldn't even trust a yellow dog to!"

He sank back upon Joe's shoulder, speechless. An open carriage had driven through the crowd, the colored driver urged by two ladies upon the back seat, and Martin Pike saw it stop by the group in the middle of the street where Joe stood, the wounded dog held to his breast by one arm, the old man, white and half fainting, supported by the other. Martin Pike saw this and more; he saw Ariel Tabor and his own daughter leaning from the carriage, the arms of both pityingly extended to Joe Louden and his two burdens, while the stunned and silly crowd stood round them staring, clouds of dust settling down upon them through the hot air.

THREE ARE ENLISTED

OW in that blazing noon Canaan looked upon a strange sight: an open carriage whirling through Main Street
behind two galloping bays; upon the
back seat a ghostly white old man
with closed eyes, supported by two pale ladies, his
head upon the shoulder of the taller; while beside
the driver, a young man whose coat and hands
were bloody, worked over the hurts of an injured
dog. Sam Warden's whip sang across the horses;
lather gathered on their flanks, and Ariel's voice
steadily urged on the pace: "Quicker, Sam, if
you can." For there was little breath left in the
body of Eskew Arp.

Mamie, almost as white as the old man, was
silent; but she had not hesitated in her daring,
now that she had been taught to dare; she had not
come to be Ariel's friend and honest follower for
nothing, and it was Mamie who had cried to Joe
to lift Eskew into the carriage. "You must come
too," she said. "We will need you." And so it

came to pass that under the eyes of Canaan Joe Louden rode in Judge Pike's carriage at the bidding of Judge Pike's daughter.

Toward Ariel's own house they sped with the stricken octogenarian, for he was "alone in the world," and she would not take him to the cottage where he had lived for many years by himself, a bleak little house, a derelict of the "early days" left stranded far down in the town between a woollen - mill and the water - works. The workmen were beginning their dinners under the big trees, but as Sam Warden drew in the lathered horses at the gate, they set down their tin buckets hastily and ran to help Joe lift the old man out. Carefully they bore him into the house and laid him upon a bed in one of the finished rooms. He did not speak or move and the workmen uncovered their heads as they went out, but Joe knew that they were mistaken. "It's all right, Mr. Arp," he said, as Ariel knelt by the bed with water and restoratives. "It's all right. Don't you worry."

Then the veteran's lips twitched, and though his eyes remained closed, Joe saw that Eskew understood, for he gasped, feebly: "Pos-i-tive-ly—no—free—seats!"

To Mrs. Louden, sewing at an up-stairs window, the sight of her stepson descending from Judge

Pike's carriage was sufficiently startling, but when she saw Mamie Pike take Respectability from his master's arms and carry him tenderly indoors, while Joe and Ariel occupied themselves with Mr. Arp, the good lady sprang to her feet as if she had been stung, regardlessly sending her work-basket and its contents scattering over the floor, and ran down the stairs three steps at a time.

At the front door she met her husband, entering for his dinner, and she leaped at him. Had he seen? What was it? What had happened?

Mr. Louden rubbed his chin-beard, indulging himself in a pause which was like to prove fatal to his companion, finally vouchsafing the information that the doctor's buggy was just turning the corner; Eskew Arp had suffered a "stroke," it was said, and, in Louden's opinion, was a mighty sick man. His spouse replied in no uncertain terms that she had seen quite that much for herself, urging him to continue, which he did with a deliberation that caused her to recall their wedding-day with a gust of passionate self-reproach. Presently he managed to interrupt, reminding her that her dining-room windows commanded as comprehensive a view of the next house as did the front steps, and after a time her housewifely duty so far prevailed over her indignation at the man's unwholesome stolidity that she followed him down the hall to preside over the meal, not, however, to partake largely of it herself.

Mr. Louden had no information of Eugene's mishap, nor had Mrs. Louden any suspicion that all was not well with the young man, and, hearing him enter the front door, she called to him that his dinner was waiting. Eugene, however, made no reply and went up-stairs to his own apartment without coming into the dining-room.

A small crowd, neighboring children, servants, and negroes, had gathered about Ariel's gate, and Mrs. Louden watched the working-men disperse this assembly, gather up their tools, and depart; then Mamie came out of the house, and, bowing sadly to three old men who were entering the gate as she left it, stepped into her carriage and drove away. The new-comers, Colonel Flitcroft, Squire Buckalew, and Peter Bradbury, glanced at the doctor's buggy, shook their heads at one another, and slowly went up to the porch, where Joe met them. Mrs. Louden uttered a sharp exclamation, for the Colonel shook hands with her stepson.

Perhaps Flitcroft himself was surprised; he had offered his hand almost unconsciously, and the greeting was embarrassed and perfunctory; but his two companions, each in turn, gravely followed his lead, and Joe's set face flushed a little. It was the first time in many years that men of their kind in Canaan had offered him this salutation.

"He wouldn't let me send for you," he told them. "He said he knew you'd be here soon without that." And he led the way to Eskew's bedside.

Joe and the doctor had undressed the old man, and had put him into night-gear of Roger Tabor's, taken from an antique chest; it was soft and yellow and much more like color than the face above it, for the white hair on the pillow was not whiter than that. Yet there was a strange youthfulness in the eyes of Eskew; an eerie, inexplicable, luminous, *live* look; the thin cheeks seemed fuller than they had been for years; and though the heavier lines of age and sorrow could be seen, they appeared to have been half erased. He lay not in sunshine, but in clear light; the windows were open, the curtains restrained, for he had asked them not to darken the room.

The doctor was whispering in a doctor's way to Ariel at the end of the room opposite the bed, when the three old fellows came in. None of them spoke immediately, and though all three cleared their throats with what they meant for casual cheerfulness, to indicate that the situation was not at all extraordinary or depressing, it was to be seen that the Colonel's chin trembled under his mustache, and his comrades showed similar small and unwilling signs of emotion.

Eskew spoke first. "Well, boys?" he said, and smiled.

That seemed to make it more difficult for the others; the three white heads bent silently over the fourth upon the pillow; and Ariel saw waveringly, for her eyes suddenly filled, that the Colonel laid his unsteady hand upon Eskew's, which was outside the coverlet.

"It's—it's not," said the old soldier, gently— "it's not on—on both sides, is it, Eskew?"

Mr. Arp moved his hand slightly in answer. "It ain't paralysis," he said. "They call it 'shock and exhaustion'; but it's more than that. It's just my time. I've heard the call. We've all been slidin' on thin ice this long time—and it's broke under me—"

"Eskew, Eskew!" remonstrated Peter Bradbury. "You'd oughtn't to talk that-a-way! You only kind of overdone a little—heat o' the day, too, and—"

"Peter," interrupted the sick man, with feeble asperity, "did you ever manage to fool me in your life?"

"No, Eskew."

"Well, you're not doin' it now!"

Two tears suddenly loosed themselves from

Squire Buckalew's eyelids, despite his hard endeavor to wink them away, and he turned from the bed too late to conceal what had happened. "There ain't any call to feel bad," said Eskew. "It might have happened any time—in the night, maybe—at my house—and all alone—but here's Airie Tabor brought me to her own home and takin' care of me. I couldn't ask any better way to go, could I?"

"I don't know what we'll do," stammered the Colonel, "if you—you talk about goin' away from us, Eskew. We—we couldn't get along—"

"Well, sir, I'm almost kind of glad to think," Mr. Arp murmured, between short struggles for breath, "that it 'll be—quieter—on the—"National House" corner!"

A moment later he called the doctor faintly and asked for a restorative. "There," he said, in a stronger voice and with a gleam of satisfaction in the vindication of his belief that he was dying. "I was almost gone then. *I* know!" He lay panting for a moment, then spoke the name of Joe Louden.

Joe came quickly to the bedside.

"I want you to shake hands with the Colonel and Peter and Buckalew.

"We did," answered the Colonel, infinitely surprised and troubled. "We shook hands outside before we came in."

"Do it again," said Eskew. "I want to see you."

And Joe, making shift to smile, was suddenly blinded, so that he could not see the wrinkled hands extended to him, and was fain to grope for them.

"God knows why we didn't all take his hand long ago," said Eskew Arp. "I didn't because I was stubborn. I hated to admit that the argument was against me. I acknowledge it now before him and before you—and I want the word of it *carried!*"

"It's all right, Mr. Arp," began Joe, tremulously. "You mustn't—"

"Hark to me"—the old man's voice lifted higher: "If you'd ever whimpered, or give backtalk, or broke out the wrong way, it would of been different. But you never did. I've watched you and I know; and you've just gone your own way alone, with the town against you because you got a bad name as a boy, and once we'd given you that, everything you did or didn't do, we had to give you a blacker one. Now it's time some one stood *by* you! Airie Tabor 'll do that with all her soul and body. She told me once I thought a good deal of you. She knew! But I want these three old friends of mine to do it, too. I was boys with them and they'll do it, I think. They've even stood up fer you against me, sometimes, but mostly fer the sake of the argument, I reckon; but now they must do it when there's more to stand against than just my talk. They saw it all to-day—the meanest thing I ever knew! I could of stood it all except that!" Before they could prevent him he had struggled half upright in bed, lifting a clinched fist at the town beyond the windows. "But, by God! when they got so low down they tried to kill your dog—"

He fell back, choking, in Joe's arms, and the physician bent over him, but Eskew was not gone, and Ariel, upon the other side of the room, could hear him whispering again for the restorative. She brought it, and when he had taken it, went quickly out-of-doors to the side yard.

She sat upon a workman's bench under the big trees, hidden from the street shrubbery, and breathing deeply of the shaded air, began to cry quietly. Through the windows came the quavering voice of the old man, lifted again, insistent, a little querulous, but determined. Responses sounded, intermittently, from the Colonel, from Peter, and from Buckalew, and now and then a sorrowful, yet almost humorous, protest from Joe; and so she made out that the veteran swore his three comrades to friendship with Joseph Louden, to lend him their countenance in all matters, to stand by him in weal and woe, to speak only good of him and defend him in the town of Canaan. Thus did Eskew Arp on the verge of parting this life render justice.

The gate clicked, and Ariel saw Eugene approaching through the shrubbery. One of his hands was bandaged, a thin strip of court-plaster crossed his forehead from his left eyebrow to his hair, and his thin and agitated face showed several light scratches.

"I saw you come out," he said. "I've been waiting to speak to you."

"The doctor told us to let him have his way in whatever he might ask." Ariel wiped her eyes. "I'm afraid that means—"

"I didn't come to talk about Eskew Arp," interrupted Eugene. "I'm not laboring under any anxiety about him. You needn't be afraid; he's too sour to accept his *congé* so readily."

"Please lower your voice," she said, rising quickly and moving away from him toward the house; but, as he followed, insisting sharply that he must speak with her, she walked out of ear-shot of the windows, and stopping, turned toward him. "Very well," she said. "Is it a message from Mamie?"

At this he faltered and hung fire.

"Have you been to see her?" she continued.

"I am anxious to know if her goodness and bravery caused her any—any discomfort at home."

"You may set your mind at rest about that," returned Eugene. "I was there when the Judge came home to dinner. I suppose you fear he may have been rough with her for taking my step-brother into the carriage. He was not. On the contrary, he spoke very quietly to her, and went on out toward the stables. But I haven't come to you to talk of Judge Pike, either!"

"No," said Ariel. "I don't care particularly to hear of him, but of Mamie."

"Nor of her, either!" he broke out. "I want to talk of you!"

There was not mistaking him; no possibility of misunderstanding the real passion that shook him, and her startled eyes betrayed her comprehension.

"Yes, I see you understand," he cried, bitterly. "That's because you've seen others the same way. God help me," he went on, striking his forehead with his open hand, "that young fool of a Bradbury told me you refused him only yesterday! He was proud of even rejection from you! And there's Norbert—and half a dozen others, perhaps, already, since you've been here." He flung out his arms in ludicrous, savage despair. "And here am I—"

"Ah yes," she cut him off, "it is of yourself that you want to speak, after all—not of me!"

"Look here," he vociferated; "are you going to marry that Joe Louden? I want to know whether you are or not. He gave me this—and this to-day!" He touched his bandaged hand and plastered forehead. "He ran into me—over me—for nothing, when I was not on my guard; struck me down—stamped on me—"

She turned upon him, cheeks aflame, eyes sparkling and dry.

"Mr. Bantry," she cried, "he did a good thing! And now I want you to go home. I want you to go home and try if you can discover anything in yourself that is worthy of Mamie and of what she showed herself to be this morning! If you can, you will have found something that I could like!"

She went rapidly toward the house, and he was senseless enough to follow, babbling: "What do you think I'm made of? You trample on me—as he did! I can't bear everything; I tell you— "

But she lifted her hand with such imperious will that he stopped short. Then, through the window of the sick-room came clearly the querulous voice.

"I tell you it was; I heard him speak just now—out there in the yard, that no-account step-brother of Joe's! What if he *is* a hired hand on the *Tocsin?* He'd better give up his job and quit, than do what he's done to help make the town think hard of Joe. And what *is* he? Why, he's worse than Cory. When that Claudine Fear first came here, 'Gene Bantry was hangin' around her himself. Joe knew it and he'd never tell, but I will. I saw 'em buggy-ridin' out near Beaver Beach and she slapped his face fer him. It ought to be *told!*"

"I didn't know that Joe knew—that!" Eugene stammered huskily. "It was—it was—a long time ago—"

"If you understood Joe," she said, in a low voice, "you would know that before these men leave this house, he will have their promise never to tell."

His eyes fell miserably, then lifted again; but in her clear and unbearable gaze there shone such a flame of scorn as he could not endure to look upon. For the first time in his life he saw a true light upon himself, and though the vision was darkling, the revelation was complete.

"Heaven pity you!" she whispered.

Eugene found himself alone, and stumbled away, his glance not lifted. He passed his own home without looking up, and did not see his mother beckoning frantically from a window. She ran to the door and called him. He did not hear her, but went on toward the *Tocsin* office with his head still bent.

XX

NORBERT WAITS FOR JOE

HERE was meat for gossip a plenty in Canaan that afternoon and evening; there were rumors that ran from kitchen to parlor, and rumors that ran from parlor to kitchen; speculations that detained housewives in talk across front gates; wonderings that held cooks in converse over shadeless back fences in spite of the heat; and canards that brought Main Street clerks running to the shop doors to stare up and down the sidewalks. Out of the confusion of report, the judicious were able by evenfall to extract a fair history of this day of revolution. There remained no doubt that Joe Louden was in attendance at the death-bed of Eskew Arp, and somehow it came to be known that Colonel Flitcroft, Squire Buckalew, and Peter Bradbury had shaken hands with Joe and declared themselves his friends. There were those (particularly among the relatives of the hoary trio) who expressed the opinion that the Colonel and his comrades were too old to be responsible and a commission ought to sit on them; nevertheless, some echoes of Eskew's last "argument" to the conclave had sounded in the town and were not wholly without effect.

Everywhere there was a nipping curiosity to learn how Judge Pike had "taken" the strange performance of his daughter, and the eager were much disappointed when it was truthfully reported that he had done and said very little. He had merely discharged both Sam Warden and Sam's wife from his service, the mild manner of the dismissal almost unnerving Mr. Warden, although he was fully prepared for bird-shot; and the couple had found immediate employment in the service of Ariel Tabor.

Those who humanly felt the Judge's behavior to be a trifle flat and unsensational were recompensed late in the afternoon when it became known that Eugene Bantry had resigned his position on the *Tocsin.* His reason for severing his connection was dumfounding; he had written a formal letter to the Judge and repeated the gist of it to his associates in the office and acquaintances upon the street. He declared that he no longer sympathized with the attitude of the *Tocsin* toward his stepbrother, and regretted that he had previously assisted in emphasizing the paper's hostility to Joe, particularly in the matter of the approaching murder trial. This being the case, he felt that his effectiveness in the service of the paper had ceased, and he must, in justice to the owner, resign.

"Well, I'm damned!" was the simple comment of the elder Louden when his step-son sought him out at the factory and repeated this statement to him.

"So am I, I think," said Eugene, wanly. "Good-bye. I'm going now to see mother, but I'll be gone before you come home."

"Gone where?"

"Just away. I don't know where," Eugene answered from the door. "I couldn't live here any longer. I—"

"You've been drinking," said Mr. Louden, inspired. "You'd better not let Mamie Pike see you."

Eugene laughed desolately. "I don't mean to. I shall write to her. Good-bye," he said, and was gone before Mr. Louden could restore enough order out of the chaos in his mind to stop him.

Thus Mrs. Louden's long wait at the window was tragically rewarded, and she became an unhappy actor in Canaan's drama of that day. Other ladies attended at other windows, or near their front doors, throughout the afternoon: the families of the three patriarchs awaiting their return, as

the time drew on, with something akin to frenzy.
Mrs. Flitcroft (a lady of temper), whose rheumatism confined her to a chair, had her grandson
wheel her out upon the porch, and, as the dusk
fell and she finally saw her husband coming at a
laggard pace, leaning upon his cane, his chin sunk
on his breast, she frankly told Norbert that although she had lived with that man more than
fifty-seven years, she would never be able to understand him. She repeated this with genuine symp-
toms of hysteria when she discovered that the
Colonel had not come straight from the Tabor
house, but had stopped two hours at Peter Bradbury's to "talk it over."

One item of his recital, while sufficiently startling to his wife, had a remarkable effect upon his
grandson. This was the information that Ariel
Tabor's fortune no longer existed.

"What's that?" cried Norbert, starting to his
feet. "What are you talking about?"

"It's true," said the Colonel, deliberately. "She
told me so herself. Eskew had dropped off into
a sort of doze—more like a stupor, perhaps,—and
we all went into Roger's old studio, except Louden
and the doctor, and while we were there, talkin',
one of Pike's clerks came with a basket full of tin
boxes and packages of papers and talked to Miss
Tabor at the door and went away. Then old Peter

blundered out and asked her point-blank what it was, and she said it was her estate, almost everything she had, except the house. Buckalew, tryin' to make a joke, said he'd be willin' to swap *his* house and lot for the basket, and she laughed and told him she thought he'd be sorry; that all there was, to speak of, was a pile of distillery stock—"

"What?" repeated Norbert, incredulously.

"Yes. It was the truth," said the Colonel, solemnly. "I saw it myself: blocks and blocks of stock in that distillery trust that went up higher'n a kite last year. Roger had put all of Jonas's good money—"

"Not into that!" shouted Norbert, uncontrollably excited.

"Yes, he did. I tell you I saw it!"

"I tell you he didn't. He owned Granger Gas, worth more to-day than it ever was! Pike was Roger's attorney-in-fact and bought it for him before the old man died. The check went through my hands. You don't think I'd forget as big a check as that, do you, even if it was more than a year ago? Or how it was signed and who made out to? It was Martin Pike that got caught with distillery stock. He speculated once too often!"

"No, you're wrong," persisted the Colonel. "I tell you I saw it myself."

"Then you're blind," returned his grandson,

disrespectfully; "you're blind or else—or else—"
He paused, open-mouthed, a look of wonder struggling its way to expression upon him, gradually
conquering every knobby outpost of his countenance. He struck his fat hands together. "Where's
Joe Louden?" he asked, sharply. "I want to see
him. Did you leave him at Miss Tabor's?"

"He's goin' to sit up with Eskew. What do you
want of him?"

"I should say you better ask that!" Mrs. Flitcroft began, shrilly. "It's enough, I guess, for one
of this family to go runnin' after him and shakin'
hands with him and Heaven knows what not! *Norbert Flitcroft!*"

But Norbert jumped from the porch, ruthlessly
crossed his grandmother's geranium-bed, and, making off at as sharp a pace as his architecture permitted, within ten minutes opened Ariel's gate.

Sam Warden came forward to meet him.

"Don't ring, please, suh," said Sam. "Dey sot
me out heah to tell inquirin' frien's dat po' ole Mist'
Arp mighty low."

"I want to see Mr. Louden," returned Norbert.
"I want to see him immediately."

"I don' reckon he kin come out yit," Sam said,
in a low tone. "But I kin go in an' ast 'em."

He stepped softly within, leaving Norbert waiting, and went to the door of the sick-room. The

door was open, the room brightly lighted, as Eskew had commanded when, a little earlier, he awoke.

Joe and Ariel were alone with him, leaning toward him with such white anxiety that the colored man needed no warning to make him remain silent in the hallway. The veteran was speaking and his voice was very weak, seeming to come from a great distance.

"It's mighty funny, but I feel like I used to when I was a little boy. I reckon I'm kind of scared—after all. Airie Tabor,—are you—here?"

"Yes, Mr. Arp."

"I thought—so—but I—I don't see very well—lately. I—wanted—to—know—to know—"

"Yes—to know?" She knelt close beside him.

"It's kind of—foolish," he whispered. "I just —wanted to know if you was still here. It—don't seem so lonesome now that I know."

She put her arm lightly about him and he smiled and was silent for a time. Then he struggled to rise upon his elbow, and they lifted him a little.

"It's hard to breathe," gasped the old man. "I'm pretty near—the big road. Joe Louden—"

"Yes?"

"You'd have been—willing—willing to change places with me—just now—when Airie—"

Joe laid his hand on his, and Eskew smiled again. "I thought so! And, Joe—"

"Yes?"

"You always—always had the—the best of that joke between us. Do you — you suppose they charge admission — up there?" His eyes were lifted. "Do you suppose you've got to—to show your good deeds to git in?" The answering whisper was almost as faint as the old man's.

"No," panted Eskew, "nobody knows. But I hope—I do hope—they'll have some free seats. It's a—mighty poor show—we'll—all have—if they—don't!"

He sighed peacefully, his head grew heavier on Joe's arm; and the young man set his hand gently upon the unseeing eyes. Ariel did not rise from where she knelt, but looked up at him when, a little later, he lifted his hand.

"Yes," said Joe, "you can cry now."

XXII

MR. SHEEHAN SPEAKS

JOE helped to carry what was mortal of Eskew from Ariel's house to its final abiding-place. With him, in that task, were Buckalew, Bradbury, the Colonel, and the grandsons of the two latter, and Mrs. Louden drew in her skirts grimly as her step-son passed her in the mournful procession through the hall. Her eyes were red with weeping (not for Eskew), but not so red as those of Mamie Pike, who stood beside her.

On the way to the cemetery, Joe and Ariel were together in a carriage with Buckalew and the minister who had read the service, a dark, pleasant-eyed young man;—and the Squire, after being almost overcome during the ceremony, experienced a natural reaction, talking cheerfully throughout the long drive. He recounted many anecdotes of Eskew, chuckling over most of them, though filled with wonder by a coincidence which he and Flitcroft had discovered; the Colonel had recently been made the custodian of his old friend's will, and it had been opened the day before the funeral. Eskew had left everything he possessed—with the regret that it was so little—to Joe.

"But the queer thing about it," said the Squire, addressing himself to Ariel, "was the date of it, the seventeenth of June. The Colonel and I got to talkin' it over, out on his porch, last night, tryin' to rec'lect what was goin' on about then, and we figgered it out that it was the Monday after you come back, the very day he got so upset when he saw you goin' up to Louden's law-office with your roses."

Joe looked quickly at Ariel. She did not meet his glance, but, turning instead to Ladew, the clergyman, began, with a barely perceptible blush, to talk of something he had said in a sermon two weeks ago. The two fell into a thoughtful and amiable discussion, during which there stole into Joe's heart a strange and unreasonable pain. The young minister had lived in Canaan only a few months, and Joe had never seen him until that morning; but he liked the short, honest talk he had made; liked his cadenceless voice and keen, dark face; and, recalling what he had heard Martin Pike vociferating in his brougham one Sunday, perceived that Ladew was the fellow who had "got to go" because his sermons did not please the Judge. Yet Ariel remembered for more than a fortnight a passage from one of these sermons. And as Joe looked at the manly and intelligent face opposite him, it did not seem strange that she should.

He resolutely turned his eyes to the open window and saw that they had entered the cemetery, were near the green knoll where Eskew was to lie beside a brother who had died long ago. He let the minister help Ariel out, going quickly forward himself with Buckalew; and then — after the little while that the restoration of dust to dust mercifully needs—he returned to the carriage only to get his hat.

Ariel and Ladew and the Squire were already seated and waiting. "Aren't you going to ride home with us?" she asked, surprised.

"No," he explained, not looking at her. "I have to talk with Norbert Flitcroft. I'm going back with him. Good-bye."

His excuse was the mere truth, his conversation with Norbert, in the carriage which they managed to secure to themselves, continuing earnestly until Joe spoke to the driver and alighted at a corner, near Mr. Farbach's Italian possessions. "Don't forget," he said, as he closed the carriage door, "I've got to have both ends of the string in my hands."

"Forget!" Norbert looked at the cupola of the Pike Mansion, rising above the maples down the street. "It isn't likely I'll forget!"

When Joe entered the "Louis Quinze room" which some decorator, drunk with power, had mingled into the brewer's villa, he found the owner and Mr. Sheehan, with five other men, engaged in a meritorious attempt to tone down the apartment with smoke. Two of the five others were prosperous owners of saloons; two were known to the public (whose notion of what it meant when it used the term was something of the vaguest) as politicians; the fifth was Mr. Farbach's closest friend, one who (Joe had heard) was to be the next chairman of the city committee of the party. They were seated about a table, enveloped in blue clouds, and hushed to a grave and pertinent silence which clarified immediately the circumstance that whatever debate had preceded his arrival, it was now settled.

Their greeting of him, however, though exceedingly quiet, indicated a certain expectancy, as he accepted the chair which had been left for him at the head of the table. He looked thinner and paler than usual, which is saying a great deal; but presently, finding that the fateful hush which his entrance had broken was immediately resumed, a twinkle came into his eye, one of his eyebrows went up and a corner of his mouth went down.

"Well, gentlemen?" he said.

The smokers continued to smoke and to do nothing else; the exception being Mr. Sheehan, who, though he spoke not, exhibited tokens of agitation and excitement which he curbed with difficulty; shifting about in his chair, gnawing his cigar, crossing and uncrossing his knees, rubbing and slapping his hands together, clearing his throat with violence, his eyes fixed all the while, as were those of his companions, upon Mr. Farbach; so that Joe was given to perceive that it had been agreed that the brewer should be the spokesman. Mr. Farbach was deliberate, that was all, which added to the effect of what he finally did say.

"Choe," he remarked, placidly, "you are der next Mayor off Canaan."

"Why do you say that?" asked the young man, sharply.

"Bickoss us here," he answered, interlocking the tips of his fingers over his waistcoat, that being as near folding his hands as lay within his power,— "bickoss us here shall try to fix it so, und so hef ditcided."

Joe took a deep breath. "Why do you want me?"

"Dot," replied the brewer, "iss someding I shall

tell you." He paused to contemplate his cigar. "We want you bickoss you are der best man fer dot positsion."

"Louie, you mustn't make a mistake at the beginning," Joe said, hurriedly. "I may not be the kind of man you're looking for. If I went in—" He hesitated, stammering. "It seems an ungrateful thing to say, but—but there wouldn't be any slackness—I couldn't be bound to anybody—"

"Holt up your hosses!" Mr. Farbach, once in his life, was so ready to reply that he was able to interrupt. "Who hef you heert speak off bounding? Hef I speakt off favors? Dit I say der shoult be slackness in der city gofer'ment? Litsen to me, Choe." He renewed his contemplation of his cigar, then proceeded: "I hef been t'inkin' it ofer, now a couple years. I hef mate up my mind. If some peobles are gombelt to keep der laws and oders are not, dot's a great atwantitch to der oders. Dot iss what iss ruining der gountry und der peobles iss commencement to take notice. Efer'veres in oder towns der iss housecleaning; dey are reforming und indieding, und pooty soon dot mofement comes here — shoo-er! If we intent to holt der pardy in power, we shoult be a leetle ahead off dot mofement, so, when it shoult be here, we hef a goot 'minadstration to fall beck on. Now, dere iss anoder brewery opened und trying to gombete mit me here in Canaan. If dot brewery owns der Mayor, all der tsaloons buying my bier must shut up at 'leven o'glock und Sundays, but der oders keep open. If I own der Mayor, I make der same against dot oder brewery. Now I am pooty sick off dot ways off bitsness und fighting all times. Also," Mr. Farbach added, with magnificent calmness, "my trade iss larchly owitside off Canaan, und it iss bedder dot here der laws shoult be enforced der same fer all. Litsen, Choe; all us here beliefs der same way. You are square. Der whole tsaloon element knows dot, und knows dot all voult be treated der same. Mit you it voult be fairness fer each one. Foolish peobles hef sait you are a law-tricker, but we know dot you hef only mate der laws brotect as well as bunish. Und at such times as dey het been broken, you hef made dem as mertsiful as you coult. You are no tricker. We are willing to help you make it a glean town. Odervise der fightin' voult go on until der mofement strikes here und all der granks vake up und we git a fool reformer fer Mayor und der town goes to der dogs. If I try to put in a man dot I own, der oder brewery iss goin' to fight like hell, but if I work fer you it will not fight so hart."

"But the other people," Joe objected, "those outside of what is called the saloon element—do you understand how many of them will be against me?"

"It iss der tsaloon element," Mr. Farbach returned, peacefully, "dot does der fightin'."

"And you have considered my standing with that part of Canaan which considers itself the most respectable section?" He rose to his feet, standing straight and quiet, facing the table, upon which, it chanced, there lay a copy of the *Tocsin*.

"Und yet," observed Mr. Farbach, with mildness, "we got some pooty risbecdable men right here."

"Except me," broke in Mr. Sheehan, grimly, 'you have."

"Have you thought of this?" Joe leaned forward and touched the paper upon the table.

"We hef," replied Mr. Farbach. "All of us. You shall beat it."

There was a strong chorus of confirmation from the others, and Joe's eyes flashed.

"Have you considered," he continued, rapidly, while a warm color began to conquer his pallor,— "have you considered the powerful influence which will be against me, and more against me now, I should tell you, than ever before? That influence, I mean, which is striving so hard to discredit me that lynch-law has been hinted for poor Fear if I should clear him! Have you thought of that? Have you thought—"

"Have we thought o' Martin Pike?" exclaimed

Mr. Sheehan, springing to his feet, face aflame and beard bristling. "Ay, we've thought o' Martin Pike, and our thinkin' of him is where he begins to git what's comin' to him! What d'ye stand there pickin' straws fer? What's the matter with ye?" he demanded, angrily, his violence tenfold increased by the long repression he had put upon himself during the brewer's deliberate utterances. "If Louie Farbach and his crowd says they're fer ye, I guess ye've got a chanst, haven't ye?"

"Wait," said Joe. "I think you underestimate Pike's influence—"

"Underestimate the devil!" shouted Mr. Sheehan, uncontrollably excited. "You talk about influence! He's been the worst influence this town's ever had—and his tracks covered up in the dark wherever he set his ugly foot down. These men know it, and you know some, but not the worst of it, because none of ye live as deep down in it as I do! Ye want to make a clean town of it, ye want to make a little heaven of the Beach—"

"And in the eyes of Judge Pike," Joe cut him off, "and of all who take their opinions from him, I *represent* Beaver Beach!"

Mike Sheehan gave a wild shout. "Whooroo! It's come! I knowed it would! The day I couldn't hold my tongue, though I passed my word I would when the coward showed the deed he didn't dare to git recorded! Waugh!" He shouted again, with bitter laughter. "Ye do! In the eyes o' them as follow Martin Pike ye stand fer the Beach and all its wickedness, do ye? Whooroo! It's come! Ye're an offence in the eyes o' Martin Pike and all his kind because ye stand fer the Beach, are ye?"

"You know it!" Joe answered, sharply. "If they could wipe the Beach off the map and me with it—"

"Martin Pike would?" shouted Mr. Sheehan, while the others, open-mouthed, stared at him. "Martin Pike would?"

"I don't need to tell you that," said Joe.

Mr. Sheehan's big fist rose high over the table and descended crashing upon it. "It's a damn lie!" he roared. "Martin Pike owns Beaver Beach!"

XXIII

JOE WALKS ACROSS THE COURT-HOUSE YARD

FROM within the glossy old walnut bar that ran from wall to wall, the eyes of the lawyers and reporters wandered often to Ariel as she sat in the packed court-room watching Louden's fight for the life and liberty of Happy Fear. She had always three escorts, and though she did not miss a session, and the same three never failed to attend her, no whisper of scandal arose. But not upon them did the glances of the members of the bar and the journalists with tender frequency linger; nor were the younger members of these two professions all who gazed that way. Joe had fought out the selection of the jury with the prosecutor at great length and with infinite pains; it was not a young jury, and *it* stared at her. The "Court" wore a gray beard with which a flock of sparrows might have villaged a grove, and yet, in spite of the vital necessity for watchfulness over this fighting case, *It* once needed to be stirred from a trancelike gaze in Miss Tabor's direction and aroused to the realization that It was there to Sit and not to dream.

The August air was warm outside the windows, inviting to the open country, to swimmin'-hole, to orchard reveries, or shaded pool wherein to drop a meditative line; you would have thought no one could willingly coop himself in this hot room for three hours, twice a day, while lawyers wrangled, often unintelligibly, over the life of a dingy little creature like Happy Fear, yet the struggle to swelter there was almost like a riot, and the bailiffs were busy men.

It was a fighting case throughout, fought to a finish on each tiny point as it came up, dragging, in the mere matter of time, interminably, yet the people of Canaan (not only those who succeeded in penetrating to the court-room, but the others who hung about the corridors, or outside the building, and the great mass of stay-at-homes who read the story in the *Tocsin*) found each moment of it enthralling enough. The State's attorney, fearful of losing so notorious a case, and not underestimating his opponent, had modestly summoned others to his aid; and the attorney for the defence, single-handed, faced "an array of legal talent such as seldom indeed had hollered at this bar"; faced it good-naturedly, an eyebrow crooked up and his head on one side, most of the time, yet faced it indomitably. He had a certain careless and disarming smile when he lost a point, which carried off the defeat as of only humorous account and not at all part of the serious business in hand; and in his treatment of witnesses, he was plausible, kindly, knowing that in this case he had no intending perjurer to entrap; brought into play the rare and delicate art of which he was a master, employing in his questions subtle suggestions and shadings of tone and manner, and avoiding words of debatable and dangerous meanings;—a fine craft, often attempted by blunderers to their own undoing, but which, practised by Joseph Louden, made inarticulate witnesses articulate to the precise effects which he desired. This he accomplished as much by the help of the continuous fire of objections from the other side as in spite of them. He was infinitely careful, asking never an ill-advised question for the other side to use to his hurt, and, though exhibiting only a pleasant easiness of manner, was electrically alert.

A hundred things had shown Ariel that the feeling of the place, influenced by "public sentiment" without, was subtly and profoundly hostile to Joe and his client; she read this in the spectators, in the jury, even in the Judge; but it seemed to her that day by day the inimical spirit gradually failed, inside the railing, and also in those spectators who, like herself, were enabled by special favor to be present throughout the trial, and that now and then a kindlier sentiment began to be manifested. She was unaware how strongly she contributed to effect this herself, not only through the glow of visible sympathy which radiated from her, but by a particular action. Claudine was called by the State, and told as much of her story as the law permitted her to tell, interlarding her replies with fervent protestations (too quick to be prevented) that she "never meant to bring no trouble to Mr. Fear" and that she "did hate to have gen'lemen starting things on her account." When the defence took this perturbed witness, her interpolations became less frequent, and she described straightforwardly how she had found the pistol on the floor near the prostrate figure of Cory, and hidden it in her own dress. The attorneys for the State listened with a somewhat cynical amusement to this portion of her testimony, believing it of no account, uncorroborated, and that if necessary the State could impeach the witness on the ground that it had been indispensable to produce her. She came down weeping from the stand; and, the next witness not being immediately called, the eyes of the jurymen naturally followed her as she passed to her seat, and they saw Ariel Tabor bow gravely to her across the railing. Now, a thou sand things not set forth by legislatures, law-men and judges affect a jury, and the slight salutation caused the members of this one to glance at one another; for it seemed to imply that the exquisite lady in white not only knew Claudine, but knew that she had spoken the truth. It was after this, that a feeling favorable to the defence now and then noticeably manifested itself in the court-room. Still, when the evidence for the State was all in, the life of Happy Fear seemed to rest in a balance precarious indeed, and the little man, swallowing pitifully, looked at his attorney with the eyes of a sick dog.

Then Joe gave the prosecutors an illuminating and stunning surprise, and, having offered in evidence the revolver found upon Claudine, produced as his first witness a pawnbroker of Denver, who identified the weapon as one he had sold to Cory, whom he had known very well. The second witness, also a stranger, had been even more intimately acquainted with the dead man, and there began to be an uneasy comprehension of what Joe had accomplished during that prolonged absence of his which had so nearly cost the life of the little mongrel, who was at present (most blissful Respectability!) a lively convalescent in Ariel's back yard. The second witness also identified the revolver, testifying that he had borrowed it from Cory in St. Louis to settle a question of marksmanship, and that on his returning it to the owner, the latter, then working his way eastward, had confided to him his intention of stopping in Canaan for the purpose of exercising its melancholy functions upon a man who had once "done him good" in that city.

By the time the witness had reached this point, the Prosecutor and his assistants were on their feet, excitedly shouting objections, which were promptly overruled. Taken unawares, they fought for time; thunder was loosed, forensic bellowings; everybody lost his temper—except Joe; and the examination of the witness proceeded. Cory, with that singular inspiration to confide in some one, which is the characteristic and the undoing of his kind, had outlined his plan of operations to the witness with perfect clarity. He would first attempt, so he had declared, to incite an attack upon himself by playing upon the jealousy of his victim, having already made a tentative effort in that direction. Failing in this, he would fall back upon one of a dozen schemes (for he was ready in such matters, he bragged), the most likely of which would be to play the peacemaker; he would talk of his good intentions toward his enemy, speaking publicly of him in friendly and gentle ways; then, getting at him secretly, destroy him in such a fashion as to leave open for himself the kind gate of self-defence. In brief, here was the whole tally of what had actually occurred, with the exception of the last account in the sequence which had proved that demise for which Cory had not arranged; and it fell from the lips of a witness whom the prosecution had no means of impeaching. When he left the stand, unshaken and undiscredited, after a frantic cross - examination, Joe, turning to resume his seat, let his hand fall lightly for a second upon his client's shoulder.

That was the occasion of a demonstration which indicated a sentiment favorable to the defence (on the part of at least three of the spectators); and it was in the nature of such a hammering of canes upon the bare wooden floor as effectually stopped all other proceedings instantly. The indignant Judge fixed the Colonel, Peter Bradbury, and Squire Buckalew with his glittering eye, yet the hammering continued unabated; and the offenders surely would have been conducted forth in ignominy, had not gallantry prevailed, even in that formal place. The Judge, reluctantly realizing that some latitude must be allowed to these aged enthusiasts, since they somehow seemed to belong to Miss Tabor, made his remarks general, with the time - worn threat to clear the room, whereupon the loyal survivors of Eskew relapsed into unabashed silence.

It was now, as Joe had said, a clear-enough case. Only the case itself, however, was clear, for, as he and his friends feared, the verdict might possibly be neither in accordance with the law, the facts, nor the convictions of the jury. Eugene's defection had not altered the tone of the *Tocsin*.

All day long a crowd of men and boys hung about the corridors of the Court - house, about the Square and the neighboring streets, and from these rose sombre murmurs, more and more ominous. The public sentiment of a community like Canaan can make itself felt inside a court-room; and it was strongly exerted against Happy Fear. The *Tocsin* had always been a powerful agent; Judge Pike had increased its strength with a staff which was thoroughly efficient, alert, and always able to strike centre with the paper's readers; and in town and country it had absorbed the circulation of the other local journals, which resisted feebly at times, but in the matter of the Cory murder had not dared to do anything except follow the *Tocsin's* lead. The *Tocsin*, having lit the fire, fed it—fed it saltpetre and sulphur—for now Martin Pike was fighting hard.

The farmers and people of the less urban parts of the country were accustomed to found their opinions upon the *Tocsin*. They regarded it as the single immutable rock of journalistic righteousness and wisdom in the world. Consequently, stirred by the outbursts of the paper, they came into Canaan in great numbers, and though the pressure from the town itself was so strong that only a few of them managed to crowd into the court-room, the others joined their voices to those sombre murmurs outdoors, which increased in loudness as the trial went on.

The *Tocsin*, however, was not having everything its own way; the volume of outcry against Happy Fear and his lawyer had diminished, it was noticed, in "very respectable quarters." The information imparted by Mike Sheehan to the politicians at Mr. Farbach's had been slowly seeping through the various social strata of the town, and though at first incredulously rejected, it began to find acceptance; Upper Main Street cooling appreciably in its acceptance of the *Tocsin* as the law and the prophets. There were even a few who dared to wonder in their hearts if there had not been a mistake about Joe Louden; and although Mrs. Flitcroft weakened not, the relatives of Squire Buckalew and of Peter Bradbury began to hold up their heads a little, after having made home horrible for those gentlemen and reproached them with their conversion as the last word of senile shame. In addition, the Colonel's grandson and Mr. Bradbury's grandson had both mystifyingly lent countenance to Joe, consorting with him openly; the former for his own purposes—the latter because he had cunningly discovered that it was a way to Miss Tabor's regard, which, since her gentle rejection of him, he had grown to believe (good youth!) might be the pleasantest thing that could ever come to him. In short, the question had begun to thrive: Was it possible that Eskew Arp had not been insane, after all?

The best of those who gathered ominously about the Court-house and its purlieus were the young farmers and field-hands, artisans and clerks; one of the latter being a pimply faced young man (lately from the doctor's hands), who limped, and would limp for the rest of his life, he who, of all men, held the memory of Eskew Arp in least respect, and was burningly desirous to revenge himself upon the living.

The worst were of that mystifying, embryonic, semi-rowdy type, the American *voyou*, in the production of which Canaan and her sister towns everywhere over the country are prolific; the young man, youth, boy perhaps, creature of nameless age, whose clothes are like those of a brakeman out of work, but who is not a brakeman in or out of work; wearing the black, soft hat tilted forward to shelter—as a counter does the contempt of a clerk—that expression which the face does not dare wear quite in the open, asserting the possession of supreme capacity in wit, strength, dexterity, and amours; the dirty handkerchief under the collar; the short black coat always double-breasted; the eyelids sooty; one cheek always bulged; the forehead speckled; the lips cracked; horrible teeth; and the affectation of possessing secret information upon all matters of the universe; above all, the instinct of finding the shortest way to any scene of official interest to the policeman, fireman, or ambulance surgeon;—a singular being, not professionally criminal; tough histrionically rather than really; full of its own argot of brag; hysterical when crossed, timid through great ignorance, and therefore dangerous. It furnishes not the leaders but the mass of mobs; and it springs up at times of crisis from Heaven knows where. You might have driven through all the streets of Canaan, a week before the trial, and have seen four or five such fellows; but from the day of its beginning the Square was full of them, dingy shuttlecocks batted up into view by the *Tocsin*.

They kept the air whirring with their noise. The news of that sitting which had caused the Squire, Flitcroft, and Peter Bradbury to risk the Court's displeasure, was greeted outside with loud and vehement disfavor; and when, at noon, the jurymen were marshalled out to cross the yard to the "National House" for dinner, a large crowd followed and surrounded them, until they reached the doors of the hotel. "Don't let Lawyer Louden bamboozle you!" "Hang him!" "Tar and feathers fer ye ef ye don't hang him!" These were the mildest threats, and Joe Louden, watching from an upper window of the Court-house, observed with a troubled eye how certain of the jury shrank from the pressure of the throng, how the cheeks of others showed sudden pallor. Sometimes "public sentiment" has done evil things to those who have not shared it; and Joe knew how rare a thing is a jury which dares to stand square against a town like Canaan aroused.

The end of that afternoon's session saw another point marked for the defence; Joe had put the defendant on the stand, and the little man had proved an excellent witness. During his life he had been many things — many things disreputable; high standards were not brightly illumined for him in the beginning of the night-march which his life had been. He had been a tramp, afterward a petty gambler; but his great motive had finally come to be the intention to do what Joe told him to do: that, and to keep Claudine as straight as he could. In a measure, these were the two things that had brought him to the pass in which he now stood, his loyalty to Joe and his resentment of whatever tampered with Claudine's straightness. He was submissive to the consequences: he was still loyal. And now Joe asked him to tell "just what happened," and Happy obeyed with crystal clearness. Throughout the long, tricky cross-examination he continued to tell "just what happened" with a plaintive truthfulness not to be imitated, and throughout it Joe guarded him from pitfalls (for lawyers in their search after truth are compelled by the exigencies of their profession to make pitfalls even for the honest), and gave him, by various devices, time to remember, though not to think, and made the words "come right" in his mouth. So that before the sitting was over, a disquieting rumor ran through the waiting crowd in the corridors, across the Square, and over the town, that the case was surely going "Louden's way." This was also the opinion of a looker-on in Canaan—a ferret-faced counsellor of corporations who, called to consultation with the eminent Buckalew (nephew of the Squire), had afterward spent an hour in his company at the trial. "It's going that young fellow Louden's way," said the stranger. "You say he's a shyster, but—"

"Well," admitted Buckalew, with some reluctance, "I don't mean that exactly. I've got an old uncle who seems lately to think he's a great man."

"I'll take your uncle's word for it," returned the other, smiling. "I think he'll go pretty far."

They had come to the flight of steps which descended to the yard, and the visitor, looking down upon the angry crowd, added, "If they don't kill him!"

Joe himself was anxious concerning no such matter. He shook hands with Happy at the end of the sitting, bidding him be of good cheer, and, when the little man had marched away, under a strong guard, began to gather and sort his papers at a desk inside the bar. This took him perhaps five minutes, and when he had finished there were only three people left in the room: a clerk, a negro janitor with a broom, and the darky friend who always hopefully accompanies a colored man holding high public office. These two approvingly greeted the young lawyer, the janitor handing him a note from Norbert Flitcroft, and the friend mechanically "borrowing" a quarter from him as he opened the envelope.

"I'll be roun' yo' way to git a box o' *se*-gahs," laughed the friend, "soon ez de campaign open up good. Dey all goin' vote yo' way, down on the levee bank, but dey sho' expecks to git to smoke a little 'fo' leckshun-day! We knows who's *ow* frien'!"

Norbert's missive was lengthy and absorbing; Joe went on his way, perusing it with profound attention; but as he descended the stairway to the floor below, a loud burst of angry shouting, outside the building, caused him to hasten toward the big front doors which faced Main Street. The doors opened upon an imposing vestibule, from which a handsome flight of stone steps, protected by a marble balustrade, led to the ground.

Standing at the top of these steps and leaning over the balustrade, he had a clear view of half the yard. No one was near him; everybody was running in the opposite direction, toward that corner of the yard occupied by the jail, the crowd centring upon an agitated whirlpool of men which moved slowly toward a door in the high wall that enclosed the building; and Joe saw that Happy Fear's guards, conducting the prisoner back to his cell, were being jostled and rushed. The distance they had made was short, but as they reached the door the pressure upon them increased dangerously. Clubs rose in the air, hats flew, the whirlpool heaved tumultuously, and the steel door clanged.

Happy Fear was safe inside, but the jostlers were outside—baffled, ugly, and stirred with the passion that changes a crowd into a mob.

Then some of them caught sight of Joe as he stood alone at the top of the steps, and a great shout of rage and exultation arose.

For a moment or two he did not see his danger. At the clang of the door, his eyes, caught by the gleam of a wide white hat, had turned toward the street, and he was somewhat fixedly watching Mr. Ladew extricate Ariel (and her aged and indignant escorts) from an overflow of the crowd in which they had been caught. But a voice warned him: the wild piping of a newsboy who had climbed into a tree near by.

"*Joe Louden!*" he screamed. "*Look out!*"

With a muffled roar the crowd surged back from the jail and turned toward the steps. "Tar and feather him!" "Take him over to the river and throw him in!" "Drown him!" "Hang him!"

Then a thing happened which was dramatic enough in its inception, but almost ludicrous in its effect. Joe walked quietly down the steps and toward the advancing mob with his head cocked to one side, one eyebrow lifted, and one corner of his mouth drawn down in a faintly distorted smile.

He went straight toward the yelling forerunners, with only a small bundle of papers in his hands, and then—while the non-partisan spectators held their breath, expecting the shock of contact— straight on through them.

A number of the bulge-cheeked formed the scattering van of these forerunners, charging with hoarse and cruel shrieks of triumph. The first, apparently about to tear Joseph Louden to pieces, changed countenance at arm's-length, swerved violently, and with the loud cry, "*Head him off!*" dashed on up the stone steps. The man next behind him followed his lead, with the same shout, strategy, and haste; then the others of this advance attack, finding themselves confronting the quiet man, who kept his even pace and showed no intention of turning aside for them, turned suddenly aside for *him*, and, taking the cue from the first, pursued their way, bellowing: "*Head him off! Head him off!*" until there were a dozen and more rowdyish men and youths upon the steps, their eyes blazing with fury, menacing Louden's back with frightful gestures across the marble balustrade, as they hysterically bleated the chorus, "*Head him off!*"

Whether or not Joe could have walked through the entire mob as he had walked through these is a matter for speculation; it was believed in Canaan that he could. Already a gust of mirth began to sweep over the sterner spirits as they paused to marvel no less at the disconcerting advance of the lawyer than at the spectacle presented by the intrepid dare-devils upon the steps; a kind of lane actually opening before the young man as he walked steadily on. And when Mr. Sheehan, leading half a dozen huge men from the Farbach brewery, unceremoniously shouldered a way through the mob to Joe's side, reaching him where the press was thickest, it is a question if the services of his detachment were needed.

The laughter increased. It became voluminous. Homeric salvos shook the air. And never one of the fire-eaters upon the steps lived long enough to live down the hateful cry of that day, "*Head him off!*" which was to become a catch-word on the streets, a taunt more stinging than any devised by deliberate invention, an insult bitterer than the ancestral doubt, a fighting-word, and the great historical joke of Canaan, never omitted in afterdays when the tale was told how Joe Louden took that short walk across the Court-house yard which made him Mayor of Canaan.

XXIV

MARTIN PIKE KEEPS AN ENGAGEMENT

N hour later, Martin Pike, looking forth from the Mansion, saw a man open the gate, and, passing between the unemotional deer, rapidly approach the house. He was a thin young fellow, very well dressed in dark gray, his hair prematurely somewhat silvered, his face prematurely somewhat lined, and his hat covered a scar such as might have been caused by a blow from a blunt instrument in the nature of a poker.

He did not reach the door, nor was there necessity for him to ring, for, before he had set foot on the lowest step, the Judge had hastened to meet him. Not, however, with any fulsomely hospitable intent; his hand and arm were raised to execute one of his Olympian gestures, of the kind which had obliterated the young man upon a certain bygone morning.

Louden looked up calmly at the big figure towering above him.

348

"It won't do, Judge," he said; that was all, but there was a significance in his manner and a certainty in his voice which caused the uplifted hand to drop limply; while the look of apprehension which of late had grown more and more to be Martin Pike's habitual expression deepened into something close upon mortal anxiety.

"Have you any business to set foot upon my property?" he demanded.

"Yes," answered Joe. "That's why I came."

"What business have you got with me?"

"Enough to satisfy you, I think. But there's one thing I don't want to do"—Joe glanced at the open door—"and that is to talk about it here—for your own sake and because I think Miss Tabor should be present. I called to ask you to come to her house at eight o'clock to-night."

"You did!" Martin Pike spoke angrily, but not in the bull-bass of yore; and he kept his voice down, glancing about him nervously as though he feared that his wife or Mamie might hear. "My accounts with her estate are closed," he said, harshly. "If she wants anything, let her come here."

Joe shook his head. "No. You must be there at eight o'clock."

The Judge's choler got the better of his uneasiness. "You're a pretty one to come ordering me around!" he broke out. "You slanderer, do you suppose I haven't heard how you're going about traducing me, undermining my character in this community, spreading scandals that I am the real owner of Beaver Beach—"

"It can easily be proved, Judge," Joe interrupted, quietly, "though you're wrong: I haven't been telling people. I haven't needed to—even if I'd wished. Once a thing like that gets out you can't stop it—ever! That isn't all: to my knowledge you own other property worse than the Beach; I know that you own half of the worst dens in the town: profitable investments, too. You bought them very gradually and craftily, only showing the deeds to those in charge—as you did to Mike Sheehan, and not recording them. Sheehan's betrayal of you gave me the key; I know most of the poor creatures who are your tenants, too, you see, and that gave me an advantage because they have some confidence in me. My investigations have been almost as quiet and careful as your purchases."

"You damned blackmailer!" The Judge bent upon him a fierce, inquiring scrutiny in which, oddly enough, there was a kind of haggard hopefulness. "And out of such stories," he sneered, "you are going to try to make political capital against the *Tocsin*, are you?"

"No," said Joe. "It was necessary in the interests of my client for me to know pretty thoroughly just what property you own, and I think I do. These pieces I've mentioned are about all you have not mortgaged. You couldn't do that without exposure, and you've kept a controlling interest in the *Tocsin* clear, too—for the sake of its influence, I suppose. Now, do you want to hear any more, or will you agree to meet me at Miss Tabor's this evening?"

Whatever the look of hopefulness had signified, it fled from Pike's face during this speech, but he asked with some show of contempt, "Do you think it likely?"

"Very well," said Joe, "if you want me to speak here." And he came a little closer to him. "You bought a big block of Granger Gas for Roger Tabor," he began, in a low voice. "Before his death you sold everything he had, except the old house, put it all into cash for him, and bought that stock; you signed the check as his attorney-in-fact, and it came back to you through the Washington National, where Norbert Flitcroft handled it. He has a good memory, and when he told me what he knew, I had him to do some tracing; did a little myself, also. Judge Pike, I must tell you that you stand in danger of the law. You were the custodian of that stock for Roger Tabor; it was transferred in blank; though I think you meant to be 'legal' at that time, and that was merely for convenience in case Roger had wished you to sell it for him. But just after his death you found yourself saddled with distillery stock, which was going bad on your hands. Other speculations of yours were failing at the same time; you had to have money—you filed your report as administrator, crediting Miss Tabor with your own stock which you knew was going to the wall, and transferred hers to yourself. Then you sold it because you needed ready money. You used her fortune to save yourself — but you were horribly afraid! No matter how rotten your transactions had been, you had always kept inside the law; and now that you had gone outside of it, you were frightened. You didn't dare come flat out to Miss Tabor with the statement that her fortune had gone; it had been in your charge all the time and things might look ugly. So you put it off, perhaps from day to day. You didn't dare tell her until you were forced to, and to avoid the confession you sent her the income which was rightfully hers. That was your great weakness."

Joe had spoken with great rapidity, though keeping his voice low, and he lowered it again, as he continued: "Judge Pike, what chance have you to be believed in court when you swear that you

sent her twenty thousand dollars out of the good-
ness of your heart? Do you think *she* believed
you? It was the very proof to her that you had
robbed her. For she knew you! Do you want
to hear more now? Do you think this is a good
place for it? Do you wish me to go over the de-
tails of each step I have taken against you, to land
you at the bar where this poor fellow your paper
is hounding stands to-day?"

The Judge essayed to answer, and could not.
He lifted his hand uncertainly and dropped it,
while a thick dew gathered on his temples. Inarticulate sounds came from between his teeth.

"You will come?" said Joe.

Martin Pike bent his head dazedly; and at that
the other turned quickly from him and went away
without looking back.

Ariel was in the studio, half an hour later, when
Joe was announced by the smiling Mr. Warden.
Ladew was with her, though upon the point of
taking his leave, and Joe marked (with a sinking
heart) that the young minister's cheeks were
flushed and his eyes very bright.

"It was a magnificent thing you did, Mr. Louden," he said, offering his hand heartily; "I saw
it, and it was even finer in one way than it was
plucky. It somehow straightened things out with

such perfect good nature; it made those people feel that what they were doing was ridiculous."

"So it was," said Joe.

"Few, under the circumstances, could have acted as if they thought so! And I hope you'll let me call upon you, Mr. Louden."

"I hope you will," he answered; and then, when the minister had departed, stood looking after him with sad eyes, in which there dwelt obscure meditations. Ladew's word of farewell had covered a deep look at Ariel, which was not to be mistaken by Joseph Louden for anything other than what it was: the clergyman's secret was an open one, and Joe saw that he was as frank and manly in love as in all other things. "He's a good fellow," he said at last, sighing. "A good man."

Ariel agreed. "And he said more to me than he did to you."

"Yes, I think it probable," Joe smiled sorrowfully.

"About *you*, I mean." He had time to fear that her look admitted confusion before she proceeded: "He said he had never seen anything so fine as your coming down those steps. Ah, he was right! But it was harder for me to watch you, I think, than for you to do it, Joe. I was so horribly afraid—and the crowd between us—if we could have got near you—but we couldn't—we—"

She faltered, and pressed her hand close upon her eyes.

"We?" asked Joe, slowly. "You mean you and Mr. Ladew?"

"Yes, he was there; but I mean"—her voice ran into a little laugh with a beatific quaver in it —"I mean Colonel Flitcroft and Mr. Bradbury and Mr. Buckalew, too—we were hemmed in together when Mr. Ladew found us—and, oh, Joe, when that cowardly rush started toward you, those three—I've heard wonderful things in Paris and Naples, cabmen quarrelling and disappointed beggars—but never anything like them to-day—"

"You mean they were profane?"

"Oh, magnificently—and with such inventiveness! All three begged my pardon afterwards. I didn't grant it—I blessed them!"

"Did they beg Mr. Ladew's pardon?"

"Ah, Joe!" she reproached him. "He isn't a prig. And he's had to fight some things that you of all men ought to understand. He's only been here a few months, but he told me that Judge Pike has been against him from the start. It seems that Mr. Ladew is too liberal in his views. And he told me that if it were not for Judge Pike's losing influence in the church on account of the Beaver Beach story, the Judge would probably have been able to force him to resign; but now he will stay."

"He wishes to stay, doesn't he?"

"Very much, I think. And, Joe," she continued, thoughtfully, "I want you to do something for me. I want you to go to church with me next Sunday."

"To hear Mr. Ladew?"

"Yes. I wouldn't ask except for that."

"Very well," he consented, with averted eyes. "I'll go."

Her face was radiant with the smile she gave him. "It will make me very happy," she said.

He bent his head and fumbled over some papers he had taken from his pocket. "Will you listen to these memoranda? We have a great deal to go over before eight o'clock."

Judge Pike stood for a long while where Joe had left him, staring out at the street, apparently. Really he saw nothing. Undoubtedly an image of blurring foliage, cast - iron, cement, and turf, with sunshine smeared over all, flickered upon the retinas of his eyes; but the brain did not accept the picture from the optic nerve. Martin Pike was busy with other visions. Joe Louden had followed him back to his hidden deeds and had read them aloud to him as Gabriel would read them on Judgment-day. Perhaps *this* was the Judgment-day.

Pike had taken charge of Roger Tabor's affairs

because the commissions as agent were not too inconsiderable to be neglected. To make the task simpler, he had sold, as time went on, the various properties of the estate, gradually converting all of them into cash. Then, the opportunity offering, he bought a stock which paid excellent dividends, had it transferred in blank, because if it should prove to Roger's advantage to sell it, his agent could do so without any formal delays between Paris and Canaan. At least, that is what the Judge had told himself at the time, though it may be that some lurking whisperer in his soul had hinted that it might be well to preserve the great amount of cash in hand, and Roger's stock was practically that. Then came the evil days. Laboriously, he had built up a name for conservatism which most of the town accepted, but secretly he had always been a gambler: Wall Street was his goal; to adventure there, as one of the great single-eyed Cyclopean man-eaters, his fond ambition; and he had conceived the distillery trust as a means to attain it; but the structure tumbled about his ears; other edifices of his crumbled at the same time; he found himself beset, his solvency endangered, and there was the Tabor stock, quite as good as gold; Roger had just died, and it was enough to save him.—Save? That was a strange way to be remembering it to-day, when

357

Fate grinned at him out of a dreadful mask contorted like the face of Norbert Flitcroft.

Martin Pike knew himself for a fool. What chance had he, though he destroyed the check a thousand times over, to escape the records by which the coil of modern trade duplicates and quadruplicates each slip of scribbled paper? What chance had he against the memories of men? Would the man of whom he had bought, forget that the check was signed by Roger's agent? Had the bank-clerk forgotten? Thrice fool, Martin Pike, to dream that in a town like Canaan, Norbert or any of his kind could touch an order for so great a sum and forget it! But Martin Pike had not dreamed that; had dreamed nothing. When failure confronted him his mind refused to consider anything but his vital need at the time, and he had supplied that need. And now he grew busy with the future: he saw first the civil suit for restitution, pressed with the ferocity and cunning of one who intended to satisfy a grudge of years; then, perhaps, a criminal prosecution. . . . But he would fight it! Did they think that such a man was to be overthrown by a breath of air? By a girl, a bank-clerk, and a shyster lawyer? They would find their case difficult to prove in court. He did not believe they *could* prove it. They would be discredited for the attempt upon him and he would win clear; these Beaver Beach scandals would die of inertia presently; there would be a lucky trick in wheat, and Martin Pike would be Martin Pike once more; reinstated, dictator of church, politics, business; all those things which were the breath of his life restored. He would show this pitiful pack what manner of man they hounded! Norbert Flitcroft. . . .

The Judge put his big hand up to his eyes and rubbed them. Curious mechanisms the eyes. . . . That deer in line with the vision—not a zebra? A zebra after all these years? And yet . . . curious, indeed, the eyes! . . . a zebra. . . . Who ever heard of a deer with stripes? The big hand rose from the eyes and ran through the hair which he had always worn rather long. It would seem strange to have it cut very short. . . . Did they use clippers, perhaps? . . .

He started suddenly and realized that his next-door neighbor had passed along the sidewalk with head averted, pretending not to see him. A few weeks ago the man would not have missed the chance of looking in to bow—with proper deference, too! Did he know? He could not know *this!* It must be the Beaver Beach scandal. It must be. It could not be *this*—not yet! But it *might* be. How many knew? Louden, Norbert, Ariel—who else? And again the deer took on the strange zebra look.

The Judge walked slowly down to the gate; spoke to the man he had employed in Sam Warden's place, a Scotchman who had begun to refresh the lawn with a garden hose; bowed affably in response to the salutation of the elder Louden, who was passing, bound homeward from the factory, and returned to the house with thoughtful steps. In the hall he encountered his wife; stopped to speak with her upon various household matters; then entered the library, which was his workroom. He locked the door; tried it, and shook the handle. After satisfying himself of its security, he pulled down the window-shades carefully, and, lighting a gas drop-lamp upon his desk, began to fumble with various documents, which he took from a small safe near by. But his hands were not steady; he dropped the papers, scattering them over the floor, and had great difficulty in picking them up. He perspired heavily: whatever he touched became damp, and he continually mopped his forehead with his sleeve. After a time he gave up the attempt to sort the packets of papers; sank into a chair despairingly, leaving most of them in disorder.

A light tap sounded on the door.

"Martin, it's supper-time."

With a great effort he made shift to answer: "Yes, I know. You and Mamie go ahead. I'm too busy to-night. I don't want anything."

MARTIN KEEPS AN ENGAGEMENT

A moment before, he had been a pitiful figure, face distraught, hands incoherent, the whole body inco-ordinate, but if eyes might have rested upon him as he answered his wife they would have seen a strange thing; he sat, apparently steady and collected, his expression cool, his body quiet, poised exactly to the quality of his reply, for the same strange reason that a young girl smiles archly and coquettes to a telephone.

"But, Martin, you oughtn't to work so hard. You'll break down—"

"No fear of that," he replied, cheerfully. "You can leave something on the sideboard for me."

After another fluttering remonstrance, she went away, and the room was silent again. His arms rested upon the desk, and his head slowly sank between his elbows. When he lifted it again the clock on the mantel-piece had tinkled once. It was half-past seven. He took a sheet of note-paper from a box before him and began to write, but when he had finished the words, "*My dear wife and Mamie*," his fingers shook so violently that he could go no further. He placed his left hand over the back of his right to steady it, but found the device unavailing: the pen left mere zigzags on the page, and he dropped it.

He opened a lower drawer of the desk and took out of it a pistol; rose, went to the door, tried it once more, and again was satisfied of his seclusion. Then he took the weapon in both hands, the handle against his fingers, one thumb against the trigger, and, shaking with nausea, lifted it to the level of his eyes. His will betrayed him; he could not contract his thumb upon the trigger, and, with a convulsive shiver, he dropped the revolver upon the desk.

He locked the door of the room behind him, crept down the stairs and out of the front-door. He walked shamblingly, when he reached the street, keeping close to the fences as he went on, now and then touching the pickets with his hand, like a feeble old man.

He had always been prompt; it was one of the things of which he had been proud: in all his life he had never failed to keep a business engagement precisely upon the appointed time, and the Court-house bell clanged eight when Sam Warden opened the door for his old employer to-night.

The two young people looked up gravely from the script-laden table before them as Martin Pike came into the strong lamplight out of the dimness of the hall, where only a taper burned. He shambled a few limp steps into the room and came to a halt. Big as he was, his clothes hung upon him loosely, like coverlets upon a collapsed bed; and he seemed but a distorted image of himself, as if (save for the dull and reddened eyes) he had been made of yellowish wax and had been left too long in the sun. Abject, hopeless, his attitude a confession of ruin and shame, he stood before his judges in such wretchedness that, in comparison, the figure of Happy Fear, facing the court-room through his darkest hour, was one to be envied.

"Well," he said, brokenly, "what are you going to do?"

Joe Louden looked at him with great intentness for several moments. Then he rose and came forward. "Sit down, Judge," he said. "It's all right. Don't worry."

XXV

THE JURY COMES IN

M RS. FLITCROFT, at breakfast on the following morning, continued a disquisition which had ceased, the previous night, only because of a provoking human incapacity to exist without sleep. Her theme was one which had exclusively occupied her since the passing of Eskew, and, her rheumatism having improved so that she could leave her chair, she had become a sort of walking serial; Norbert and his grandfather being well assured that, whenever they left the house, the same story was to be continued upon their reappearance. The *Tocsin* had been her great comfort: she was but one helpless woman against two strong men; therefore she sorely needed assistance in her attack upon them, and the invaluable newspaper gave it in generous measure.

"Yes, young man," she said, as she lifted her first spoonful of oatmeal, "you *better* read the *Tocsin!*"

"I *am* reading it," responded Norbert, who was almost concealed by the paper.

"And your grandfather better read it!" she continued, severely.

"I already have," said the Colonel, promptly. "Have you?"

"No, but you can be sure I will!" The good lady gave the effect of tossing her head. "And you better take what it says to heart, you and some others. It's a wonder to me that you and Buckalew and old Peter don't go and hold that Happy Fear's hand durin' the trial! And as for Joe Louden, his step-mother's own sister, Jane, says to me only yesterday afternoon, 'Why, law! Mrs. Flitcroft,' she says, 'it's a wonder to me,' she says, 'that your husband and those two other old fools don't lay down in the gutter and let that Joe Louden walk over 'em.'"

"Did Jane Quimby say 'those two other old fools'?" inquired the Colonel, in a manner which indicated that he might see Mr. Quimby in regard to the slander.

"I can't say as I remember just precisely her exact words," admitted Mrs. Flitcroft, "but that was the sense of 'em! You've made yourselves the laughin'-stock of the whole town!"

"Oh, we have?"

"And I'd like to know"—her voice became shrill

and goading—"I'd like to know what Judge Pike thinks of you and Norbert! I should think you'd be ashamed to have him pass you in the street."

"I've quit speaking to him," said Norbert, coldly, "ever since I heard he owned Beaver Beach."

"That story ain't proved yet!" returned his grandmother, with much irascibility.

"Well, it will be; but that's not all." Norbert wagged his head. "You may be a little surprised within the next few days."

"I've been surprised for the *past* few!" she replied, with a bitterness which overrode her satisfaction in the effectiveness of the retort. "Surprised! I'd like to know who wouldn't be surprised when half the town acts like it's gone crazy. People *praisin'* that fellow, that nobody in their sober minds and senses never in their lives had a good word for before! Why, there was more talk yesterday about his doin's at the Court-house— you'd of thought he was Phil Sheridan! It's 'Joe Louden' here and 'Joe Louden' there, and 'Joe Louden' this and 'Joe Louden' that, till I'm sick of the name!"

"Then why don't you quit saying it?" asked the Colonel, reasonably.

"Because it'd *ought* to be said!" she exclaimed, with great heat. "Because he'd ought to be held up to the community to be despised. You let me have that paper a minute," she pursued, vehemently; "you just let me have the *Tocsin* and I'll read you out some things about him that 'll show him in his true light!"

"All right," said Norbert, suddenly handing her the paper. "Go ahead."

And after the exchange of a single glance the two gentlemen composed themselves to listen.

"Ha!" exclaimed Mrs. Flitcroft. "Here it is in head-lines on the first page. 'Defence Scores Again and Again. Ridiculous Behavior of a Would-Be Mob. Louden's—'" She paused, removed her spectacles, examined them dubiously, restored them to place, and continued: "'Louden's Masterly Conduct and Well-Deserved—'" she paused again, incredulous—"'Well-Deserved Triumph—'"

"Go on," said the Colonel, softly.

"Indeed I will!" the old lady replied. "Do you think I don't know sarcasm when I see it? Ha, ha!" She laughed with great heartiness. "I reckon I *will* go on! You listen and try to *learn* something from it!" She resumed the reading:

"'It is generally admitted that after yesterday's sitting of the court, the prosecution in the Fear-Cory murder trial has not a leg to stand on. Louden's fight for his client has been, it must be confessed, of a most splendid and talented order, and the bottom has fallen out of the case for the State, while a verdict of Not Guilty, it is now conceded, is the general wish of those who have attended and followed the trial. But the most interesting event of the day took place after the session, when some miscreants undertook to mob the attorney for the defence in the Court-house yard. He met the attack with a coolness and nerve which have won him a popularity that—'" Mrs. Flitcroft again faltered.

"Go on," repeated the Colonel. "There's a great deal more."

"Look at the editorials," suggested Norbert. "There's one on the same subject."

Mrs. Flitcroft, her theory of the *Tocsin's* sarcasm somewhat shaken, turned the page. "We Confess a Mistake" was the rubric above the leader, and she uttered a cry of triumph, for she thought the mistake was what she had just been reading, and that the editorial would apologize for the incomprehensible journalistic error upon the first page. "'The best of us make mistakes, and it is well to have a change of heart sometimes.'" (Thus Eugene's successor had written, and so Mrs. Flitcroft read.) "'An open confession is good for the soul. The *Tocsin* has changed its mind in regard to certain matters, and means to say so freely and frankly. After yesterday's events in connection with the murder trial before our public, the evidence being now all presented, for we understand that neither side has more to offer, it is generally conceded that all good citizens are hopeful of a verdict of acquittal; and the *Tocsin* is a good citizen. No good citizen would willingly see an innocent man punished, and that our city is not to be disgraced by such a miscarriage of justice is due to the efforts of the attorney for the defendant, who has gained credit not only by his masterly management of this case, but by his splendid conduct in the face of danger yesterday afternoon. He has distinguished himself so greatly that we frankly assert that our citizens may point with pride to—'" Mrs. Flitcroft's voice, at the beginning pitched to a high exultation, had gradually lowered in key and dropped down the scale till it disappeared altogether.

"It's a wonder to me," the Colonel began, "that the *Tocsin* doesn't go and hold Joe Louden's hand."

"I'll read the rest of it for you," said Norbert, his heavy face lighting up with cruelty. "Let's see — where were you? Oh yes — 'point with pride'? 'Our citizens may point with pride to ...'"

Let us not linger to observe the unmanly behavior of an aged man and his grandson left alone at the breakfast-table by a defenceless woman.

The *Tocsin's* right-about-face undermined others besides Mrs. Flitcroft that morning, and rejoiced greater (though not better) men than the Colonel. Mr. Farbach and his lieutenants smiled, yet stared, amazed, wondering what had happened. That was a thing which only three people even certainly knew; yet it was very simple.

The *Tocsin* was part of the Judge's restitution.

"The controlling interest in the paper, together with the other property I have listed," Joe had said, studying his memoranda under the lamp in Roger's old studio, while Martin Pike listened with his head in his hands, "make up what Miss Tabor is willing to accept. As I estimate it, their total value is between a third and a half of that of the stock which belonged to her."

"But this boy—this Flitcroft," said Pike, feebly; "he might—"

"He will do nothing," interrupted Joe. "The case is 'settled out of court,' and even if he were disposed to harass you, he could hardly hope to succeed, since Miss Tabor declines either to sue or to prosecute."

The Judge winced at the last word. "Yes—yes, I know; but he might—he might—tell."

"I think Miss Tabor's influence will prevent. If it should not—well, you're not in a desperate case by any means; you're involved, but far from stripped; in time you may be as sound as ever. And if Norbert tells, there's nothing for you to do but to live it down." A faint smile played upon Joe's lips as he lifted his head and looked at the other. "It can be done, I think."

It was then that Ariel, complaining of the warmth of the evening, thought it possible that Joe might find her fan upon the porch, and as he departed, whispered hurriedly: "Judge Pike, I'm not technically in control of the *Tocsin*, but haven't I the right to control its policy?"

"I understand," he muttered. "You mean about Louden—about this trial—"

"That is why I have taken the paper."

"You want all that changed, you mean?"

She nodded decisively. "From this instant. Before morning."

"Oh, well, I'll go down there and give the word." He rubbed his eyes wearily with big thumbs. "I'm through fighting. I'm done. Besides, what's the use? There's nothing more to fight."

"Now, Judge," Joe said, as he came in briskly, "we'll go over the list of that unencumbered property, if you will."

This unencumbered property consisted of Beaver Beach and those other belongings of the Judge which he had not dared to mortgage. Joe had somehow explained their nature to Ariel, and these with the *Tocsin* she had elected to accept in restitution.

"You told me once that I ought to look after my own property, and now I will. Don't you see?" she cried to Joe, eagerly. "It's my work!" She resolutely set aside every other proposition; and this was the quality of mercy which Martin Pike found that night.

There was a great crowd to hear Joe's summing-up at the trial, and those who succeeded in getting into the court-room declared that it was worth the struggle. He did not orate, he did not "thunder at the jury," nor did he slyly flatter them; he did not overdo the confidential, nor seem so secure of understanding beforehand what their verdict would be that they felt an instinctive desire to fool him. He talked colloquially but clearly, without appeal to the pathetic and without garnitures, not mentioning sunsets, birds, oceans, homes, the glorious old State, or the happiness of liberty; but he made everybody in the room quite sure that Happy Fear had fired the shot which killed Cory to save his own life. And that, as Mr. Bradbury remarked to the Colonel, was "what Joe was *there* for!"

Ariel's escort was increased to four that day: Mr. Ladew sat beside her, and there were times when Joe kept his mind entirely to the work in hand only by an effort, but he always succeeded. The sight of the pale and worshipping face of Happy Fear from the corner of his eye was enough to insure that. And people who could not get near the doors, asking those who could, "What's he doin' now?" were answered by variations of the one formula, "Oh, jest walkin' away with it!"

Once the court-room was disturbed and set in an uproar which even the Judge's customary threat failed to subdue. Joe had been talking very rapidly, and having turned the point he was making with perfect dexterity, the jury listening eagerly, stopped for a moment to take a swallow of water. A voice rose over the low hum of the crowd in a delirious chuckle: "Why don't somebody '*head him off!*'" The room instantly rocked with laughter, under cover of which the identity of the sacrilegious chuckler was not discovered, but the voice was the voice of Buckalew, who was incredibly surprised to find that he had spoken aloud.

The jury were "out," after the case had been given to them, seventeen minutes and thirty seconds by the watch Claudine held in her hand. The little man, whose fate was now on the knees of the gods, looked pathetically at the foreman and then at the face of his lawyer and began to shake violently, but not with fright. He had gone to the jail on Joe's word, as a good dog goes where his master bids, trustfully; and yet Happy had not been able to keep his mind from considering the horrible chances. "Don't worry," Joe had said. "It's all right. I'll see you through." And he had kept his word.

The little man was cleared.

It took Happy a long time to get through what he had to say to his attorney in the anteroom, and even then, of course, he did not manage to put it in words, for he had "broken down" with sheer gratitude. "Why, damn *me*, Joe," he sobbed, "if ever I—if ever you—well, by God! if you ever—" This was the substance of his lingual accomplishment under the circumstances. But Claudine threw her arms around poor Joe's neck and kissed him.

Many people were waiting to shake hands with Joe and congratulate him. The trio, taking advantage of seats near the rail, had already done that (somewhat uproariously) before he had followed Happy, and so had Ariel and Ladew, both, necessarily, rather hurriedly. But in the corridors he found, when he came out of the anteroom, clients, acquaintances, friends: old friends, new friends, and friends he had never seen before —everybody beaming upon him and wringing his hand, as if they had been sure of it all from the start.

"*Know* him?" said one to another. "Why, I've knowed him sence he was that high! *Smart* little feller he was, too!" This was a total stranger.

"I said, years ago"—thus Mr. Brown, the "National House" clerk, proving his prophetic vision —"that he'd turn out to be a big man some day."

They gathered round him if he stopped for an instant, and crowded after him admiringly when he went on again, making his progress slow. When he finally came out of the big doors into the sunshine, there were as many people in the yard as there had been when he stood in the same place and watched the mob rushing his client's guards. But to-day their temper was different, and as he paused a moment, looking down on the upturned, laughing faces, with a hundred jocular and congratulatory salutations shouted up at him, somebody started a cheer, and it was taken up with thunderous good-will.

There followed the interrogation customary in such emergencies, and the anxious inquirer was informed by four or five hundred people simultaneously that Joe Louden was all right.

"*Head him off!*" bellowed Mike Sheehan, suddenly darting up the steps. The shout increased, and with good reason, for he stepped quickly back within the doors; and, retreating through the building, made good his escape by a basement door.

He struck off into a long détour, but though he managed to evade the crowd, he had to stop and shake hands with every third person he met. As he came out upon Main Street again, he encountered his father.

"Howdy do, Joe?" said this laconic person, and offered his hand. They shook, briefly. "Well," he continued, rubbing his beard, "how are ye?"

"All right, father, I think."

"Satisfied with the verdict?"

"I'd be pretty hard to please if I weren't," Joe laughed.

Mr. Louden rubbed his beard again. "I was there," he said, without emotion.

"At the trial, you mean?"

"Yes." He offered his hand once more, and again they shook. "Well, come around and see us," he said.

"Thank you. I will."

"Well," said Mr. Louden, "good-day, Joe."

"Good-day, father."

The young man stood looking after him with a curious smile. Then he gave a slight start. Far up the street he saw two figures, one a lady's, in white, with a wide white hat; the other a man's, wearing recognizably clerical black. They seemed to be walking very slowly.

It had been a day of triumph for Joe; but in all his life he never slept worse than he did that night.

XXVI

"ANCIENT OF DAYS"

H E woke to the chiming of bells, and, as his eyes slowly opened, the sorrowful people of a dream, who seemed to be bending over him, weeping, swam back into the darkness of the night whence they had come, and returned to the imperceptible, leaving their shadows in his heart. Slowly he rose, stumbled into the outer room, and released the fluttering shade; but the sunshine, springing like a golden lover through the open window, only dazzled him, and found no answering gladness to greet it, nor joy in the royal day it heralded.

And yet, to the newly cleaned boys on their way to midsummer morning Sunday-school, the breath of that cool August day was as sweet as stolen apples. No doubt the stir of far, green thickets and the twinkle of silver-slippered creeks shimmered in the longing vision of their minds' eyes; even so, they were merry. But Joseph

Louden, sighing as he descended his narrow stairs, with the bitterness still upon his lips of the frightful coffee he had made, heard the echo of their laughter with wonder.

It would be an hour at least before time to start to church, when Ariel expected him; he stared absently up the street, then down, and, after that, began slowly to walk in the latter direction, with no very active consciousness, or care, of where he went. He had fallen into a profound reverie, so deep that when he had crossed the bridge and turned into a dusty road which ran along the river-bank, he stopped mechanically beside the trunk of a fallen sycamore, and, lifting his head, for the first time since he had set out, looked about him with a melancholy perplexity, a little surprised to find himself there.

For this was the spot where he had first seen the new Ariel, and on that fallen sycamore they had sat together. "*Remember, across Main Street bridge at noon!*" And Joe's cheeks burned, as he recalled why he had not understood the clear voice that had haunted him. But that shame had fallen from him; she had changed all that, as she had changed so many things. He sank down in the long grass, with his back against the log, and stared out over the fields of tall corn, shaking in a steady wind all the way to the horizon.

"Changed so many things?" he said, half aloud. "Everything!" Ah, yes, she had changed the whole world for Joseph Louden—at his first sight of her! And now it seemed to him that he was to lose her, but not in the way he had thought.

Almost from the very first, he had the feeling that nothing so beautiful as that she should stay in Canaan could happen to him. He was sure that she was but for the little while, that her coming was like the flying petals of which he had told her.

He had lain upon the earth; and she had lifted him up. For a moment he had felt the beatific wings enfolding him with gentle protection, and then saw them lifted to bear the angel beyond his sight. For it was incredible that the gods so loved Joe Louden that they would make greater gifts to him than this little time with her which they had granted him.

"Changed so many things?"

The bars that had been between him and half of his world were down, shattered, never more to be replaced; and the ban of Canaan was lifted. Could this have been, save for her? And upon that thought he got to his feet, uttering an exclamation of bitter self - reproach, asking himself angrily what he was doing. He knew how much she gave him, what full measure of her affection! Was not that enough?—Out upon you, Louden!

Are you to sulk in your tent, dour in the gloom, or to play a man's part, and if she be happy, turn a cheery face upon her joy?

And thus this pilgrim recrossed the bridge, emerging to the street with his head up, smiling, and his shoulders thrown back so that none might see the burden he carried.

Ariel was waiting on the porch for him. She wore the same dress she had worn that Sunday of their tryst; that exquisite dress, with the faint lavender overtint, like the tender colors of the beautiful day he made his own. She had not worn it since, and he was far distant when he caught the first flickering glimpse of her through the lower branches of the maples, but he remembered. . . . And again, as on that day, he heard a far-away, ineffable music, the Elf-land horns, sounding the mysterious reveille which had wakened his soul to her coming.

She came to the gate to meet him, and gave him her hand in greeting, without a word—or the need of one—from either. Then together they set forth over the sun-flecked pavement, the maples swishing above them, heavier branches crooning in the strong breeze, under a sky like a Della Robbia background. And up against the glorious blue of it, some laughing, invisible god was blowing small, rounded clouds of pure cotton, as children blow thistledown.

When he opened her parasol, as they came out into the broad sunshine beyond Upper Main Street, there was the faintest mingling of wild roses and cinnamon loosed on the air.

"Joe," she said, "I'm very happy!"

"That's right," he returned, heartily. "I think you always will be."

"But, oh! I wish," she went on, "that Mr. Arp could have lived to see you come down the Court-house steps."

"God bless him!" said Joe. "I can hear the 'argument'!"

"Those dear old men have been so loyal to you, Joe."

"No," he returned; "loyal to Eskew."

"To you both," she said. "I'm afraid the old circle is broken up; they haven't met on the 'National House' corner since he died. The Colonel told me he couldn't bear to go there again."

"I don't believe any of them ever will," he returned. "And yet I never pass the place that I don't see Eskew in his old chair. I went there last night to commune with him. I couldn't sleep, and I got up, and went over there; they'd left the chairs out; the town was asleep, and it was beau tiful moonlight—"

"To commune with him? What about?"

"You."

"Why?" she asked, plainly mystified.

"I stood in need of good counsel," he answered, cheerfully, "or a friendly word, perhaps, and—as I sat there—after a while it came."

"What was it?"

"To forget that I was sodden with selfishness; to pretend not to be as full of meanness as I really was! Doesn't that seem to be Eskew's own voice?"

"Weren't you happy last night, Joe?"

"Oh, it was all right," he said, quickly. "Don't you worry."

And at this old speech of his she broke into a little laugh of which he had no comprehension.

"Mamie came to see me early this morning," she said, after they had walked on in silence for a time. "Everything is all right with her again; that is, I think it will be. Eugene is coming home. And," she added, thoughtfully, "it will be best for him to have his old place on the *Tocsin* again. She showed me his letter, and I liked it. I think he's been through the fire—"

Joe's distorted smile appeared. "And has come out gold?" he asked.

"No," she laughed; "but nearer it! And I think he'll try to be more worth her caring for.

She has always thought that his leaving the *Tocsin* in the way he did was heroic. That was her word for it. And it *was* the finest thing he ever did."

"I can't figure Eugene out." Joe shook his head. "There's something behind his going away that I don't understand." This was altogether the truth; nor was there ever to come a time when either he or Mamie would understand what things had determined the departure of Eugene Bantry; though Mamie never questioned, as Joe did, the reasons for it, or doubted those Eugene had given her, which were the same he had given her father. For she was content with his return.

Again the bells across the Square rang out their chime. The paths were decorously enlivened with family and neighborhood groups, bound church-ward; and the rumble of the organ, playing the people into their pews, shook on the air. And Joe knew that he must speak quickly, if he was to say what he had planned to say, before he and Ariel went into the church.

"Ariel?" He tried to compel his voice to a casual cheerfulness, but it would do nothing for him, except betray a desperate embarrassment.

She looked at him quickly, and as quickly away. "Yes?"

"I wanted to say something to you, and I'd

better do it now, I think—before I go to church for the first time in two years!" He managed to laugh, though with some ruefulness, and continued stammeringly: "I want to tell you how much I like him—how much I admire him—"

"Admire whom?" she asked, a little coldly, for she knew.

"Mr. Ladew."

"So do I," she answered, looking straight ahead. "That is one reason why I wanted you to come with me to-day."

"It isn't only that. I want to tell you—to tell you—" He broke off for a second. "You remember that night in my office before Fear came in?"

"Yes; I remember."

"And that I—that something I said troubled you because it—it sounded as if I cared too much for you—"

"No; not too much." She still looked straight ahead. They were walking very slowly. "You didn't understand. You'd been in my mind, you see, all those years, so much more than I in yours. I hadn't forgotten *you*. But to you I was really a stranger—"

"No, no!" he cried.

"Yes, I was," she said, gently but very quickly. "And I—I didn't want you to fall in love with me at first sight. And yet — perhaps I did! But I hadn't thought of things in that way. I had just the same feeling for you that I always had—always! I had never cared so much for any one else, and it seemed to me the most necessary thing in my life to come back to that old companionship— Don't you remember—it used to trouble you so when I would take your hand? I think I loved your being a little rough with me. And once, when I saw how you had been hurt, that day you ran away—"

"Ariel!" he gasped, helplessly.

"Have you forgotten?"

He gathered himself together with all his will. "I want to prove to you," he said, resolutely, "that the dear kindness of you isn't thrown away on me; I want you to know what I began to say: that it's all right with me; and I think Ladew—" He stopped again. "Ah! I've seen how much he cares for you—"

"Have you?"

"Ariel," he said, "that isn't fair to me, if you trust me. You could not have helped seeing—"

"But I have not seen it," she interrupted, with great calmness. After having said this, she finished truthfully: "If he did, I would never let him tell me. I like him too much."

"You mean you're not going to—"

"ANCIENT OF DAYS"

Suddenly she turned to him. *"No!"* she said, with a depth of anger he had not heard in her voice since that long - ago winter day when she struck Eugene Bantry with her clenched fist. She swept over him a blinding look of reproach. "How could I?"

And there, upon the steps of the church, fell the burden of him who had made his sorrowful pilgrimage across Main Street bridge that morning.

A manifold rustling followed them as they went down the aisle, and the sibilance of many whisperings; but Joe was not conscious of that, as he took his place in Ariel's pew beside her. For him there was only the presence of divinity; the church was filled with it.

They rose to sing:

"Ancient of days, Who sittest, throned in glory,
    To Thee all knees are bent, all voices pray;
Thy love has blest the wide world's wondrous story
    With light and life since Eden's dawning day."

And then, as they knelt to pray, there were the white heads of the three old friends of Eskew Arp; and beyond was the silver hair of Martin Pike, who knelt beside his daughter. Joe felt that people should be very kind to the Judge.

387

The sun, so eager without, came temperately through the windows, where stood angels and saints in gentle colors, and the face of the young minister in this quiet light was like the faces in the windows. . . .

"Not only to confront your enemies," he said; "that is not enough; nor is it that I would have you bluster at them, nor take arms against them; you will not have to do that if, when they come at you, you do not turn one inch aside, but with an assured heart, with good nature, not noisily, and with steadfastness, you keep on your way. If you can do that, I say that they will turn aside for you, and you shall walk straight through them, and only laughter be left of their anger!"

There was a stir among the people, and many faces turned toward Joe. Two years ago he had sat in the same church, when his character and actions had furnished the underlying theme of a sermon, and he had recognized himself without difficulty: to-day he had not the shadow of a dream that the same thing was happening. He thought the people were turning to look at Ariel, and he was very far from wondering at that.

She saw that he did not understand; she was glad to have it so. She had taken off her gloves, and he was holding them lightly and reverently in his hands, looking down upon them, his thin cheeks a little flushed. And at that, and not knowing the glory that was in his soul, something forlorn in his careful tenderness toward her gloves so touched her that she felt the tears coming to her eyes with a sudden rush. And to prevent them.

"Not the empty gloves, Joe, she whispered.

THE END

Popular Copyright Books

AT MODERATE PRICES

Ask your dealer for a complete list of
A. L. Burt Company's Popular Copyright Fiction.

Abner Daniel. By Will N. Harben.
Adventures of A Modest Man. By Robert W. Chambers.
Adventures of Gerard. By A. Conan Doyle.
Adventures of Sherlock Holmes. By A. Conan Doyle.
Ailsa Page. By Robert W. Chambers.
Alternative, The. By George Barr McCutcheon.
Ancient Law, The. By Ellen Glasgow.
Angel of Forgiveness, The. By Rosa N. Carey.
Angel of Pain, The. By E. F. Benson.
Annals of Ann, The. By Kate Trumble Sharber.
Anna the Adventuress. By E. Phillips Oppenheim.
Ann Boyd. By Will N. Harben.
As the Sparks Fly Upward.. By Cyrus Townsend Brady.
At the Age of Eve. By Kate Trimble Sharber.
At the Mercy of Tiberius. By Augusta Evans Wilson.
At the Moorings. By Rosa N. Carey.
Awakening of Helen Richie, The. By Margaret Deland.
Barrier, The. By Rex Beach.
Bar 20. By Clarence E. Mulford.
Bar-20 Days. By Clarence E. Mulfird.
Battle Ground, The. By Ellen Glasgow.
Beau Brocade. By Baroness Orczy.
Beechy. By Bettina von Hutten.
Bella Donna. By Robert Hichens.
Beloved Vagabond, The. By William J. Locke.
Ben Blair. By Will Lillibridge.
Best Man, The. By Harold McGrath.
Beth Norvell. By Randall Parrish.
Betrayal, The. By E. Phillips Oppenheim.
Better Man, The. By Cyrus Townsend Brady.
Beulah. (Illustrated Edition.) By Augusta J. Evans.
Bill Toppers, The. By Andre Castaigne.
Blaze Derringer. By Eugene P. Lyle, Jr.
Bob Hampton of Placer. By Randall Parrish.
Bob, Son of Battle. By Alfred Ollivant.
Brass Bowl, The. By Louis Joseph Vance.
Bronze Bell, The. By Louis Joseph Vance.
Butterfly Man, The. By George Barr McCutcheon.
By Right of Purchase. By Harold Bindloss.
Cab No. 44. By R. F. Foster.
Calling of Dan Matthews, The. By Harold Bell Wright.
Call of the Blood, The. By Robert Hichens.
Cape Cod Stories. By Joseph C.Lincoln.
Cap'n Eri. By Joseph C. Lincoln.
Captain Warren's Wards. By Joseph C. Lincoln.
Caravaners, The. By the author of "Elizabeth and Her German
    Garden."
Cardigan. By Robert W. Chambers.
Carlton Case, The. By Ellery H. Clark.
Car of Destiny, The. By C. N. and A. M. Williamson.
Carpet From Bagdad, The. By Harold MacGrath.
Cash Intrigue, The. By George Randolph Chester.
Casting Away of Mrs. Lecks and Mrs. Aleshine. Frank S. Stockton.
Castle by the Sea, The. By H. B. Marriot Watson.
Challoners, The. By E. F. Benson.
Chaperon, The. By C. N. and A. M. Williamson.
City of Six, The. By C. L. Canfield.

Popular Copyright Books

AT MODERATE PRICES

Ask your dealer for a complete list of
A. L. Burt Company's Popular Copyright Fiction.

Circle, The. By Katherine Cecil Thurston (author of "The Masquerader," "The Gambler.")
Colonial Free Lance, A. By Chauncey C. Hotchkiss.
Conquest of Canaan, The. By Booth Tarkington.
Conspirators, The. By Robert W. Chambers.
Cynthia of the Minute. By Louis Joseph Vance.
Dan Merrithew. By Lawrence Perry.
Day of the Dog, The. By George Barr McCutcheon.
Depot Master, The. By Joseph C. Lincoln.
Derelicts. By William J. Locke.
Diamond Master, The. By Jacques Futrelle.
Diamonds Cut Paste. By Agnes and Egerton Castle.
Divine Fire, The. By May Sinclair.
Dixie Hart. By Will N. Harben.
Dr. David. By Marjorie Benton Cooke.
Early Bird, The. By George Randolph Chester.
Eleventh Hour, The. By David Potter.
Elizabeth in Rugen. (By the author of "Elizabeth and Her German Garden.")
Elusive Isabel. By Jacques Futrelle.
Elusive Pimpernel, The. By Baroness Orczy.
Enchanted Hat, The. By Harold McGrath.
Excuse Me. By Rupert Hughes.
54-40 or Fight. By Emerson Hough.
Fighting Chance, The. By Robert W. Chambers.
Flamsted Quarries. By Mary E. Waller.
Flying Mercury, The. By Eleanor M. Ingram.
For a Maiden Brave. By Chauncey C. Hotchkiss.
Four Million, The. By O. Henry.
Four Pool's Mystery, The. By Jean Webster.
Fruitful Vine, The. By Robert Hichens.
Ganton & Co. By Arthur J. Eddy.
Gentleman of France, A. By Stanley Weyman.
Gentleman, The. By Alfred Ollivant.
Get-Rick-Quick-Wallingford. By George Randolph Chester.
Gilbert Neal. By Will N. Harben.
Girl and the Bill, The. By Bannister Merwin.
Girl from His Town, The. By Marie Van Vorst.
Girl Who Won, The. By Beth Ellis.
Glory of Clementina, The. By William J. Locke.
Glory of the Conquered, The. By Susan Glaspell.
God's Good Man. By Marie Corelli.
Going Some. By Rex Beach.
Golden Web, The. By Anthony Partridge.
Green Patch, The. By Bettina von Hutten.
Happy Island (sequel to "Uncle William"). By Jennette Lee.
Hearts and the Highway. By Cyrus Townsend Brady.
Held for Orders. By Frank H. Spearman.
Hidden Water. By Dane Coolidge.
Highway of Fate, The. By Rosa N. Carey.
Homesteaders, The. By Kate and Virgil D. Boyles.
Honor of the Big Snows, The. By James Oliver Curwood.
Hopalong Cassidy. By Clarence E. Mulford.
Household of Peter, The. By Rosa N. Carey.
House of Mystery, The. By Will Irwin.
House of the Lost Court, The. By C. N. Williamson.
House of the Whispering Pines, The. By Anna Katherine Green.

Popular Copyright Books

AT MODERATE PRICES

Ask your dealer for a complete list of
A. L. Burt Company's Popular Copyright Fiction.

House on Cherry Street, The. By Amelia E. Barr.
How Leslie Loved. By Anne Warner.
Husbands of Edith, The. By George Barr McCutcheon.
Idols. By William J. Locke.
Illustrious Prince, The. By E. Phillips Oppenheim.
Imprudence of Prue, The. By Sophie Fisher.
Inez. (Illustrated Edition.) By Augusta J. Evans.
Infelice. By Augusta Evans Wilson.
Initials Only. By Anna Katharine Green.
In Defiance of the King. By Chauncey C. Hotchkiss.
Indifference of Juliet, The. By Grace S. Richmond.
In the Service of the Princess. By Henry C. Rowland.
Iron Woman, The. By Margaret Deland.
Ishmael. (Illustrated.) By Mrs. Southworth.
Island of Regeneration, The. By Cyrus Townsend Brady.
Jack Spurlock, Prodigal. By Horace Lorimer.
Jane Cable. By George Barr McCutcheon .
Jeanne of the Marshes. By E. Phillips Oppenheim.
Jude the Obscure. By Thomas Hardy.
Keith of the Border. By Randall Parrish.
Key to the Unknown, The. By Rosa N. Carey.
Kingdom of Earth, The. By Anthony Partridge.
King Spruce. By Holman Day.
Ladder of Swords, A. By Gilbert Parker.
Lady Betty Across the Water. By C. N. and A. M. Williamson.
Lady Merton, Colonist. By Mrs. Humphrey Ward.
Lady of Big Shanty, The. By Berkeley F. Smith.
Langford of the Three Bars. By Kate and Virgil D. Boyles.
Land of Long Ago, The. By Eliza Calvert Hall.
Lane That Had No Turning, The. By Gilbert Parker.
Last Trail, The. By Zane Grey.
Last Voyage of the Donna Isabel, The. By Randall Parrish.
Leavenworth Case, The. By Anna Katharine Green.
Lin McLean. By Owen Wister.
Little Brown Jug at Kildare, The. By Meredith Nicholson.
Loaded Dice. By Ellery H. Clarke.
Lord Loveland Discovers America. By C. N. and A. M. Williamson.
Lorimer of the Northwest. By Harold Bindloss.
Lorraine. By Robert W. Chambers.
Lost Ambassador, The. By E. Phillips Oppenheim.
Love Under Fire. By Randall Parrish.
Loves of Miss Anne, The. By S. R. Crockett.
Macaria. (Illustrated Edition.) By Augusta J. Evans.
Mademoiselle Celeste. By Adele Ferguson Knight.
Maid at Arms, The. By Robert W. Chambers.
Maid of Old New York, A. By Amelia E. Barr.
Maid of the Whispering Hills, The. By Vingie Roe.
Maids of Paradise, The. By Robert W. Chambers.
Making of Bobby Burnit, The. By George Randolph Chester.
Mam' Linda. By Will N. Harben.
Man Outside, The. By Wyndham Martyn.
Man in the Brown Derby, The. By Wells Hastings.
Marriage a la Mode. By Mrs. Humphrey Ward.
Marriage of Theodora, The. By Molly Elliott Seawell.
Marriage Under the Terror, A. By Patricia Wentworth.
Master Mummer, The. By E. Phillips Oppenheim.
Masters of the Wheatlands. By Harold Bindloss.

Popular Copyright Books

AT MODERATE PRICES

Ask your dealer for a complete list of
A. L. Burt Company's Popular Copyright Fiction.

Max. By Katherine Cecil Thurston.
Memoirs of Sherlock Holmes. By A. Conan Doyle.
Millionaire Baby, The. By Anna Katharine Green.
Missioner, The. By E. Phillips Oppenheim.
Miss Selina Lue. By Maria Thompson Daviess.
Mistress of Brae Farm, The. By Rosa N. Carey.
Money Moon, The. By Jeffery Farnol.
Motor Maid, The. By C. N. and A. M. Williamson.
Much Ado About Peter. By Jean Webster.
Mr. Pratt. By Joseph C. Lincoln.
My Brother's Keeper. By Charles Tenny Jackson.
My Friend the Chauffeur. By C. N. and A. M. Williamson.
My Lady Caprice (author of the "Broad Higway"). Jeffery Farnol.
My Lady of Doubt. By Randall Parrish.
My Lady of the North. By Randall Parrish.
My Lady of the South. By Randall Parrish.
Mystery Tales. By Edgar Allen Poe.
Nancy Stair. By Elinor Macartney Lane.
Ne'er-Do-Well, The. By Rex Beach.
No Friend Like a Sister. By Rosa N. Carey.
Officer 666. By Barton W. Currie and Augustin McHugh.
One Braver Thing. By Richard Dehan.
Order No. 11. By Caroline Abbot Stanley.
Orphan, The. By Clarence E. Mulford.
Out of the Primitive. By Robert Ames Bennett.
Pam. By Bettina von Hutten.
Pam Decides. By Bettina von Hutten.
Pardners. By Rex Beach.
Partners of the Tide. By Joseph C. Lincoln.
Passage Perilous, The. By Rosa N. Carey.
Passers By. By Anthony Partridge.
Paternoster Ruby, The. By Charles Edmonds Walk.
Patience of John Moreland, The. By Mary Dillon.
Paul Anthony, Christian. By Hiram W. Hays.
Phillip Steele. By James Oliver Curwood.
Phra the Phoenician. By Edwin Lester Arnold.
Plunderer, The. By Roy Norton.
Pole Baker. By Will N. Harben.
Politician, The. By Edith Huntington Mason.
Polly of the Circus. By Margaret Mayo.
Pool of Flame, The. By Louis Joseh Vance.
Poppy.. By Cynthia Stockley.
Power and the Glory, The. By Grace McGowan Cooke.
Price of the Prairie, The. By Margaret Hill McCarter.
Prince of Sinners, A. By E. Phillis Oppenheim.
Prince or Chauffeur. By Lawrence Perry.
Princess Dehra, The. By John Reed Scott.
Princess Passes, The. By C. N. and A. M. Williamson.
Princess Virginia, The. By C. N. and A. M. Williamson.
Prisoners of Chance. By Randall Parrish.
Prodigal Son, The. By Hall Caine.
Purple Parasol, The. By George Barr McCutcheon.

Popular Copyright Books

AT MODERATE PRICES

Ask your dealer for a complete list of
A. L. Burt Company's Popular Copyright Fiction.

Reconstructed Marriage, A. By Amelia Barr.
Redemption of Kenneth Galt, The. By Will N. Harben.
Red House on Rowan Street. By Roman Doubleday.
Red Mouse, The. By William Hamilton Osborne.
Red Pepper Burns. By Grace S. Richmond.
Refugees, The. By A. Conan Doyle.
Rejuvenation of Aunt Mary, The. By Anne Warner.
Road to Providence, The. By Maria Thompson Daviess.
Romance of a Plain Man, The. By Ellen Glasgow.
Rose in the Ring, The. By George Barr McCutcheon.
Rose of Old Harpeth, The. By Maria Thompson Daviess.
Rose of the World. By Agnes and Egerton Castle.
Round the Corner in Gay Street. By Grace S. Richmond.
Routledge Rides Alone. By Will Livingston Comfort.
Running Fight, The. By Wm. Hamilton Osborne.
Seats of the Mighty, The. By Gilbert Parker.
Septimus. By William J. Locke.
Set in Silver. By C. N. and A. M. Williamson.
Self-Raised. (Illustrated.) By Mrs. Southworth.
Shepherd of the Hills, The. By Harold Bell Wright.
Sheriff of Dyke Hole, The. By Ridgwell Cullum.
Sidney Carteret, Rancher. By Harold Bindloss.
Simon the Jester. By William J. Locke.
Silver Blade, The. By Charles E. Walk.
Silver Horde, The. By Rex Beach.
Sir Nigel. By A. Conan Doyle.
Sir Richard Calmady. By Lucas Malet.
Skyman, The. By Henry Ketchell Webster.
Slim Princess, The. By George Ade.
Speckled Bird, A. By Augusta Evans Wilson.
Spirit in Prison, A. By Robert Hichens.
Spirit of the Border, The. By Zane Grey.
Spirit Trail, The. By Kate and Virgil D. Boyles.
Spoilers, The. By Rex Beach.
Stanton Wins. By Eleanor M. Ingram.
St. Elmo. (Illustrated Edition.) By Augusta J. Evans.
Stolen Singer, The. By Martha Bellinger.
Stooping Lady, The. By Maurice Hewlett.
Story of the Outlaw, The. By Emerson Hough.
Strawberry Acres. By Grace S. Richmond.
Strawberry Handkerchief, The. By Amelia E. Barr.
Sunnyside of the Hill, The. By Rosa N. Carey.
Sunset Trail, The. By Alfred Henry Lewis.

Popular Copyright Books

AT MODERATE PRICES

Ask your dealer for a complete list of
A. L. Burt Company's Popular Copyright Fiction.

Susan Clegg and Her Friend Mrs. Lathrop. By Anne Warner.
Sword of the Old Frontier, A. By Randall Parrish.
Tales of Sherlock Holmes. By A. Conan Doyle.
Tennessee Shad, The. By Owen Johnson.
Tess of the D'Urbervilles. By Thomas Hardy.
Texican, The. By Dane Coolidge.
That Printer of Udell's. By Harold Bell Wright.
Three Brothers, The. By Eden Phillpotts.
Throwback, The. By Alfred Henry Lewis.
Thurston of Orchard Valley. By Harold Bindloss.
Title Market, The. By Emily Post.
Torn Sails. A Tale of a Welsh Village. By Allen Raine.
Trail of the Axe, The. By Ridgwell Cullum.
Treasure of Heaven, The. By Marie Corelli.
Two-Gun Man, The. By Charles Alden Seltzer.
Two Vanrevels, The. By Booth Tarkington.
Uncle William. By Jennette Lee.
Up from Slavery. By Booker T. Washington.
Vanity Box, The. By C. N. Williamson.
Vashti. By Augusta Evans Wilson.
Varmint, The. By Owen Johnson.
Vigilante Girl, A. By Jerome Hart.
Village of Vagabonds, A. By F. Berkeley Smith.
Visioning, The. By Susan Glaspell.
Voice of the People, The. By Ellen Glasgow.
Wanted—A Chaperon. By Paul Leicester Ford.
Wanted: A Matchmaker. By Paul Leicester Ford.
Watchers of the Plains, The. Ridgwell Cullum.
Wayfarers, The. By Mary Stewart Cutting.
Way of a Man, The. By Emerson Hough.
Weavers, The. By Gilbert Parker.
When Wilderness Was King. By Randall Parrish.
Where the Trail Divides. By Will Lillibridge.
White Sister, The. By Marion Crawford.
Window at the White Cat, The. By Mary Roberts Rhinehart.
Winning of Barbara Worth, The. By Harold Bell Wright.
With Juliet in England. By Grace S. Richmond.
Woman Haters, The. By Joseph C. Lincoln.
Woman in Question, The. By John Reed Scott.
Woman in the Alcove, The. By Anna Katharine Green.
Yellow Circle, The. By Charles E. Walk.
Yellow Letter, The. By William Johnston.
Younger Set, The. By Robert W. Chambers.